CW00740602

CAN YOU KEEP A SECRET?

JO LOVETT

Boldwood

First published in Great Britain in 2024 by Boldwood Books Ltd.

Copyright © Jo Lovett, 2024

Cover Design by Head Design Ltd

Cover Illustration: Shutterstock

The moral right of Jo Lovett to be identified as the author of this work has been asserted in accordance with the Copyright, Designs and Patents Act 1988.

All rights reserved. No part of this book may be reproduced in any form or by any electronic or mechanical means, including information storage and retrieval systems, without written permission from the author, except for the use of brief quotations in a book review.

This book is a work of fiction and, except in the case of historical fact, any resemblance to actual persons, living or dead, is purely coincidental.

Every effort has been made to obtain the necessary permissions with reference to copyright material, both illustrative and quoted. We apologise for any omissions in this respect and will be pleased to make the appropriate acknowledgements in any future edition.

A CIP catalogue record for this book is available from the British Library.

Paperback ISBN 978-1-78513-509-5

Large Print ISBN 978-1-78513-510-1

Hardback ISBN 978-1-78513-508-8

Ebook ISBN 978-1-78513-511-8

Kindle ISBN 978-1-78513-512-5

Audio CD ISBN 978-1-78513-503-3

MP3 CD ISBN 978-1-78513-504-0

Digital audio download ISBN 978-1-78513-506-4

Boldwood Books Ltd
23 Bowerdean Street
London SW6 3TN
www.boldwoodbooks.com

To Liz and Daniel

1

GEORGIE

Georgie James leaned back in her chair and beamed at her three best friends. She bloody loved them. And she loved this pub, with its low beams, squishy leather sofas and roaring log fire, not to mention a roomful of regulars, most of whom she'd known her whole life. You didn't get this in a city wine bar. Doing New Year's Eve together again at the Duck and Grapes was *amazing*.

She reached out to place her glass on the table in front of her, whoops, missed first time, no, got it on now, oops, no, nearly spilled it, no it was definitely safely on now, she was a glass-placing *genius*, and then angled herself back in towards the others.

'You're the best best friends ever,' she told them. 'Thank you for being here.'

'No, thank *you* for organising us.' Beth was shaking her head, her blonde curls bobbing manically around her head.

'It wasn't me.' Georgie leaned in even further and beckoned, so that the others drew closer. 'Obviously it was inspired by Poppy being back from Australia. But also it was my hair.'

'Your hair?' asked Beth, frowning.

'Yes.' Georgie nodded. 'Specifically, a grey hair. It made me feel nostalgic for our youth, so I thought we should do New Year again. I found one the day before my birthday right on the top of my head. Then I looked carefully and there were loads. Dozens. And obviously I was already feeling old, because thirty-four's only a year away from thirty-five, next stop forty.'

'Then fifty.' Poppy's face drooped.

'That's right.' Ankita did a comedy eye roll. 'It's only sixteen years from thirty-four to fifty, and then only twenty years until we're seventy, so we're totally knocking on the door of old age. *Not.*' She put her arm round Poppy and hugged her. 'Honestly, Pops, you're letting the drink get to you.' She pointed at Georgie. 'And you, Georgie. We are *not* old. Forty's the new thirty and we are nowhere near forty. So we're actually extremely young. We do not need to be melodramatic about our age.'

Georgie shook her head. 'Easy for you to say. There's no way a grey hair would *dare* to show its face on your head.' They all knew that Ankita's beautiful, glossy, sleek, *perfect*, mahogany bobbed hair was tended to fortnightly – at a minimum – by a famous Central London hairdresser at about three hundred quid a throw (Ankita had a very hotshot City job that she said she hated but did have the advantage of paying her an absolute fortune).

'Now that—' Ankita waved her glass at them, slopping Prosecco over the rim '—is where you're wrong. I've been having my hair dyed since we were twenty-nine.'

Beth's jaw literally dropped. 'Nooooo. But you said that you'd never done *anything* to your hair. Remember, when we went to the spa?'

'That was a white lie. There were all those WAGs listening,' said Ankita.

'*Oh.* But I thought we didn't lie to each other.' Beth looked like a bewildered eight-year-old.

'Apparently, almost no adult is capable of holding a ten-minute conversation without lying.' Raf, the bartender-for-the-night, was manoeuvring past them holding three packets of smoky bacon and anchovy popcorn and balancing a tray with two pints and a glass of red on the fingers of his other hand. Georgie was impressed; he'd told them earlier he'd never worked in a pub before.

'That can't be true.' Beth's wide-eyed bewildered look had morphed into wide-eyed horror.

'She's right, it can't be,' Ankita agreed. 'I mean, I lie, but that's my job for

you. Beth probably never does. And Georgie neither, except about chocolate consumption. Same for Poppy. So there you go: it's nonsense.'

'It's definitely true.' Raf was on his way back past. He stopped in front of
them and opened one of the bags he was carrying. 'Think about it. Think
about the last ten minutes.' He held the bag out. 'Popcorn?'

'It depends what you mean by lying,' Georgie mused out loud, thinking
of how much possible-lying-by-omission she'd been doing over the past ten
days. 'Because there are different kinds of lies, aren't there? Like sometimes
people's lives can turn into one big, constant lie.'

Everyone's eyes swivelled to her.

Fuck. Why had she said that? Had she lost her mind?

'What do you mean?' Beth cocked her head to one side, her hair only
narrowly missing the inside of Poppy's glass as she reached for some
popcorn.

Georgie took a massive slurp of Prosecco while her mind flipped
around desperately, searching for a straw to grasp. 'Well, like people who
always tell white lies. People who automatically compliment everyone they
see. Like when someone's wearing a top that really doesn't suit them and
you tell them it looks lovely.' She smiled, pleased with herself. That was a
nice recovery.

'Do you mean *my* top?' Poppy pulled it down at the hem. 'I knew I
shouldn't have worn it. I'm so fat now. The baby weight's never going to go. I
should have bought something new in a huge size.'

'*No,*' said Georgie, appalled. 'Really, no. You look lovely. Beautiful. Stunning. The shape's great for you. And the colour really suits you. Genuinely.
Not a white lie. The total truth.'

Being honest, the top would have looked better if it hadn't had baby
food on the left shoulder, but no *way* was Georgie going to mention that
right now and oh, there she went again, lying by omission. That was a tiny
lie, though.

'It really does look good on you, Poppy.' Beth nodded furiously, and
Ankita chimed in with an, 'It really does, Pops. Honestly. You look
blooming.'

'I shouldn't be blooming.' Poppy's face was drooping again. 'Daniel's seven months old. Pregnant people should be blooming. Women who gave birth seven months ago should be back to normal.'

'No, they shouldn't.' Georgie did an authoritative head shake. 'I read somewhere last week that the average British woman doesn't lose all her baby weight until her baby's seventeen months old.'

'I think you look beautiful, Poppy.' Raf produced a megawatt smile for her.

Poppy's lips immediately turned up at the corners and her shoulders visibly lifted.

Which was ridiculous. To be fair, Raf was possibly the most gorgeous man ever to set foot in the whole of Gloucestershire, even including all the celebs who flocked to the Cotswolds in their very un-muddy 4x4s to install solar-powered swimming pools and cinema complexes on their organic farms. His liquid chocolate eyes and slightly lopsided smile could persuade a lot of people to do a *lot* of things. And so far he'd seemed like very good company. But he was a stranger. And he had succeeded where all Poppy's actual best friends had failed. And that was just not right.

'But,' Raf continued, pulling a stool up and pointing the open bag of popcorn at Georgie, 'that weight loss statistic was totally invented. Aka a lie. I can see it in your eyes. Which *totally* proves my point.'

'You cannot see it in her eyes,' scoffed Ankita.

'I can,' said Raf. 'I'm a divorce lawyer and it's my USP. I can always tell when people are lying. Which, as I said, they do at least once every ten minutes.'

Honestly. He might *look* like actual sex-on-legs, but in fact he was a tactless idiot. The mood she was in, Poppy would definitely take that the wrong way.

Georgie sneaked a quick look at her. Yep, she looked as though she was on the brink of tears; she was definitely not her usual self. Poppy had always been very positive, very upbeat. It was probably all the post-baby sleep deprivation getting to her.

'Poppy.' She reached for Poppy's hands. 'I *did* invent the details of that statistic, but the big picture of it is one hundred per cent true. Hardly anyone goes back to their pre-pregnancy weight within years of giving birth. Look at me. I'm literally a stone and a half heavier than I was before I had Max and I'm obviously not going to lose the weight now, because he's *eleven*. And I never manage to do any exercise. And I never get enough sleep. And I really don't mind. I never think about any of it all.'

She *totally* minded. She'd love to get a full eight hours at night, at least occasionally, but it was difficult getting to bed on time when combining full-time work and single-motherhood. And she'd like to lose a bit of weight. If only she had any willpower to do some proper exercise and give up chocolate and cake. And crisps, obviously. Speaking of which, she could murder a packet of salt and vinegar right now.

She looked up and caught Raf smirking at her. The look on his face totally implied he thought she was lying.

'Seriously,' Georgie said. 'Does anyone *like* you when you do the Mr Human-Lie-Detector thing?'

'Lots of people do.' He gave a pantomime wink.

Georgie raised her eyes to the ceiling. Ow. That hurt, and the ceiling looked all swirly. It must be because she wasn't used to still being up at 2 a.m.

'But Georgie, it suits you,' said Poppy. 'You've got the whole Marilyn Monroe amazing hourglass figure and beautiful face thing going on. I haven't. Oh. I've just realised. You think I should buy bigger clothes.'

'No, I really, really don't.' Georgie put her hand on her forehead. It was still hurting a bit, even now she wasn't looking upwards. 'You look great. Honestly. You do.'

'You really do,' Beth and Ankita agreed simultaneously.

'You've always looked like you should be a model,' said Beth, 'and you still do.'

'An ugly, plus-sized one.' Poppy sniffed. 'With falling-out hair and bags under her eyes.'

'They're all telling the truth.' Raf was megawatt-smiling again. Not too megawatt, though. Just the right amount. 'You do look fantastic.'

And, again, Poppy produced an actual smile of her own.

'So who's made any New Year's resolutions?' asked Georgie. It was definitely time to change the subject. 'I have. Lots.'

'Me too,' said Ankita, 'which I don't normally do.'

'There's no point.' Poppy's smile had gone. 'I wouldn't keep them. I'm too tired and too bored.'

'Poppy, darling.' Beth put her arms round her, causing some of her hair to dip into the wine in Poppy's glass. 'Do you think you'd be happier if you went back to work?'

'I said I'd take a year's maternity leave. I can't desert Daniel.'

'What about just a day or two a week?' said Georgie. 'It wouldn't be deserting him. I started teaching three days a week when Max was six months old and he loved nursery. And it was fantastic for me because we still spent the majority of the week together but I got to have that break from full-time parenting when I was at work. I bet you could find a one- or two-day-a-week locum job. Maybe at the village surgery with Declan?'

Poppy shook her head. 'I don't think so.'

'Why don't you make it your New Year's resolution just to think about it and make a couple of enquiries?' suggested Raf. 'You don't have to *do* it. Just ask.'

'Maybe I will.' Poppy's forehead was wrinkled a bit, like she was actually thinking about it. Seriously. The Raf effect was ridiculous. 'Maybe just one day a week would be okay for Daniel.'

'I think it definitely would. And I don't think we should have *maybes* about our resolutions this year.' Georgie reached for the Prosecco and topped up all their glasses. Wow, they'd finished *another* bottle. 'I think we should *definitely* do them.'

She really did want to sort herself out with a healthier lifestyle before she turned thirty-five, which was only just over ten months away.

'Oh, oh, oh, I know!' she said. 'We should *make* each other do them.'

'How, though?' Ankita asked.

Georgie waved her empty glass at her. 'Write them down and make each other stick to them. Simple.'

Ankita shook her head. 'We've tried that before. It doesn't work. We need a penalty of some kind. Something that will properly *make* us.'

'I've been on my feet for hours. I need a rest.' Noah, who was the landlord and Raf's cousin, and who they'd all known forever, put two more bottles of Prosecco and two of red wine down on the table, and squeezed his giant frame into the corner of the three-seater sofa that Beth and Ankita were sitting on. 'What are we talking about?'

'Resolutions.' Beth smiled at him. 'We all want to make some and we're trying to work out how to make ourselves keep them.'

'What are yours?' asked Noah.

Beth screwed up her face. 'I don't totally want to say.'

'Beth,' said Raf. 'Are you saying that you have a *secret*?'

'Kind of.'

'Which is akin to lying by omission?' Raf smirked.

'Not always,' Georgie said. She knew that because she was fast becoming the queen of actual lying by omission *and* secrets, and she didn't like it.

Raf raised his eyebrows at her. Like he could almost tell what she was thinking.

Georgie raised her own eyebrows right back at him. He did *not* know what she was thinking.

'Okay.' Noah finished topping up everyone's glasses. 'What's the Failed Resolution Penalty going to be?'

'Don't know.' Ankita's brow was furrowed in thought. 'It has to be a proper punishment.'

'Obviously,' said Raf, 'it should be secret-related. Everyone has to divulge their biggest secret if they don't keep their resolutions.'

'That could work.' Ankita reached for the red wine. She always liked to mix her drinks because she always maintained that it stopped hangovers (it never did). 'But how will we do that practically?'

'Brainwave, brainwave, brainwave,' yelled Poppy, looking a lot livelier all of a sudden. 'We write our secrets down and put them in envelopes and give them to someone else.'

'Yes, yes, yes.' Georgie was very impressed. 'And if we don't keep our resolutions the secret envelope gets opened and the secret is read out.'

'Another brainwave,' Poppy screeched. 'We should all address an envelope to ourselves and then pass the envelope to the left and put our secrets in, seal the envelopes and then—' she paused and everyone stared at her in anticipation '—*post* them.'

'Nice.' Raf nodded.

'And we have to record the resolutions now and then prove we kept them,' Noah said. 'Photographic evidence.'

'We can set up a chat and send the photos to it.' Poppy was still shouting very excitably.

'Clever.' Beth nodded. 'And we reconvene here in exactly one year's time to open the envelopes.'

'We need to drink to this,' commanded Ankita.

Noah filled everyone's glasses, again, and then they all went for a down-in-one, just as Declan, Poppy's husband, pushed open the pub's main door and made his way over to them.

'Just finished my on-call shift,' he said.

Amazingly, it took Declan no time at all to understand what they were doing, even though everyone was talking at once. Maybe it was because he was incredibly clever, or maybe it was because he was incredibly sober.

'Let's get writing.' Beth did a little burp.

'Wait.' Ankita held a finger up. 'They have to be SMART.'

'Smart?' repeated Poppy, except it sounded like *Shmart*.

'Specific, Measurable, Achievable, Relevant and Timely,' dictated Ankita.

Georgie nodded. Ow, that hurt her head again.

Poppy sighed. 'I'll never manage that.'

Beth smiled and said, 'You're very wise, Ankita.'

Raf grinned at them all.

Noah, who'd always been an opening-his-throat expert, had already downed a pint and returned from getting paper, pens, envelopes and stamps while everyone else was still drinking. 'The stamps are so that we can post them to each other tonight so we don't renege in the morning,' he said, handing stationery out to everyone.

'We have to write our resolutions down too,' Ankita instructed. 'We can seal those all together in a separate envelope.'

Georgie wrote her address carefully on her envelope. She was pleased that she could focus enough to write, because just now she'd been struggling to see only one of everybody and the floor had seemed a really long way away.

The fire's flames were nice, though. Very flamey. And fiery. And flamey. Nice. Very nice.

Right, she needed to think of a secret.

Well, she didn't need to *think* of a secret. Because for the past week and a half she'd had the *mother* of all secrets.

It only took about a minute to write it down and seal the envelope. It was easy to write her resolutions too, because they were the same every year:

Lose exactly one stone. Run a minimum of two miles a minimum of twice a week for an entire year. Give up chocolate completely. Only eat two packets of crisps and two slices of cake a week. And only one pizza a month. Go to bed by eleven at least four nights a week. Plus stop pulling grey hairs out in case it was true that about three million grew in the place of each one. And finally, because Poppy had been looking miserable on each of the three times she'd seen her this week, she wrote that she had to cheer her up. By Valentine's Day (six weeks seemed like a reasonable length of time to do it in), to make it SHMART.

And then she added an extra final one for good measure: she was going to take up yoga. It needed to be measurable. She was going to go once every two weeks.

And, actually, she wouldn't mind learning Italian. Beth had suggested camping next summer. It would be *amazing* to camp in Italy and be able to speak Italiano. Or Italiana. Or whatever it was. She'd *know* what it was soon. Exciting. They could go on a city break to Rome or Florence or Venice too. What would make it measurable and timely? Oh, she could take a GCSE in it before the end of the year. She could totally manage that if she only had one subject to focus on. Sixteen-year-olds often did eight or more subjects at once. She tapped her head as she was sitting there, pleased with her own clever thinking.

And finally, really finally, she wouldn't mind learning to ice skate. It needed to be measurable. Okay, she was going to learn to do a jump on ice before the end of the year. Torvill and Dean, here she came.

Okay. Finished.

She sealed her secret in the envelope that Raf, who was sitting on her right, had just handed her, and said, 'Done. Who's ready to come to the postbox?'

Everyone else except Raf was still writing, or thinking. Georgie started laughing.

'I'll come with you.' Raf stood up. 'What's funny?'

'People have got their thinking faces on,' Georgie hiccupped. 'They look very, very funny.'

Raf smiled at her. She thought he did, anyway, because neither of the images she could see of him were that clear. 'Come on. Maybe some fresh air will stop your hiccups.'

They opened the door and discovered that for once the weather forecast had been right. It had been snowing while they were inside.

'It's beautiful.' Georgie concentrated hard on walking down the steps. 'The snowflakes are very flakey.'

Oops, it was a lot more slippery than she'd expected. And she was wearing her favourite wedge-heeled ankle boots, which had zero grip. Raf stood her up straight and held out his arm for her to take.

'Thank you, kind sir.' He was very tall. 'Your arm's very strong,' she said, as they walked round the village green to the postbox on the opposite side from the pub. 'It's got very nice muscles.' She gave them a little squeeze.

Raf was laughing. 'I'm going to get you a nice pint of water when we get back inside,' he said.

It was very slippery again next to the postbox.

'Slide, slide, slide.' Georgie was swishing her feet backwards and forwards. Raf caught her just as she started to spin through the air.

'You should only have swished one foot at a time.'

'You're very wise.' Georgie wagged a finger at him. 'I'm going to remember that for next time.' She looked up at him.

She hadn't kissed anyone since Max's conception, exactly twelve years ago to the night. Raf had very kissable-looking lips.

'I like you,' she said.

'I like you too. And you are very, very drunk, so we're going to have a little walk all the way round the green and then we're going to get you some water.'

By the time they got back inside, everyone except Beth had finished.

'She's writing a bloody essay.' Ankita was tapping the table a little impatiently with her pen. 'She's on her third side of A4.'

'It's important to explain things fully,' said Beth. 'And I've almost finished now.'

'Here you go.' Raf placed two pint glasses of water down in front of Georgie. 'I think you might feel better in the morning if you drink this now.'

'Thank you,' said Georgie happily. 'You're very nice.'

She downed the first one.

'That was quite watery,' she said.

'That's water for you,' said Raf, grinning. 'Have the other one.'

'Okay.' Georgie downed that one too, a bit more slowly. Then she slid down onto the sofa next to the fire and closed her eyes.

* * *

'Georgie, wake up,' she heard Ankita say some time later through a bit of a fog.

'Mmph.' Georgie dragged her eyes open. 'Ow, my head hurts.'

'Mine too.' Ankita pulled her arm. 'Beth's finished. Time to go home.'

'Okay.'

Wow. When they got outside, the air was so cold it was like it was biting into your forehead.

Georgie took a couple of steps along the icy path and then suddenly *remembered*. She stopped still and Beth bumped into her from behind.

Oh fuck. Fuck, fuck *fuck*.

'Are you okay?' Beth asked.

No. She really was not. She'd made a monumental mistake.

Fuck.

'Fine,' she said in a strangled voice. 'Night.'

And she dashed off across the village green to her mum's house as fast as she could, only nearly breaking her ankle on the ice about five times on the way.

New Year's Day was *not* going to be Happy.

2

GEORGIE

Seven hours later, Georgie typed '*And...*' into a note on her phone, and then paused with her finger in the air. And *what*? She was *sure* there was one more resolution she was missing. She'd obviously put her usual ones down. But then she'd put some more down. She remembered thinking that she was very cunning and that if someone was going to make her stick to her resolutions this year she might as well take full advantage.

She'd definitely written yoga down.

And learning a language, she was pretty sure. She'd thought about holidays. She and Beth had been talking earlier in the evening about camping together in the summer holidays in France, Spain or Italy, and she was sure she'd written down French, Spanish or Italian. Which one, though?

And then there was something else. She had a feeling it had been something to do with her surroundings. What, though? Something related to the pub? The date? What they'd been drinking? The decor? Who knew?

She shook her head in frustration and winced as an invisible clamp seemed to settle around her forehead.

What was she going to *do*?

It would be a disaster if she couldn't remember all the resolutions. There was no way Ankita would let any of them get away with this. There was no question that they'd all be sitting in the pub next thirty-first of December reading out their lists, which could be a very bad thing.

Even worse, what if someone somehow opened the envelope *now*?

Her mind was whirling from the many possible ramifications – all bad.

She needed so much to work out whether her secret was *true*, and as soon as possible. How, though?

She typed *language* and *surroundings* into her phone and then lay back and stared at the ceiling above the bed.

Okay. She needed to clear her head so she could *think*.

She needed to get hold of the resolutions envelope and check what she'd written. *Or* she needed to get the secret envelope back somehow. Because whether or not it was right it wasn't a good thing to have written it down and put it out there. What if Raf opened it out of curiosity? He was Noah's cousin, and she'd known Noah forever, and he *seemed* nice and trustworthy, but what if he wasn't? Or what if, somehow, someone *else* opened it?

Eurgh, she'd vomited bile into her mouth at that thought.

Right. She needed to do something.

Going for a run would be the best way to clear her head *and* it would tick one thing off the resolutions list. At the very least she had to make sure she wouldn't have to read the secret out next New Year's Eve. So she needed to ignore her throbbing head and churning stomach and get herself into her Lycra and go and get some of those endorphins that fit people raved about, and then make a plan.

She opened her barely used running app, mapped out an exactly two-mile-long circular route starting from the front door, pushed her duvet down and swung her legs round and off the bed. And nearly threw up.

Yep, realistically, no amount of endorphins would be enough of a miracle drug to make her feel good today.

It was lucky she'd packed her as-new Lycra for the weekend. She always took it if she and Max went away for New Year's, just in case. Obviously in normal years she never put it on in the end because you never felt up to a run on New Year's Day. Or the next day. And so on, until before you knew it another year of no running had gone by. But this was not a normal year.

Actually getting her running tights on turned out to be a challenge in itself. Sitting on the edge of her bed, with the tights dragged up just above her knees, she pulled the waistband as far round towards the front as she could and squinted at the label. Yep, they were a good two sizes too small. *Maybe* with all the resolutions she was about to keep they'd actually fit her soon.

Her Met Office app told her that it was two degrees outside, so she could wear her puffer jacket to hide her unappealingly squished thighs and only-halfway-up-her-bottom leggings. Ideal.

Once she'd manhandled herself into her sports bra and poured herself into her running top, her childhood full-length wall mirror confirmed that head-to-toe too-small Lycra was indeed not her best look. It made her limbs look very... dimply.

She stepped closer to the mirror and peered at her head. Yep, she had a couple more grey hairs. She reached up and... did not pull them out. Instead, she angled her phone camera and took a photo of them and her empty hand for the resolution record, then posted it to the 'Resolutions' chat they'd set up last night, noting smugly that she was the first person to post anything on there.

Nice. And wow she was pretty sure that she had a tiny rush of endorphins from the smugness.

Okay. Time to go. She'd better act normal and say morning to everyone even though there was a hideous possible sword of Damocles poised above her aching head.

Max, her mother and stepfather were all eating a fry-up in the kitchen.

'Happy New Year,' she said, trying not to gag at the smell of oil.

'Bacon and eggs?' asked her stepfather.

'Actually, I wouldn't mind a bacon sandwich.' She never mentioned bacon in her resolutions, so she was totally fine to have it, and there was no hangover that a bacon sarnie couldn't help. 'In about fifteen minutes, if that's okay.' Fifteen minutes. Two miles. Nope, not a hope in hell. 'Actually, probably in about half an hour. Maybe forty minutes. I'm just popping out first.'

'Mum, are you wearing *running kit*?' Max was staring at her.

'Yep.' Georgie gave what was hopefully a nonchalant-looking shrug.

'Sick,' said Max.

Sick was about right. Georgie hadn't felt this nauseous since she was pregnant.

'Happy New Year.' Her mother looked up from her magazine. 'Enjoy your... What? Where are you going now?'

Georgie winced. Her family's voices were *really* hurting her head.

'Just a run,' she said.

Max and her stepfather were both staring at her. Fair enough; neither of them had ever witnessed her go for a run before.

'Oh.' Her mother frowned. 'You'll be back to look after Max, though, won't you? We're having a family New Year's lunch.'

'Yes, I will.' Georgie spoke loudly to try to divert Max's attention but it didn't work.

'Do you mean you're having a family lunch without us?' he asked.

'Yes. An all-day thing, actually. Evening, too.' Her mother wasn't even *looking* at him – her grandson – as she spoke; she was concentrating on her magazine again. 'Us and the girls and Alfie.'

The girls were her other two daughters, Georgie's half-sisters, Lauren and Lottie, and Alfie was Lauren's baby.

'But we're in your family,' Max persisted.

'Not in *our* family.' Georgie's mum turned a page. 'I mean just our little nuclear family.'

'You can come if you like,' Georgie's stepfather said after a pause, during which Georgie's mother had continued to read her magazine.

Georgie battled with herself not to say *How dare you treat my son like that* and just about won.

'That's a *really* lovely invitation.' She knew her voice was laced with anger and she didn't care. 'But we're meeting our friends in the pub. My best friends. A different kind of family.' She looked at Max. She *really* didn't want to leave him now but for his sake as much as anyone's, she had to attempt to stick to her resolutions. 'I'll be back soon,' she told him. 'You can play FIFA while I'm out if you like. I love you.'

She had to try very hard not to slam the kitchen door shut behind her. If there was one thing she hated even more than being second best to both her parents' new families, it was them making Max feel second best. How *could* they? Thank goodness for her friends, who were more like family than her actual family had ever been.

And because she loved her friends, she was going to get out there now and run her two miles and then make a plan.

After a bit more severe pain, whilst she bent down to do up the laces of her pristine, never-before-used, at least five-year-old running shoes, her waistband digging into her bladder area and her head feeling as though it was going to explode, she let herself out of the house. As she went, she took a quick selfie and posted it to the chat, feeling smug all over again when she saw that still no one else had posted anything in there.

If you had to go running, it was a beautiful day for it: frosty, with light, powdery snow falling, but with a blue sky and the sun peeping through from behind pale grey cotton-wool clouds. The setting was amazing too. Georgie hadn't really appreciated it when she was growing up, but as an adult she recognised every time she visited how chocolate-box perfect Melting Bishop was. All the houses were eighteenth- and nineteenth-century honey-coloured Cotswold stone, set either round the village green or in windy little roads off the green. Her mother and stepfather's house, where she and Max were staying for the weekend, was wide, low and double-fronted, with views across the green from the front, and over their garden and open fields from the back windows.

Her eye alit on the postbox on the edge of the green.

She should google whether it was legal for posties to give letters back to you if you lay in wait for them when they came to collect mail. Although she'd need to think about that because, since the address on the envelope was in Raf's handwriting, it would be tricky to prove that she'd written it without showing Jack, the postman, the letter itself, which she obviously wasn't going to do; he'd been the village postman as long as she could remember and knew everyone.

Maybe it would be safer to convince Raf to give the letter back to her unopened after it was delivered. *How*, though? He lived in *New York*.

She heard herself moan out loud. It was all so complicated.

She jogged across the green and around the pond in its centre, enjoying her trainered feet crunching the lovely, untouched, crisp snow, and really not enjoying the way that every step caused her head to pound. By the time she got to the pub opposite, her heart was pounding too, she was boiling, and every step felt like an effort. She ran round the corner of the pub and straight into a much larger person.

Her feet lost their grip and she started to fall, until strong arms caught her and stood her upright. Raf's voice, sounding a little sniggery, said, 'Morning. Would running be one of your resolutions?'

Georgie had a flashback to last night and the same strong arms stopping her from falling over next to the postbox. And, oh no, no, no, she'd *commented* on his arms, and his muscles. In fact, she'd practically sexually harassed him. He was a lawyer and therefore probably litigious.

She could see the headlines in the *Bristol Telegraph* now. 'School deputy head loses job after drunkenly sexually harassing New York lawyer.' If she'd had any breath left for it, she'd have groaned. She should say something, apologise maybe, but she really couldn't talk. She also needed to keep running or she'd never get going again.

'Resolution,' she managed to say. 'Got to go.'

'I'm out for a run, too. Want to run together?'

She so, so didn't.

'Too slow for you.'

'Not at all. It would be nice to have the company.'

'Great.' Georgie tried to smile.

They jogged together down the lane, with Raf, not sounding in any way as if he was making any physical effort or as if he was hungover, chatting about the snow and the village, and Georgie grunting on her side of the conversation.

The lane was long. Really, really long. Georgie's chest was *so* hot; it was like it had a clamp round it. She was sure she was going to vomit. This was what marathon runners must feel like twenty-six miles in.

At the end of the lane was a stile and on the other side of the stile was a hill. And Raf was still next to her. He climbed over it, giving her an excellent view of his toned legs, which, despite all the thoughts whirring in her head, she could still appreciate.

'Want a hand?' He turned round and held an arm out towards her.

'I'm fine, thanks,' she panted.

'You sure? I'm very *strong*.' He was outright laughing now. '*Muscly*.'

She should just be grateful that he probably wasn't going to sue her. She gave what she hoped was a dignified smile.

'Honestly, I really am fine, thanks. You go.' She waved vaguely at the hill.

'No, this is nice.' He was still laughing. 'Companionable.'

Georgie didn't have the energy to care now. She was too busy putting one foot in front of the other and not throwing up. The hill was really, really steep. Her thighs were already aching and, weirdly – and not pleasantly – so were her bum cheeks. Raf seemed absolutely fine.

The one good thing about his presence was that it meant that Georgie had to keep on running. Eventually they arrived at the top of the hill and started going down the other side. That was a lot better, until Georgie's stitch set in.

'You okay?' asked Raf.

'Stitch.'

'You need to keep on running through it.'

Georgie didn't answer. She couldn't speak.

Eventually, they arrived back at the pub. Georgie stopped and nearly fell over, her legs now turned to jelly. She was unbelievably hot but she absolutely couldn't take her coat off in front of Raf. Her head was miraculously better so maybe some of those endorphins had indeed kicked in. Or maybe it was only better relative to the rest of her.

'Well done,' Raf said.

Georgie couldn't reply.

She was so hot now that any minute she was going to have to give in and take her jacket off. And everything was swimming in front of her eyes. Her stomach was going like a washing machine on top spin cycle. And... No. No, no, no. She put her hands to her mouth but nothing could have made a difference at that point. Her stomach gave a huge heave.

She and Raf both stood staring for a while at the lumpy vomit covering his legs and previously blue and green trainers.

She should definitely chew her food more. Especially sweetcorn.

'Better out than in,' said Raf eventually.

* * *

Obviously, the first person Georgie saw when she walked into the pub three hours later was Raf.

'How's your head?' he asked, with a definite smirk. But also a twinkle in his eye, which was good, because there was a strong chance she was going to need him on side, and after the vomit this morning he'd scarpered quite quickly and she'd wondered if he might avoid her forevermore.

'Surprisingly, totally fine. The run and vomit plus some carbs worked wonders. I feel completely normal and I haven't even had to take any paracetamol. How are your trainers?'

'They're totally fine.'

Hmm. They couldn't be, even if they were washable. She was definitely going to have to buy him some new ones. She hoped they weren't super expensive ones but had a suspicion they might be. Raf just *looked* expensive.

'When did you vomit?' Max asked from behind her.

'Hello. I'm Raf.' Raf put out his hand.

In two seconds flat, Max seemed to grow about three inches in height, a couple of inches across the shoulders and four years in age. He put his own hand out and shook Raf's. 'I'm Max.'

And he'd deepened his voice, too.

'Max is my son.' Georgie did not want to discuss the vomit with either of them. 'Max, why don't you go and find the others?'

'So Mum vomited?'

Georgie looked at Raf. Raf looked back at her and raised an eyebrow. Georgie sighed, and waited to see what he'd say.

'Only a little bit,' said Raf. 'And it was understandable.'

'Why?'

'I got the impression it was your mum's first run for a while. It's always hard work the first time. Next time she goes it'll be a lot easier.'

Georgie mouthed, 'Thank you,' and sighed at the thought of *next time* she went running.

She really needed to chat more to Raf to try to gauge whether or not she could maybe just ask for her envelope. But not in front of anyone else.

'How long are you over here for?' she asked instead.

'Another few days. Why, do you fancy going running together again?' He chuckled at his own (weak) joke and Georgie rolled her eyes at him.

'Really not. Just wondered. You need to tell me your shoe size so I can get you new trainers.'

'You are not buying me new trainers.'

'Obviously, I *am* going to buy you new trainers, so you might as well tell me which ones you want so I don't buy ones that you *don't* want, because that would be a total waste of money and you'd feel really bad about being ungrateful and wasteful if you didn't wear them.'

'No, I'd just think you were silly to have bought them when I told you it was completely unnecessary.'

She'd have to ask Noah to sneak a look at Raf's shoes and tell her his size. Although that would mean admitting she'd vomited on the trainers.

That would have been an appropriate level of secret to have written down, had it already happened before last night. *I once vomited on someone's trainers.* A small, non-earth-shattering kind of secret. There were so many things she could happily have put. Eating chocolate spread straight out of the jar with a spoon every evening when Max was in bed. Lying about stealing her mother's lipstick when she was nine. Lusting after Simon Cowell.

Why had she been so stupid?

'Why do you want to buy new trainers for Raf?' asked Max. 'And why did you ask if they go in the washing machine? Mum. Did you *vomit* on Raf's trainers?'

'*Did* you?' Ankita, who'd just appeared from behind Max, sounded very gleeful.

'Did she what?' Poppy, Declan and Daniel were behind Ankita.

'Vomit on Raf's trainers.' Ankita could be very annoying at times.

'Unfortunate.' Raf shook his head sorrowfully. 'You shouldn't have persisted about buying new ones.'

'Yes, I vomited on Raf. Why don't we go and find our table?' Georgie started to edge towards the dining part of the pub to try to stop all the *hilarious* vomit-related chat.

'Can I bring drinks to your table?' asked Raf. 'Hair of the dog, Georgie?'

'I'm drinking water.' She could still hear Raf laughing even when she'd walked away and sat down with her back to him.

'So, did anyone else go for a run this morning?' she asked. 'Why haven't any of you added any photos to the chat yet?'

Ankita and Declan had both been running, but that was no surprise, because they were both regular exercisers; Ankita hadn't even bothered with any fitness-related resolutions.

'So neither of you had running as one of your resolutions?' she asked Poppy and Beth. 'I thought you had an exercise resolution every year? I've spent my entire adult life wanting to be about a billion times fitter than I actually am, so it's always on my list.'

'Me too, normally.' Poppy was looking no less gloomy than she had last night. 'But next year. I hope. I'm still breastfeeding for the next few months. And I feel so unfit that I don't think I could even work my way up to a jog at the moment. And obviously I wouldn't fit into any of my running kit.'

'No, honestly, if I can go for a run, so can you. I mean, I actually vomited at the end, that's how unfit I am. And my running kit's way, *way* too small. I *know* that I'm going to sound like a slap-me-now-instant-fitness-evangelist, but we could go together. When we've both bought some new kit. You honestly *cannot* be more unfit than I am.'

'I don't think so. I'm *unbelievably* unfit.'

'So am I. I *vomited*. And it wasn't because I was hungover, it was because of the run and because I was too hot.' Georgie looked round but there was no sign of Raf. She was fairly sure that if he told Poppy she could run she'd be in her jogging kit within the hour.

'I'm sure you could go running, sweetheart.' Declan was smiling at his wife. 'The most surprising people can work their way up to running very long distances from a very low starting point.'

'Thank you.' Poppy did not return his smile. 'A very low starting point. The most surprising people. Thank you.'

Georgie stared at her, alarmed. Poppy never sounded bitter like this.

'No.' Declan shook his head, looking as alarmed as Georgie felt. 'I didn't mean it in a bad way. Just that you've just had a baby so you haven't had the opportunity to do any running recently.'

Poppy didn't smile at all. What had happened?

Declan was still shaking his head, looking a bit swivel-eyed worried.

'What about you, Beth?' Georgie asked, panicked. Running was clearly too contentious a topic.

'I decided to do swimming and yoga instead. And I don't have any other resolutions other than one big one, which is also my secret so I can't tell you about it.' Beth was *not* good with secrets; she'd tell them all by the end of the month, if not the week, Georgie was sure.

'Is Dominic joining us?' asked Ankita. Dominic was Beth's fiancé. He wasn't the kindest person and Ankita had been quite vocal about how she didn't think he was right for Beth.

'No.' Beth's face clouded over for a moment. 'He changed his mind. I think he wants to catch up on some work.'

Ankita raised one eyebrow and pursed her lips, clearly not impressed.

'Speaking of which, I just came for five minutes to say hi.' Declan stood up. 'I need to go and get on with some admin. The amount of paperwork GPs have to complete seems to increase exponentially year on year.'

Georgie snuck a look at Poppy. She in her turn was taking a sideways look at Declan. She was slightly frowning with her eyes narrowed, like she was kind of sizing him up. Really odd. Georgie wasn't exactly a relationship expert, never having actually had a long-term one herself, but in her experience couples did not usually look at each other like that. Although, equally, all couples did argue at times, everyone knew that, and having a baby was a prime time for arguing, with all the pressure of lack of sleep and childcare. That was probably what it was.

'Okay,' she said, to take Poppy's mind off whatever was going on between her and Declan. 'I'm going to talk you all through my vomiting incident in detail now.'

And it worked. Everyone laughed and everything was fine all the way through their roasts.

And then Ankita said, 'Who's got space for pudding?'

'Definitely me.' Georgie reached for the menu. 'I earnt it with that run.'

'I can't,' Poppy said. 'Resolution.'

'What? No puddings at all?' Ankita asked. 'For a year?'

'No. None.'

'Wow.'

'It's easy for you to look incredulous,' Poppy snapped, 'with your model metabolism.'

'I...' It was rare for Ankita to be lost for words.

'I don't want one,' Beth rushed in.

'Me neither.' Georgie pushed her menu away. She didn't know what was going on with Poppy but it was clearly more important than the sticky toffee pudding she'd been planning to have.

'Oh, Ankita, I'm so sorry.' Poppy's eyes were filling. 'I'm a witch. Ignore me.'

'*No*,' they all chorused. 'Not a witch.'

Georgie was casting around in her mind for something to say to diffuse the emotion when Raf came over.

'Noah's told me to have a rest.' He drew up a chair. 'And I said yes. Bar work is *hard*.' He turned to Poppy. 'Daniel is ridiculously cute.'

Poppy actually beamed. Seriously. The Raf Effect was ridiculous.

And then Poppy's smile dropped again and she pushed her chair back. 'I should go. Daniel should go down for his afternoon sleep.'

'He looks quite happy at the moment,' said Ankita.

They all looked over at Daniel. He and Max were on the floor together. Max was doing monkey imitations and Daniel was laughing and laughing. Georgie's heart clenched with worry.

'Max is lovely with Daniel, isn't he?' Poppy said, sounding quite sentimental. Georgie nodded. She was starting to feel really sick again. 'But, no, we have to go. Routine is everything with babies. Apparently. And it's one of my resolutions and I am *not* revealing my secret. Yet, anyway.'

Wow. From the look on Poppy's face it looked as though her secret could almost rival Georgie's. Georgie frowned, grappling with that thought, and then shook her head.

'Photos, then.' She pulled a face and pointed her phone at Poppy. 'Hold the pudding menu and look worthy.' She snapped and then sent the photo to the chat. 'And when you have Daniel in his buggy and you're on your way out I'll take one of you then too.'

As Raf stood to help Poppy out of the door and down the steps with the buggy, Ankita stage-whispered, 'Georgie, he's gorgeous and I think he might like you.'

'Yes.' Beth nodded vigorously. 'I think he might be over his wife.'

Raf had very tragically lost his wife to cancer about five years ago and had moved to New York quite soon afterwards.

No way was Georgie going to contemplate any kind of involvement with someone who was probably still grieving – that was a second-best situation straight off – and also he lived in the US, and she lived in Bristol.

'Nonsense,' she said briskly.

'No, I really think he does,' Ankita insisted. 'You *must* like him, too? Like, who wouldn't?'

'No,' Georgie began. And then she stopped. She really needed to get her envelope back from him. Which would involve her convincing him to post it to her. Or just bin it. But how would she get proof that he'd definitely done that? If she *did* need to spend any time with him trying to convince him, her friends thinking that she liked him would be an excellent smoke-screen. And she was *sure* he wouldn't like her in that way, so it wasn't like she'd be leading him on. 'A bit,' she said, aiming for coyness.

'No *way*,' Ankita screeched.

'No way what?' Raf asked, back from helping Poppy.

'Nothing.' Ankita fluttered her eyelashes at him, which would have made anyone else look, just, odd, but she actually managed to pull it off.

Raf laughed. 'Right.'

'Max, show Ankita and Beth our Christmas Day photos,' Georgie said. And then, as they both turned towards Max, she said to Raf, 'Are you free later? I have kind of a big favour to ask you in private. Max and I are going home tomorrow, so I wondered if we could meet this evening?'

Her mother's cleaner had told her that she was up for babysitting any time this week and she always let Max stay up late and eat a lot of choco-late, so he'd be ecstatic if Georgie went out this evening and left him with her while his grandparents were still out with their 'nuclear family'.

'Let me guess. You want to discuss becoming permanent running partners.'

Georgie laughed. 'Exactly.'

'Yep, no problem. I'm sure Noah will be fine without me this evening. Everyone'll be staying home nursing the remnants of their hangovers and feeling miserable about having to go to work tomorrow. Want to meet here?'

That was a good question. On balance, it would probably be better if they met in a very public place. No one would ever think they would do anything cloak and dagger here in the pub. Also – her mind was working overtime – Raf had said he was staying with Noah, so maybe she could somehow, while she was here, go into Noah's living quarters and get the resolutions envelope *and* check out Raf's trainers so she knew what to buy as a replacement.

'Perfect,' she said. 'Nine p.m.?'

'Great.'

3

POPPY

Poppy's phone pinged and she parked the buggy on the cobbled pavement outside the pub for a moment to check her messages. Maybe it was Declan.

She couldn't decide whether she was pleased or disappointed when she saw that it was actually Ankita. She'd posted a picture of a coffee cup captioned with the word *Decaf* and a strong-arm emoji in their 'Resolutions' chat.

Poppy posted a heart in return. She followed it with a sweaty-brow-big-smile-phew emoji, which was really for herself, because thank goodness *she* hadn't chosen a no-caffeine resolution; without some serious coffee she'd never get through these no-sleep months (and it was definitely going to be months and not years; she was *sure* she'd be able to get Daniel sleeping through the night soon. Fingers strongly crossed).

She frowned. How was she going to manage the next year – year! – without pudding, though? Hmm. She should really have thought that through better. She wondered what everyone else was giving up; some of the others' lists seemed to have extended to *pages*.

Daniel whimpered and then started to up his decibel level and she hastily put her phone back into her bag with one hand and began to jiggle the buggy with the other.

She was actually a bit of a buggy-jiggling superstar now, if she said it herself, because Daniel had a thing for motion.

He also had a deeply impressive sixth sense for those nanoseconds when Poppy might be feeling like an actual human rather than a nappy-changing milk machine. Like the second she sat on the loo, just hoping to wee for twenty seconds in peace, he'd start yelling. Or when she had a jam-no-butter (because that was the quickest to make) sandwich halfway to her mouth and truly believed she was going to chew in peace, maybe even sitting down, he'd start yelling.

The crying was building now. Understandably, because they'd had a long lunch and it was now way past his afternoon sleep time. It was kind of annoying that the only part of the day where he did have a routine was the afternoon, so she had no choice but to go back to the house and get him into his cot, but she'd have plenty of time to go out in the afternoon when he was older.

She bent down to smile at him and nearly fell over (she really did need to get fitter again).

'Home soon and I'll feed you and then you can sleep.'

He reached out for her and cooed and her heart squeezed at the sheer perfection of him. She made the face that always made him laugh and he gurgled and then went for a full-on chortle as she continued pulling faces. She was pretty sure that if she could bottle his laugh she could make a lot of people happy; it was literally the best sound ever created and you couldn't fail to feel cheerier while you were listening to it.

They carried on with the faces and the gorgeous laughter until her knees started hurting and she had to stand up. Daniel immediately resumed his yelling and she immediately started re-jiggling the buggy until he quietened down. Her bending-down abilities might not be up to much right now but her arm muscles definitely had to be benefiting from all the buggy-pushing.

Ouch. Her head hurt and bumping the buggy over the cobbles was not helping. She actually had a bit of a perma-headache nowadays, which was almost certainly because she never got more than a couple of hours' sleep in a row. It was usually low-level but every so often it flared up into a proper, full-on, desperate-for-darkness-and-a-cold-flannel-and-complete-silence monster one, bordering on a proper migraine, a word which, as a GP, she didn't bandy about lightly.

She was heading into monster ache territory now. For a number of reasons. In no particular order:

1. Hangover. Her first big night out for over seven months, accompanied by too much Prosecco, was always going to make her feel bad the next day.

2. Even more sleep deprivation than usual. She normally slept like the dead between Daniel's feeds but last night she'd had so much to think about that she'd lain awake for hours trying to sort through the thoughts jumbling against each other in her head. The idea that they all had secrets from each other. Even though it wasn't really a surprise, it was kind of shocking to articulate it. They didn't see each other as much as they used to, given that she'd been living in Australia for three years before Daniel was born, and she, Declan and Daniel had only arrived back in the UK a couple of weeks ago, and obviously Georgie, Beth and Ankita were busy with their own lives too, but they were still best friends. Who all had big enough secrets that they'd keep usually unkeepable resolutions for a whole year to avoid divulging the secrets. It was sad to think that however much you loved your best friends you could get to a point where you were too busy or too miserable to confide in them any more. Which brought her on to Declan. Was he or was he not having an affair?

3. Stress. Because, again, was Declan having an affair? Writing down '*I think Declan's having an affair*' and sealing it in an envelope had felt huge, and once she'd written it she'd spent last night revisiting all the moments where he'd been behaving *really* weirdly around her. It had started a few days after they got back to the UK. Sometimes he was really distracted and sometimes he was his usual lovely self, in fact even lovelier than usual, like, for example, husbands reputedly were when they were feeling guilty about an affair.

4. Resolutions. More stress. If she didn't keep them she'd have to admit that she'd written down her Declan-affair worry. Which – obviously – might by next Christmas be common knowledge, if it was true. But on the off chance that it *wasn't*, what a terrible thing to have written, and it should remain secret forever. So this year she couldn't have any desserts *at all* and she had to lose two stone, she had to get Daniel to sleep through the night by his first birthday in May, she had to cook a new dish every week (so ridiculously over-ambitious) and she had to learn to hula and *do the splits* (life lesson: never promise to achieve an unachievable life ambition).

5. Declan. Just, Declan.

Also:

1. Was she going mad? Talking to herself in numbered points in her head.
2. Ha, yes, she probably was. Ridiculous.

The buggy suddenly lurched, and the front stopped while the back carried on going with the impetus of her pushing. For a split second she thought the whole thing was going to flip over onto the ground with Daniel underneath and her on top, but then she managed to stop herself and pull the buggy back towards her.

As she bent, heart racing, in front of Daniel to check that he was alright (he seemed completely unfazed, thank heavens), she heard Beth call from the pub doorway.

'Are you okay, Pops darling? I heard you scream.' Beth was always so sweet.

'Oh, thank you, lovely Beth. Yes, we're fine. I just caught one of the buggy's wheels in a cobble and we nearly fell over, but all good.'

'Oh my goodness. I'm glad you didn't fall. Are you sure you're okay? Can I tempt you back into the pub to help you recover? I'm *sure* there'll be a loophole in your resolutions so you can eat pudding if you've just had an incident.'

Poppy laughed. 'I'd love to come back but Daniel should go down for his sleep.' Did that sound lame? 'And I've got lots to do.'

She did not have lots to do. Nothing interesting, anyway. She did have a mountain of laundry and a lot of tidying to do but those were a permanent feature of her life nowadays. It was hard to keep on top of things when you were always tired. Why *was* she going home, actually? Did it really matter if Daniel missed a bit of sleep as a one-off given that at night he essentially had no routine? And she'd been enjoying herself. Okay, yes, she was going to go back in.

But as she opened her mouth to say so, Beth flew down the steps, gave her a huge hug, and said, 'Love you, Pops. I'm so glad you're back. Let's get together again very soon,' and then said, 'Wow, it's cold without a coat,' before running back up the steps.

Georgie appeared behind her.

'Is everything okay?' Georgie poked her head round Beth's. 'I remember what it was like when Max was little. You're always desperate for them to have a sleep and you're shit scared, oops, sweary—' she made a silly face and did a big eye swivel in Daniel's direction, definitely on purpose for a bit of comic effect, which suddenly made Poppy feel as though Georgie felt she needed to be cheered up; did *everyone* think she was miserable? '—of ruining their routine.'

Georgie was always so nice and so comforting. Except it wasn't comforting because firstly Poppy did not want people to think she needed to be comforted and secondly, unlike your average baby – and Poppy really should know this, because it was the kind of thing that GPs knew – Daniel did not have a frigging routine outside his afternoon sleep. Unless you could call going ballistic when he was tired and religiously waking up a minimum of every two hours at night a routine.

'It must be so difficult.' Ankita was in the doorway too now, with a very soft un-Ankita-like expression on her face. Poppy looked at her perfect hair, perfect make-up, perfect pale grey cashmere jumper, beautifully tailored navy cigarette pants and mega-expensive-looking navy suede boots. If Ankita ever did motherhood, it would be Notting Hill yummy-mummy style and her baby would be in an amazing sleep routine immediately.

Poppy nearly sighed out loud in envy of Ankita's not-yet-even-conceived perfectly sleeping baby.

'Come here.' Ankita stepped forward and gave her a hug. Oh no. Poppy felt the tiredness-related (and maybe Declan-related) tears that had recently seemed to be regularly bubbling away just under the surface rise towards the rim of her eyes. She sniffed, hard. She couldn't ruin the exclusive cashmere jumper with tears, plus it would be embarrassing to cry. 'Are you sure you're okay?'

'Yes, of course.' Poppy smiled brightly, hoping that the smile looked convincing.

Raf had been right about the lying-every-ten-minutes thing. When had she started lying to her friends?

And *why* was she lying now? Why couldn't she just admit that occasionally she wasn't sure that she was alright? That sometimes she was absolutely desperate for some proper sleep and that she was worried, actually terrified, almost out of her mind, that Declan was having an affair. When they were younger, she'd have just told the others, they'd have hugged her, they'd have said lovely things, and everything would have felt a lot better. But now... No, she just couldn't get the words out.

She *should* tell them that actually she was going to wheel Daniel around until he went to sleep and then carry the buggy into the pub and have fun with her friends while he slept next to her. Except what if someone said something about Declan or sleep and she cried or something? Yep, no, she was going back to the house.

'Bye. Happy New Year!' She blew kisses at her friends, determined not to look miserable. She *wasn't* miserable, apart from about Declan. Daniel was beyond wonderful. Motherhood was also wonderful. Just a little bit tiring and occasionally a little bit lonely, that was all.

'Love you, Pops,' they all chorused.

'Love you all.' And, eek. Her voice had actually wobbled there. She'd better go quickly.

By the time she'd got over the cobbles without mishap and had negotiated the un-buggy-friendly village green (backwards: a lot easier than forwards over rough terrain), she had her tears pushed firmly back down.

* * *

Declan was in his office when she and Daniel got inside. Poppy hesitated and then decided not to go and tell him they were back, in case he was in one of his distracted moods again. Recently, he'd just seemed... well, not quite *present*. As though, while he was with her in body, he was somewhere else in mind. And she didn't want to assume bad things but she just really felt as though he was thinking about someone else.

Like yesterday, just before she'd gone to the pub, she'd inadvertently been standing behind him while he was at his laptop and he'd closed it really fast and almost snapped at her, and Declan *never* snapped. It had been like he felt guilty about what was on the screen. And then five minutes later he'd been *so* loving and kind as she went out, almost weirdly so. Like he felt guilty. That was part of the reason she'd made the mistake of having so much to drink last night; she'd been drowning her sorrows because she really was beginning to think that it seemed very likely that he'd gone down the clichéd have-an-affair-when-your-wife's-just-had-a-baby route.

A month ago she would never have believed that Declan of all people would do that, but probably a lot of cheated-on new mothers thought that.

An image of him suddenly pushed into her mind, of him sitting in their home office sexting or sex-mailing or whatever it was people did when they had affairs.

She felt tears rise again and sniffed hard, shaking her head and forcing a huge smile for Daniel. She was not going to give in to this misery. *If* Declan was having an affair, she was going to find out, she was going to kick him out and she was going to make an amazing life for her son.

And right now, this afternoon, she wasn't going to think about it any more.

She started singing 'The Wheels on the Bus' to Daniel again as she carried him in the direction of the stairs. Such a sexist song. *The mummies on the bus go chatter, chatter, chatter.* Why was she even singing it? Well, because she was too tired to remember the words of any other nursery rhyme except for 'Three Blind Mice' and that one wasn't exactly child-friendly when you thought about it. What had been *wrong* with all the nursery-rhyme composers of yore?

'Hello, darling,' Declan called.

Poppy stopped walking and waited, despising herself for the fact that, despite her suspicions, she still got a little heart-rush just from the sound of his voice.

And... No. He didn't bother to come and say hello and give her a kiss like he always used to until they'd come back to the UK.

Funny how – even when you still fancied them rotten like you always had and hankered so much after the good times (*wonderful* times) you used to have together – you could really start to almost dislike someone you used to love.

Fatherhood was a lot easier than motherhood. You got to have your gorgeous, perfect baby but you didn't have to get fat, shove the baby out of your vagina, have stitches, breastfeed it, never sleep, stay fat and spend your maternity leave bored out of your mind *and* seemingly lose your husband in the process.

Maybe she'd just pop into the kitchen once Daniel was down for his nap and have a sneaky little Tunnock's Caramel. It wasn't like breaking a resolution was up there with breaking wedding vows, and, yes, Declan, looking at you.

* * *

'Fire!' Poppy tried to scream but she couldn't get the sound out. Then she realised that she must have nodded off in the armchair in the corner of the kitchen. There was something wrong with the washing machine and she'd been trying to find a YouTube video to see if she could fix it herself, and had decided just to have a two-second sit-down before she carried on.

She'd obviously been dreaming about a fire.

Except... She sniffed. Smoke. Her eyes pinged open and she blinked.

On the other side of the room, Declan, wearing his previously-unworn-and-unwanted-Christmas-present butcher's apron and covered (apron, face and arms) in red, brown, green and yellow splodges, was manically looking between Daniel, who was trying to pull himself up to standing on a kitchen chair, and the hob, where he was wafting a tea towel above flames, feeding them rather than putting them out.

Poppy leapt out of her chair, dodged round the table, grabbed another apron from the back of the kitchen door, elbowed Declan out of the way, and smothered the fire with the apron. And then she ran a jugful of water and chucked it on top for good measure.

'Oh, thank God for that,' Declan said. 'You're a genius.'

Poppy nodded slowly as she looked around the insanely messy kitchen. 'Apparently I am. Or you're the worst cook ever born.'

'I mean, maybe a bit of both.' Declan grinned at her and, despite everything she'd been thinking recently, she found herself smiling back at him. He pointed upwards and said with incredulity, 'I got it on the ceiling.'

'Yep.'

'Sorry.' Declan was still looking at her, into her eyes. His expression grew gradually more serious as he continued to gaze at her, for all the world as though he had eyes only for her. A silence, a kind of loaded one, like a maybe-we-kiss moment, grew between them. The moment lengthened and Poppy bit her lip, wondering what she wanted to happen next, and Declan leaned a little closer to her. She was holding her breath, she realised. Was he, were they...

They hadn't kissed a lot since Daniel was born – she'd had a bad birth and the thought of sex had been utterly terrifying initially – and then recently, just as she'd thought that now they were back in England and things might get better for her having her mum and friends nearby, and they might start having sex regularly again, Declan had just been so odd with her that she hadn't been able to bring herself to give in to any temptation to get at all intimate.

He reached his hand round her waist and pulled her gently against him and she felt the same thrill that she always did at his touch and the way he was looking intently into her eyes. Was he really having an affair? Could he really be this duplicitous? Would he really look at her like that if he was seeing someone else? Maybe she *could*...

And then his phone vibrated on the counter next to them and he whipped his arm away from Georgie to snatch up the phone and push it straight into his pocket.

And... *what*? He *never* used to behave like that.

That was *such* a guilty gesture.

The utter humiliation. She'd been about to allow herself to give in to the temptation to kiss him exactly as another woman was probably messaging him.

'Who was that?' she heard herself asking.

'No one.'

'No one? A phantom messager?' She didn't like the way her laugh sounded so horribly brittle.

'Ha. Yes. No. Obviously not *no one*. But no one important. Just Mikey.'

Mikey was his brother. And it was clearly nonsense because why would Declan act like that about a message from him.

'I...' This was the moment. She could *demand* the truth. She *wanted* to demand the truth.

If she weren't so tired and didn't have Daniel to consider, she would.

'I think...' No, she couldn't right now. She needed to work out first what exactly she thought. A side part of her brain wondered at the new woman she'd become; the old Poppy would have just asked. The old Poppy had never felt this drained by life, though.

'Poppy.' Declan reached towards her again and she took a big step away from him and banged her hip hard on the table.

'Oh!' he said, as she said, 'Ouch.'

'Are you okay?' His face showed a mix of concern and slight misery. 'Poppy?'

Could he really be this good an actor?

And then his eyes slid away from hers in a way that was new, and just... suspicious.

She turned to the worktop so that she could close her suddenly tear-filled eyes without him seeing her do it, and heaped the nearest pieces of dirty cutlery into a bowl and put it on the work surface above the dishwasher.

After a pause, Declan said, 'Poppy.' Unbelievably, his tone had returned to normal. It was like Jekyll and Hyde. 'Obviously you are not lifting a finger to clear this mess up. The whole reason I was cooking – *trying* to cook – was to give you a break from constant housework. Obviously I didn't totally succeed but, you know, beans on toast is a great alternative. And before I make the gourmet beans and heated bread, I'm going to have the kitchen sparkling.' He was being so *nice*. But then everyone always said that cheating men often behaved like wonderful partners, to assuage some of their guilt.

'You can't do all of this yourself.' Avoiding looking directly at Declan, she picked Daniel up and kissed him before putting him in his – miraculously still quite clean – highchair and strapping him in and handing him a rattle to distract him while he was waiting for his food. 'It would take you hours.'

'I have hours. No work this evening. I'll do Daniel's tea too.'

'Well... Thank you.' She would, she supposed, feel better for a rest, which could only benefit Daniel, and to give Declan his due, he was an amazing father.

'Okay. I'm going in.' Declan took the destroyed apron off the hob.

They both stared at the pan for quite a long time.

'What *was* that?' Poppy asked eventually, not wanting to engage with him but really curious.

'It was similar to your creamy chicken and cider dish. And I was doing a tomato and olive compote and some green beans with a curry dressing.'

Wow. That would have been a *lot* of flavours on the same plate. Poppy wondered whether it would have all come together deliciously, or... not. It was the thought that counted, of course. But only if the thought came from a place of love and not a place of guilt.

'Sounds as though it would have been lovely,' she said with an effort. 'Thank you.'

'I mean... *Would* have been. Not looking so lovely now.' Declan grimaced in the direction of where something orange had splatted on the wall next to the hob.

Again, *how* could he be acting so normally?

The bone-tired half of Poppy that just wanted a nice life and to pretend that none of the Declan-probably-having-an-affair thing was happening suddenly took over.

'Honestly, it's the thought that counts. Really, thank you.' She looked again at the pan and thought about the contents of their fridge. There had definitely been chicken in there. But cream... 'Where did you find the cream?'

'Those little tubs in the fridge. Looked as though they needed to be used up.'

'Those were *breast milk*.' She'd thought Daniel might need them while she was out yesterday evening but he'd been fine, so she'd been planning to freeze them for a rainy day but hadn't got round to it because of the washing machine.

'*Eurgh*. No offence, but I don't want to drink your breast milk.'

Poppy screwed her face up. 'No. I don't want you to and I also really don't want to drink it myself.'

'That's my genius,' Declan said. 'That's why I started the fire. So we wouldn't have to.'

Poppy rolled her eyes and nearly succeeded in producing a proper 'ha ha, you made a weak joke' smile. 'Of course.'

'I'm going to have it cleared up *so* quickly. I'm going to put the kettle on so you can sit in that chair and I will entertain Daniel and feed him and then do his bath and then you and I will have our beans on toast and I will make them genuinely delicious with the addition of some grated cheddar.'

'Thank you.'

'You probably won't be too happy to hear that one of my resolutions was making new meals regularly,' he told her, seemingly oblivious to the 'are you having an affair because if so I *hate* you' vibes that had to be emanating from her.

'Wow,' she said, not bothering now to smile because the mention of the resolutions was reminding her so strongly of her secret about him cheating. 'I had the same one.'

She glanced at him and discovered that he had his lips slightly pressed together and the beginnings of a frown. Not a look he usually wore. Had the mention of resolutions reminded him of the secrets too? Had he written down the counterpart to hers – that he was having an affair?

She closed her eyes for a moment.

Declan's voice interrupted her misery. 'I need to record my first new meal for the chat.' He pulled his phone from his pocket and took a photo.

Poppy's own phone buzzed and she looked at the picture he'd just sent.

Yep, objectively it was funny. The others would probably laugh a lot when they saw it.

It wasn't funny, though. From the moment they'd met, Declan had literally never once attempted anything more ambitious than beans on toast, his pasta 'special' (literally just pasta with peas, tinned tuna and parmesan) and heating up ready meals. It felt like this had been a guilt-resolution and guilt-cookery.

Looking at his back as he began to scrub at the hob, she couldn't work out which emotion was greater: anger, hurt or just sadness.

Thank heavens she had her friends.

4

GEORGIE

'What would you like to drink?' Raf stood up as Georgie walked towards the fireside armchair he'd been lounging in.

'I'll get them.' She got her purse out of her bag. 'I definitely owe you.'

Raf opted for a pint of bitter. Georgie contemplated a glass of white wine for a second and then ordered a half of lime and soda instead. Her hangover headache still hadn't totally gone and she'd never been a hair-of-the-dog woman.

'Not a hardened drinker, then?' asked Raf, when she sat down opposite him with her drink.

'No. I like a drink, but I don't actually drink that much normally.'

'I got that.'

'Yep. Anyway, Happy New Year.'

'Happy New Year to you too,' he said. 'How are your resolutions going?'

'Pretty good so far. I've kept all of them all day. As you will have seen from the chat. Only three hundred and sixty-four days to go.'

'You're on fire.'

'I know. How are yours going?'

'Also good.' He raised his glass and smiled.

She wondered what he'd written down. She *more* wondered, though, how she was going to get her secret back. Should she just go for it? Just ask him if he could send the envelope back to her?

'So, speaking of the secrets—' obviously they hadn't really been, but she *had* to ask '—I have a little favour to ask...'

She stopped talking. Raf was looking at her, one eyebrow raised.

'Georgie James. Are you...?' He narrowed his eyes at her. 'Are you asking me to return your secret?'

Shit. *Yes*. But, no, now she felt like she couldn't admit she was. What if it made him decide to look at it? She'd known him vaguely most of her life but she didn't actually know him properly at all. She had no idea what he'd do. He might think it would be funny to look at it or something.

'No!' she said. 'Secret? Did I say secret? I meant resolutions.'

'Oh. Right. So, speaking of the resolutions?'

'What?'

'You meant to say, "speaking of the resolutions"?'

'Oh yes.' Eek. Okay. 'Yes, I was just going to say what a great idea the whole thing was.'

Raf nodded. 'Yeah.'

Georgie narrowed her eyes at him and he grinned at her.

'Never seen anyone look so miserable while they say something's a great idea,' he said. 'You're a terrible liar.'

'Excuse me. No, I'm not.' She could totally lie. She did a little head roll and stretch of her shoulders and said, 'You know, I felt really good after our run this morning.' True. 'I really enjoyed it.' Lie. 'If you're still up for it I'd like to go again tomorrow morning, maybe a bit further?' Lie.

'Yep, sure, if you're up for it.'

'Of course I'm bloody not.' She did a comedy exaggerated-eyebrow-raise and eye-roll at him. 'This morning I felt like I was going to pass out and I vomited on you. It was torture. I'm going to torture myself in private next time. I lied and you believed me.'

'Haha, nice lying. I'm impressed.'

'Thank you.'

'Also pleased.' He grinned at her.

'Because everyone lies at least once every ten minutes?'

'Exactly.'

Georgie rolled her eyes at him again and then realised that the conversation was going in the wrong direction. She needed to focus. And, actually, what had she been thinking? It would be completely safe to tell the truth about having forgotten her resolutions. Getting a look at them would be a big step in the right direction.

'Sooooo.' She smiled at him. 'I was a teensy bit drunk last night.'

'No way.'

'Ha. Yes, I was. Anyway, I can't actually remember what I wrote down for my resolutions. I did my usuals but also some extras.'

'Oh, so you really aren't going to be able to stick to them.'

'Exactly.'

'So everyone's going to hear your secret in a year's time.'

It was weird to hear someone say something so potentially horrifying in such a cheerful voice.

'Yes, and I don't want that to happen.' Georgie miraculously had her voice completely steady despite the sudden churning of her stomach. 'Because...' She searched for inspiration. 'Because basically it's very, very embarrassing. Very embarrassing indeed. Extremely embarrassing.'

'I'm not quite sure I get what you're saying.' Raf smiled and she fake-made-a-face at his sarcasm, internally cheering because he *totally* believed the embarrassing thing. 'Would you be embarrassed if we all heard your embarrassing secret?'

'Yes, my embarrassing secret is embarrassing—' she was *good* at this '— and no I do not want anyone to hear what it is. *So*, I need to open the resolutions envelope and check my list.'

'Okay. Obviously having a drink together is lovely but also... we're here in the pub now because?'

'Because you seem very kind and helpful and you're staying with Noah who has the envelope.' Oh. Dammit. She could just have explained all of this to Noah instead. 'And...'

Gaaah, Raf was wearing his raised-eyebrows look again. She did her best shut-up look, the one that worked on naughty kids at school.

'Basically, it's extremely embarrassing and I don't really know you and you live in New York, whereas I see Noah quite a lot. And it's embarrassing. As I mentioned.' She tried to make one of those faces that you made at work when you wanted to pretend that something was period-related so none of your male colleagues would question you further.

'You wouldn't have had to tell him that, though?'

Oh, for feck's sake. Bloody lawyers.

Georgie did not gnash her teeth like she wanted to. Instead, she said, 'Oh, yes. Duh. I did not think of that.'

'So shall we just tell him now?'

Georgie stared at him. 'That my secret is embarrassing?'

'Er, no? That you need to check your resolutions?'

Oh.

Having a lawyerly brain herself would have been handy right now. As would having had a good night's sleep last night.

'I suppose so,' she said eventually.

Raf laughed. 'Don't worry. No actual need since he's busy serving at the moment.' He finished up his pint and said, 'Want to go now?'

'Great.' Georgie stood up so fast she knocked over her stool.

* * *

The pub was seventeenth century. Noah had converted an adjacent, also very old, barn a few years ago into a house for himself and there was a door directly into it on the far side of the main tap room.

'We're just going to go and have a coffee,' Raf called to Noah as they went past the end of the bar.

'My favourite pub ever,' Georgie added to Noah. She didn't want him to feel hurt that they were leaving so soon.

Noah gave them both a massive pantomime-style wink and a thumbs up. Several of the people in the bar went further and they exited to a chorus of catcalls. People in Melting liked to make a fuss at any crumb of a hint of possible romance. Apparently the two of them exiting the pub together was like a whole loaf to them.

As they entered the house, Georgie reminded herself that, as well as the resolutions, she needed to remember to check Raf's trainers if she could. That would be easier than having to ask Noah's help in finding out the size.

'We'd better have actual coffee,' she said, when they got into the huge, stainless-steel-applianced kitchen, 'so Noah doesn't suspect anything.'

'Remember it doesn't matter if he does?' Raf was looking all raised-eyebrows yet again.

'Oh yes.' Lying was so confusing.

'I'll put the kettle on anyway.'

'I might pop to the loo then.'

She could have a little hunt for the trainers on her way.

No hunting was necessary, as it turned out. They were drying on the surprisingly funky towel rail on the wall of the loo. Georgie took a moment to admire its corkscrew-like design and then whipped her phone out and took photos of both the trainers' style and their size label. Raf definitely needed new ones. The bright blue and green of the upper section had run slightly onto the white bit round the bottom, plus they looked duller than they had done pre-vomit. And weirdly twisted round the front. He'd probably put them on too high a spin cycle.

Back in the kitchen, Raf had the coffees ready.

'I've made myself decaf.' He took a photo of the mug on his phone and posted it to the chat.

'Well done,' Georgie said.

'Thank you.' He grinned. 'Now, look what I just found.' He handed her a big white envelope with *Resolutions* scrawled on the front.

'Yesssss.'

Georgie could have *kissed* him.

Actually...

She looked at him.

He really was properly gorgeous. She really liked the way he wore his dark, wavy hair slightly long and tousled, curled over his shirt collar. And he had his shirt sleeves rolled up and she could see his forearms. *Strong* had definitely been the right word for his arms.

She really *could* kiss him. Except, she wouldn't. She basically never kissed anyone, despite her friends' best attempts to set her up, and she was not going to start with a by all accounts still-grieving widower who – from what she'd heard on the village grapevine – was a serial one-dater.

'Maybe I should steam it open and then re-stick it,' she said.

'Or we could just open it normally and tell Noah why and he wouldn't mind?'

Georgie shook her head. 'I feel like we've been a bit break-and-entery about it. I feel like we'd have to tell him first if we were going to do that. And now that I have the envelope in my hands, I just want to do it. Because what if we asked and he said *no*?' She pulled her phone out to google envelope steaming and then stood up. 'Do you know where the saucepans are? I need to boil water.'

Five minutes later, they were gently easing the envelope open.

'Wow.' Georgie carefully pulled the wadge of lists out. 'That was so *easy*. And satisfying.' And handy. If she could get her hands on the letter addressed to Raf, she'd be able to use her steaming skills to swap her secret too. 'It's a shame really that people don't post important documents so much any more.'

'Because you won't have much opportunity to develop a career as a master criminal specialising in envelope steaming?'

'Yes, or private investigator.'

Raf nodded very seriously and Georgie tried hard not to notice that he was now standing very close to her and she could see dark hairs where the top button of his shirt was undone. Not too many, he wasn't super hairy. But also some. Just the right amount, in fact. She felt like Goldilocks. Her gaze travelled up his thick but not too thick neck (still Goldilocks) and to his very firm jawline and to his lips. She was extremely sober now and she agreed with her drunk self that his lips looked very kissable. She swallowed and looked further up, and *oh*... He was looking at her.

His eyes were on hers. And now they were on her lips. She found herself moistening them with her tongue and...

What was she doing? When he got back to New York, Raf was going to be unwittingly (or wittingly, if he sneakily looked) in possession of her truly devastating secret. She *needed* to get a photo of her resolution list and then re-stick this envelope and here she was just standing here licking her lips and fantasising about kissing him.

She was an idiot.

'So I'm just going to take a photo of my resolutions.' Ridiculously, her voice sounded a bit squeaky.

'Of course.' Raf's voice was about three octaves below hers, bordering on uncomfortably gravelly.

They stood and just... *looked* at each other for a moment, and then Georgie dragged her eyes away from his and rustled the papers she was holding.

'The resolutions,' she said, holding the papers in front of her as if they'd protect her from the kiss-me-now vibes that were coming off him as strongly as she was feeling them herself.

'The resolutions,' Raf repeated.

'Yep. Okay.' She took a step backwards and then another step and then walked over to the table and sat down. What had that just *been*? She really didn't spend enough time with attractive men. Stick one in front of her and apparently she just turned to jelly.

Right. Her resolutions.

She turned the pile of papers over and said, 'Eek,' and turned them face down again.

'Eek?'

'I don't want to read anyone else's list. It feels really intrusive.'

'I do get that, but you've come this far? Maybe just cross your eyes or something or just don't read them? Or just forget what you read?'

'Yep. Okay. I can do that.'

The first list was Ankita's. Georgie managed to turn it over without seeing anything. Yesss.

The second was Beth's. The letters *IVF* leapt out at her from the page before she fumbled it over. IVF what? She was going to have a baby with Dominic? Dominic the Tosser, as Ankita (accurately) called him. What? Bloody hell.

The third was Raf's and she only saw the word caffeine, thank *goodness*.

The fourth was Poppy's and oh shit the words *Declan* and *bastard* leapt out at her before she managed to slam it over. Fuck. It seemed like Poppy really might genuinely hate Declan. Was she planning to leave him? That would be terrible. Georgie didn't know Declan well but it had sounded as though Poppy had a great relationship with him.

The fifth one was Georgie's, so she hadn't seen anything from Noah or Declan at least.

She took a photo of the – really very long – list and then shoved all the pieces of paper back in the envelope so there was no possibility she'd see any more snippets of shock revelations from her friends.

'Are you okay?' Raf asked.

'Yes, yes, totally fine,' she said, her mind racing. Beth and Dominic were going to have a baby? Poppy thought Declan was a bastard?

'How are we going to stick it back?' Raf asked.

Oh, yes. Good point.

'Glue?' she suggested.

'Glue, though? Does anyone actually own glue?'

'Noah's a pub landlord,' Georgie said. 'Landlords own everything.'

'*Really?*'

Raf was annoyingly sceptical about a lot of things, it seemed.

'Yes, really.' Georgie looked around. 'Where, though?'

Raf stood up and pulled open a couple of drawers.

'I can't look,' Georgie told him. 'I've already intruded too much today. I can't hunt through Noah's house.'

'Yeah, we can't look anywhere else.' Raf had finished checking kitchen drawers.

Georgie googled *How do you make glue*.

'Look, though.' She showed him her screen. 'You can make glue yourself from water, vinegar, skimmed milk and bicarb of soda.'

'We could do that *or* we could put the envelope back where it was, unsealed, and I will buy some glue tomorrow and stick it down then, and if Noah checks it in the meantime, he'll just think the envelope wasn't great.'

'That is a very good plan,' Georgie said approvingly. 'You'd make a good private investigator too.'

While Raf took the envelope and placed it back on the side where he'd found it, Georgie had a quick look at the photo she'd taken of her resolution list.

'Nooooooo,' she said.

'What?'

Georgie shook her head, still staring at her screen. Running, chocolate, crisps, cake, pizza, grey hairs, early-to-bed: they were all doable if not enjoyable. Yoga: she didn't really have time, but she'd have to find a class in it and in fact she'd probably enjoy it once she made herself squeeze it into her schedule. Italian GCSE before the end of the year, though? And learning how to do a jump while ice skating? And, maybe most challenging of all, she had to manage to cheer up Poppy by Valentine's Day.

Fucking fucking fucking hell.

'Are you okay?' Raf asked.

'Yep, all good,' she said. 'I just wrote quite a lot of resolutions and I have a busy life, so I'm going to struggle to fit them in.'

Maybe she could combine some of them. Find an Italian yoga teacher. And maybe she could ask Poppy to go to yoga, skating or Italian lessons with her to cheer her up: two birds, one stone.

'Yep, all totally fine,' she said. 'I might just get going now though.' She really needed to think. And get a good night's sleep. 'I need to relieve the babysitter.'

'Of course. I'll walk you back.'

'Oh, honestly, no need.'

'Not a problem. I like an evening stroll. And better safe than sorry?'

'Well, thank you.'

It actually *could* be a bit scary in the dark in the village due to no streetlights and the fact that everyone still remembered that someone had been mugged there about five years ago.

* * *

Within three steps of Noah's front door, Georgie, for the second evening running, was massively regretting her choice of boot. It was impossible to stand up on the ice that the cold, dry day had turned the top layer of snow into.

Although... it turned out that it was just as nice to be caught by Raf while sober as it had been when she was drunk. His arms really were very strong and she loved the way she could feel his muscles flexing as he held her. He was warm but not too hot, just right, in fact (Goldilocks again) and she *really* liked his aftershave.

Once he had her steady, after her third legs-spiralling-arms-flailing situation, he held his right arm out to her.

'I'm thinking this might be safest?' he said.

Georgie put her left arm through his. 'I think you're right. Thank you.'

And now she was hugged up against his nicely solid side, her head just level with his shoulder. Obviously he wouldn't be interested in her – he was a widower for goodness' sake, plus so gorgeous *and* funny he could probably have his pick of anyone he liked – and she had no intention of allowing herself to develop feelings for anyone and get upset down the line, plus she had a lot on her mind at the moment... But, right now, just for this moment, this was *nice*.

5

GEORGIE

Halfway across the green, Georgie was laughing at an anecdote Raf was telling her about Noah, a squirrel and a ruby engagement ring when she heard a miserable-sounding miaow from somewhere very high up. She stopped dead, and Raf stopped too, because of their linked arms.

'That cat sounds miserable.' Georgie pointed upwards with her free arm.

'I'm sure it's fine.' Raf tugged her linked arm slightly.

'I think it's in trouble.' Georgie was standing firm.

'Cats go up trees all the time.'

'Not that high.'

'Maybe it's trying to catch a bird or something.'

'That would be stupid though, wouldn't it, given that birds can fly and cats can't. It sounds like it's crying. I think we might need to help it.' She could see Raf's face in the moonlight, gorgeous even when he was grimacing.

'I thought you'd think that,' he said.

Georgie smiled at him. He was like a marshmallow covered in crisp, bitter chocolate. Underneath his cynical human-lie-detector hard exterior, he was really soft inside. He was totally going to help her rescue the cat.

Raf had his finger on his lips and was cocking his head up towards the top of the tree. The cat was still miaowing.

'Let's go and see if Noah has a ladder,' he said.

Noah didn't have a ladder long enough but he knew a man who did. Soon, the three of them plus about five of the pub regulars were traipsing up the lane on the left-hand side of the pub towards the cottage of Barry Johnson, the local builder.

Barry did have a ladder that was long enough, and he was very slurred-speech vocal about his keenness to use it himself.

'Haven't done any roofing for ages,' he said, staggering as he fumbled for his garage door key.

As he jabbed madly with it in the direction of the lock, Georgie said, reeling slightly from the fumes on his breath, 'I'm not sure you should go up. In fact, you know what—' she was starting to feel queasy about the whole thing '—maybe we should actually spend a bit more time checking on the cat from the bottom of the tree, and if it's still distressed we should call the fire brigade.'

'Nonshense,' said Barry. 'I'm going up.'

'I think not,' said Noah. 'We don't want a broken neck on our hands.'

'I'll do it,' said Raf. 'We definitely don't want any alcohol-fuelled ladder-climbing.'

'I really don't think you should,' said Georgie. 'Like, I *really* don't. That ladder looks *really* rickety. And I totally bullied you into it. If anyone should go, it should be me.' She very much did not want to. But she also didn't want Raf to, or anyone other than maybe a trained firefighter with a very sturdy ladder.

'Honestly, I'll be fine,' said Raf. And next thing he, Noah and two of the pub regulars were wedging the ladder against the tree and he was setting off up it at an extremely nippy pace. His bum was lit up *very* nicely by the moonlight, which was a ridiculous thing to be thinking at this moment in time.

His thighs weren't bad either. Nicely muscly.

'Nearly there.' Raf was so high that his voice sounded slightly muffled.

'Be careful,' shouted Georgie.

Raf took one foot off the ladder and gave it a wave to the side. Georgie screamed, one of the regulars gasped and Raf laughed. He put his foot back onto the ladder and carried on.

'I can see it,' he called.

There was some scuffling around in the tree, accompanied by more miaowing, a couple of *Fucks* from Raf and more screams from Georgie, and then Raf was coming back down the ladder with the cat wrapped up in his coat under his arm.

'She was stuck towards the end of a too-thin branch, very high up,' he told them as he approached the bottom. 'At least she had the common sense to realise that she didn't have much chance of getting down by herself, so she wasn't moving, but she wasn't exactly grateful to see me.'

When he reached the ground, to general clapping, Raf did a little bow and carefully started to unwind his coat from the cat. Apparently he wasn't careful enough, though; as soon as its head was free, the cat bit his finger.

'Shit,' yelled Raf.

Noah lunged forward to help him and tripped up one of the ladder-holding regulars, which caused the ladder to lurch away from the tree. Noah flung himself back towards the ladder, his leg clipping Raf's, and Raf then tripped. His bitten hand shot up and the cat flew off it and landed in a heap on the ground and didn't move.

'Fucking *hell*,' said Raf. 'I climb a tree and rescue a cat, who bites me, and now I've probably fucking killed her. Seriously. Way to go.'

'I think she might be okay.' Georgie was on her knees next to the cat, stroking her delicate little body. Her rib cage was very prominent through her silky fur. 'I think she might have been stuck up there for a while and be very hungry. She's very thin.'

'Not too thin not to have a very strong bite,' said Raf.

'Raf!' said Georgie. 'She's injured.'

'Sorry.'

He didn't *sound* sorry.

Georgie was cradling the cat in her arms now. Although, shit, you weren't supposed to move people who'd had blows to the head and body, in case of fractures, so probably you weren't supposed to move cats either.

'Please be okay, little kitty,' she said, stroking her under her chin. And then the cat miaowed, moved her head and sunk her very, *very* sharp teeth into the side of Georgie's hand.

After what seemed like literally minutes, the cat withdrew her fangs – seriously, she was like a bloody vampire – and dashed straight off to the last cottage on the row on the far side of the green.

The pub regulars took Barry and his ladder home, and Noah took Georgie and Raf over to the pub to check out their bites.

An hour and a quarter later, after a lot of arguing over whether the enormous swelling and blueness of Raf's finger and the fact that Georgie couldn't remember the last time she'd had a tetanus jab *mattered*, Noah won the argument. They set off for the hospital, Noah very loudly pleased with himself about the being-able-to-drive-and-not-having-to-call-a-cab upside of his no alcohol resolution, and soon they were sitting in A&E.

'I think we're looking at quite a long wait,' said Raf. 'Like, hours. This place is full of people with much bigger problems than ours.'

'You do need to see a doctor, though,' Noah said.

'Could have been worse,' Georgie pointed out. 'You could have fallen out of the tree and broken your neck.'

'Could have been better,' said Raf. 'I could have left the bloody cat to its own devices.'

'You were never going to do that.' Georgie smiled at him and he rolled his eyes in response.

'He wasn't,' agreed Noah. 'He's always had to do the hero thing. And he never hurts himself. But you should be careful, mate. You aren't getting any younger. You're nearly forty.'

'Shut up,' muttered Raf.

* * *

Forty-five minutes later, after Raf and Georgie had persuaded Noah to go home and get some sleep, the two of them were absolutely astonished. Apparently the doctors thought that *they* were the ones with the big problems. Georgie was given two stitches, a tetanus jab and a course of antibiotics. And Raf was told by a plastic surgeon that he'd need to have a one-hour operation under a general to clean out his wound, because apparently the cat's bite had punctured his knuckles and injected bacteria straight into his bloodstream. He was going to have to stay in hospital for a few days to have the wound washed regularly with iodine, plus he needed IV antibiotics. They'd have a bed on the ward ready for him soon, and in the meantime he should wait in A&E.

'That's the most ridiculous thing I've ever heard. I'm self-discharging.' Raf stood up, shaking his head.

'Fine. And I'll see you back here in the next few days and I'll be amputating your finger. At best.' The consultant had a nice way with words.

'I love your shoes,' Georgie told the consultant before the woman left them, Raf finally having agreed, with extreme reluctance, to be admitted.

'Thank you.' The consultant beamed at her, looking an entirely different woman from the one who'd been so doom-mongering about the finger. 'They're new and you're the first person who's noticed them.' She was still smiling as she pushed through the swing doors on the other side of the room.

'Love her shoes?' Raf was staring at Georgie. 'The woman's a complete tyrant and totally OTT and I'm having a general anaesthetic for probably no good reason and you love her shoes?'

'It's important to thank people and be nice to them. Make them feel good. Also, you heard her – you're having a general for a very good reason.'

'She doesn't need to be made to feel good. She's at work. She's a professional. She's an NHS consultant. She knows she's doing an amazing job.'

'It's always worth being nice to people. I've seen you being nice. You're very nice to lots of people.'

'That's different. They don't force me to have stupid operations. But fine. *Obviously* I am in fact very grateful to the mean consultant. Anyway, you should go.'

Georgie shook her head. 'I'm staying. You can't just sit here by yourself.'

'No, you should go.'

'No.' She smiled at him sunnily, and he laughed.

'Okay. Thank you. I'm grateful for the company.' He looked around. 'I'm hungry. Shall we see if there's any food?'

'You can't eat. You're about to have a general anaesthetic, you muppet.'

'Bloody hell.'

'Are you supposed to be going back to New York soon? Is this going to mess up your flights?' she asked, delighted to have a natural opportunity to delve into his plans and possibly work out how to get her envelope back.

'I have a flexible ticket. And I'm kind of flexible work-wise. So it isn't a problem.' He smiled at her and she was momentarily distracted from the annoyance of still not knowing about his plans by how his hospital gown actually suited him. Like, how was that possible? Maybe it was the whiteness against his olive skin and dark hair.

'What about you?' His eyes crinkled when he smiled. He *did* look trustworthy. Maybe she *could* just ask him to send her secret back. No. Insanity. That must be the painkillers talking.

'We can stay on an extra couple of days. I'm not due back at work until Thursday and if my mother and stepfather don't want us with them, Poppy's parents will have us.'

'Is...' He looked completely serious for once. That suited him too. Georgie worried for a moment that she'd just sighed out loud at the gorgeousness of him. 'Is everything okay with your parents?'

'Yes, yes, totally,' she lied.

When her parents split up, her mother had been pregnant by the head-teacher at Georgie's school (to be fair, they were still happily married now) and her father immediately moved in with his much younger boyfriend (being fair again, they were also still happily together and recently married, and now the proud fathers to two very gorgeous little boys). It was too humiliating to tell anyone who didn't already know about how there'd been the exact opposite of normal custody battles; they'd basically fought *not* to have Georgie living with them, and still did not really want her company or, worse, Max's.

Why did she have such an urge to tell Raf about it now? She never talked about it. Amongst her friends, only Poppy, Beth and Ankita knew all the details. And that's because they were the people she considered her real family.

'We have a bed on the ward for you now,' a very jolly nurse interrupted them. 'Visiting hours are over, I'm afraid, so I'll give you two love birds five minutes to say goodnight and then I'm going to walk you up there, Raf.'

'Oh, no, we—'

'Thank you so much.' Raf spoke at the same time as Georgie. As the nurse walked away, he said, 'Ha, ha, ha, your face. I think maybe I should be offended that it's clearly such a great hardship someone assuming we're *love birds.*'

'It's a huge hardship.' Georgie smiled at him.

'How are you getting back to Melting?'

'I'll get a cab.'

'Okay. I think I have your number from the "Resolutions" chat but just in case let's swap numbers properly and you can text me to let me know when you're back safely. And tell the taxi driver you're giving me his registration number. Just in case.'

'That's very sweet, but—'

'You can't argue with me. I'm feeling tetchy, remember, because I have to have an operation soon,' he said, very un-tetchily.

'Okay. Thank you.' Georgie took her phone out. She should not be feeling so borderline teenage-giggly-happy about this, like the hottest boy in the school had just asked for her number. The real reason she should be happy was that having his number would help her in getting her secret back.

'Night, then,' she said, when they'd done their number exchange. 'Good luck with the op. I'll... visit you.'

Because of the secret letter, obviously, and because she felt guilty about the cat thing. And because, while he'd been in the loo, she'd placed an order for replacement trainers and she'd need to hand them over when they arrived.

No other reason, obviously.

6

POPPY

Poppy nudged Declan's fried eggs into place on his plate and then adjusted the bacon rashers, tomatoes and mushrooms next to them before balancing toast in the rack his mother had given her for Christmas (she'd given her other daughter-in-law a nice bracelet, which had annoyed Poppy quite a lot before she'd managed to laugh about it).

She took a photo of the plate. She could post that to the chat later. There were so many photos being pinged there every day that no one would ask her why she'd put a picture of a fried breakfast on there on top of the one she'd posted of her own breakfast.

The truth was that she'd had a better night's sleep and woken up more refreshed than usual, and she'd decided while showering that she wasn't going to take whatever Declan was doing lying down. If he was going to leave her – or she was going to ask him to leave – she was first going to make him realise what he was missing (maybe that was petty, but it wasn't as bad as having an affair). And Declan was a man who loved his food.

So this morning she'd made him his favourite breakfast, a full English.

As he crashed through the door into the kitchen, she gave him a big, wide smile. He'd always said he loved the way she smiled. For her own self-respect, she wanted him to remember that.

'Morning, morning.' He crouched and dropped a kiss on Daniel's head where he was snoozing on his playmat and then stepped over to Poppy and dropped a kiss on her forehead. Without looking at the table at all, said, 'That *noise* last night. Outside on the green. Something to do with a cat. Woke me up about twenty minutes after I'd nodded off and then I couldn't get back to sleep for *hours*—' actually not true; Poppy *had* been awake a lot and he'd been sound asleep next to her most of the night '—so I missed my alarm so now I'm running late. I'll have to grab breakfast later in the morning. Have a good day. I love you.'

And off he dashed, still without looking at the table.

The second Declan closed the front door, Daniel's eyes popped wide open and he started a big yell. Bloody hell.

Poppy picked Daniel up and stuck him on her boob, and then sat staring at the redundant fried breakfast. It was a challenge not to lean forward over Daniel and pick it up and chuck the whole lot at the wall.

She was better than that, though. She was.

Plus the day ahead was looking boringly chore-filled enough as it was. She didn't need to be scrubbing walls and the floor. There was no point cutting off her nose to spite her face.

So when she'd finished feeding Daniel she just tipped all the food from the plate into the kitchen bin and sniffed hard and wondered whether it was some kind of metaphor for her marriage.

* * *

Georgie texted halfway through the morning, as Poppy was chopping butternut squash for a puree for Daniel.

You around for coffee?

Poppy wasn't sure. It would be lovely to see Georgie, but after feeling quite energetic first thing she was now struggling to keep her eyes open. It was like the extra sleep she'd had had made her *more* tired.

Thought you were going home today?

Staying longer. Tell you why later. See you at 11? Yours or the pub?

Georgie obviously wasn't going to take no for an answer.

Mine if you don't mind the mess.

Poppy my middle name is mess. See you at 11.

Poppy found herself smiling. Other than Daniel, obviously, Georgie was maybe her favourite person in the world to spend time with right now, with Declan being so weird. You needed friends who made you feel happy.

* * *

Georgie rolled up at ten past eleven, and that made Poppy smile too. Georgie *loved* the idea of punctuality but was terrible at it in practice.

'Sorry, sorry, sorry, got caught up,' she said as she always did, as she barrelled into the kitchen and flung herself down at the table.

'Where's Max?' Poppy turned the tap on to fill the kettle.

'With my stepfather playing FIFA, and we all know that'll end in tears when Richard walks out in the middle of the game because he's suddenly bored, but I couldn't do anything about it. That's why I was late, trying to persuade Max to come here instead. Anyway, there's an upside. Obviously Max is perfect, but it's nice to be able to talk without an eleven-year-old listening.'

'What do you want?' Poppy gestured at the kettle.

'Coffee. Fully caffeinated. It's about the only resolution I *didn't* make.' Georgie gave an exaggerated eye roll and Poppy laughed. 'Speaking of which, one of my resolutions was taking up yoga and I really don't want to go alone so I wondered if you'd come with me?'

'Oh, I don't know,' Poppy said automatically. It was tricky leaving Daniel for too long.

'We could find one with a creche or we could go in the evening and Declan could babysit. I'm very happy to come over in this direction so you don't have to travel. I only have to go once a fortnight, thank goodness. Pleeeeease.'

'Okay, yes, maybe, if I can work things out with Daniel.' In theory, Poppy would actually like to go, now she thought about it. She'd love to spend the time with Georgie, it sounded like a nice, gentle way to get fit *and* – petty or not, it was how she felt right now – she would enjoy showing Declan that she could very happily enjoy herself without him.

'Thank you, thank you, thank you. I'll find somewhere and book it. I'll try to get Beth to come too.'

'Have you ever done yoga before?' Poppy couldn't totally imagine Georgie doing yoga. Obviously Ankita probably did it all the time but Georgie was less... serene.

'No, and that's why it's such a great resolution. Well, actually it's a shit resolution because when I'm sober I really don't want to do it, but there you go. It will be good for me and it will be good for you too because apparently it's good for all people ever, so we'll both benefit, so really you should be grateful to me.'

Poppy laughed and reached for a biscuit, but then quickly withdrew her hand and pushed the plate away.

'Resolution?' asked Georgie. 'Do you want to re-do the no-biscuit-taking so I can video you doing it?'

'Not when I'm dressed like this!' It wasn't so much her hoodie and trackie bottoms as the fact that she had no make-up on at all and her hair had gone slightly mad overnight and she hadn't done anything about it this morning other than brushing it, which had just made it seem even wirier.

'You look lovely,' Georgie told her. 'As always.'

Poppy made a face.

Georgie said, 'Okay, I'll video just your hand.'

Video done and posted, she said, 'Let me tell you a story about a cat with sharp teeth, a tree and A&E.'

The story was a good one, and soon Poppy had actual tears in her eyes from laughter.

'And that's why we're here for longer than expected,' Georgie finished. 'I have to go back to the hospital walk-in centre and get my wound checked.'

'And how long's Raf going to be in hospital?'

'Not sure. I still can't believe it's caused him so much hassle.'

'I remember learning that the only animal bite that's more likely to cause sepsis than a cat one is a human one,' Poppy said.

'Wow.'

'Yep.' Poppy gave it a moment and then ventured, 'Do you…?'

She knew that Ankita and Beth would want her to ask whether Georgie and Raf had anything going between them, but she also knew as well as anyone that no one liked being hassled. So she just did one of those eyebrow waggles that people did when they were talking about people's love lives.

Georgie did a huge eye roll. 'Do I like him? My friends are *so* predictable.'

'We all just want you to be happy.' Poppy felt desperately sad for a moment thinking how happy she *used* to be with Declan before they got back to England, before pushing the thought away. They were talking about Georgie right now, not her.

'Excuse me. I am happy with no man and I do not need one.'

'I know, I know.' Poppy waited a second and then said, '*Do* you, though?'

'Honestly.' Georgie rolled her eyes again and then – in a weird way, although maybe Poppy was imagining the weirdness because she was so tired, but it was like she was being very careful about her words – said, 'I mean, he *is* gorgeous.'

'Wow.' Poppy couldn't remember the last time Georgie had admitted to finding anyone remotely attractive.

Georgie nodded. 'Yeah.' Her eyes went a bit swivelly, like she was trying to think of something to say to get away from talking about Raf. 'Anyway, let's google yoga places. And then let's take Daniel for a walk round the village.'

* * *

By the time Georgie left, Poppy was feeling so much cheerier that she made and ate a salad for her lunch *and*, once she'd put a photo of it on the chat, did *not* then secretly have any chocolate or cake for pudding.

And then, just as she was getting bored mid-afternoon, Ankita turned up and suggested another walk, which turned out to be very nice.

Declan got home while Poppy was bathing a butternut-squash-and-parsnip-covered Daniel (she wasn't giving him the spoon again any time soon, whatever NHS guidance was. Did the people who wrote that actually have babies of their own?) and came straight into the bathroom and gave her a kiss on the cheek. As she made herself smile at him, because she just wasn't ready yet to tackle him about what was happening, she realised that that was the first time he'd given her a home-from-work-kiss since they'd arrived back in the UK. It was so obvious that whatever was going on had begun then. Had he met someone at work? Had he hooked up with an ex shortly after arriving back?

'Why don't you put your feet up while I finish his bath?' Declan's voice cut through her spiralling.

She took a deep internal breath and looked at him and then at Daniel.

Declan had been working all day but he didn't seem tired. He looked genuinely excited at the prospect of bath time. Given how good he apparently was at acting in other ways, he clearly might be good at acting about this. But while he might be a shit, unfaithful husband he'd always been wonderful with Daniel, so on balance it was probably genuine, and she had to minimise Daniel's suffering if she and Declan separated.

'Thank you,' she said.

Declan kissed her on the cheek again, a bit closer to her mouth this time. And for one mad moment she almost wanted just to forget about everything and turn round and press herself against him like she would have in the past except... She suddenly froze, because he smelled... different. Like... was he wearing someone else's *perfume*? Had he been with someone *else* before coming home?

'I have to do the dishwasher.' She pushed past him and out of the room and almost stumbled along the landing.

She tripped and nearly fell down the stairs before she managed to pull herself together.

Okay. She couldn't carry on like this. She needed to find out for certain what was going on, *who* Declan was seeing. Maybe she could look at his phone or his laptop.

She closed her eyes for a second as she went into the kitchen. How could her life have come to this? She didn't *want* to be the kind of person who spied on her husband. She also didn't want to be the kind of person whose husband was unfaithful to her, though.

Okay. Right now she was going to clean the kitchen to within an inch of its life. She needed something to do so that she wouldn't just wallow in miserable thoughts.

Fifteen minutes later, she'd worked like a demon and achieved the amount a non-angry-and-betrayed person might have achieved in an hour. She decided to have a little sit-down for two seconds. They'd managed to squeeze an armchair into the corner of the kitchen and it was the most comfortable seat in the house. She sat down in it and...

'Hey.' Declan was kneeling on the floor in front of her, holding Daniel and smiling at her in a way that he hadn't smiled for a while and... Oh, she must have been asleep again.

'Why don't I get us dinner while you feed him, and then we could watch TV together?' he suggested.

Poppy blinked, her mind still sleep-fogged, but certain that she didn't want a repeat of the fire. 'I don't want to sound ungrateful but I don't think...'

'You don't want another kitchen fire.' Declan nodded. 'What about we cook together?'

Properly awake now, Poppy felt her eyes grow hot and moist. If only everything was okay and they *could* cook together. But, again, *why* was he suggesting it? They'd literally never once actually done that. They did lots of nice things together, but not cooking.

'Why don't I cook while you watch TV?' she said.

'I'd feel guilty,' he told her.

'Guilty?' Of what, though? '*Guilty*?' She could feel her heart rate picking up. 'Wow.'

Declan stared at her for a long moment and then said, 'Thanks for cooking,' and walked out of the room. A few seconds later, she heard the TV come on.

Right.

She had some thinking time while she was making carbonara for them.

She'd nearly blurted out there and then that she knew about his affair.

Did she *want* to do that, though?

She needed to think more first.

She had to consider Daniel.

If it had been a short affair, begun since they got back to England, and Declan promised to stop now, could she get over it? Move on? Trust him again? Rebuild their relationship?

She wasn't sure. Probably not.

She stuck a knife viciously into an onion.

She should make sure that she was completely certain before she did anything irrevocable.

She shouldn't say anything until she knew for definite what she wanted. And she should also – if she could – find out exactly what had happened before she confronted him.

In the meantime, she needed to try to act a little more normally around him.

* * *

'Let's start *Succession*?' Declan suggested, when she told him that the carbonara was ready. They'd been saying for months and months that they wanted to see what everyone had raved about when it came out, but they'd never found the time to watch it.

'Okay.' She forced a smile out. 'Good idea.'

It was good TV, at least.

'This is nice,' Declan said to her at the end of the first episode, moving towards her and hugging her.

'Yep,' she said.

'I love you.' He lifted his hand and gently turned her face towards his and leaned to kiss her.

Poppy allowed herself to kiss him back for a second. If he remembered how good they'd always been together maybe that would cause him to rethink. Maybe he'd just had a moment of madness. Maybe everything could be okay.

The kiss continued somehow, and she began to feel her whole body sigh into it.

It was actually lovely. Long and deep. She could feel Declan's body responding as much as her – traitorous – one was. Good. He needed to know what he was missing.

'Poppy.' His voice had gone hoarse and her whole body *zinged* at the sound of it. That was the way he always used to sound when they were about to have sex, and he was desperate for her and she for him. She missed that. So much, actually. She missed *him*. If only things could be the way they'd always been. If only he hadn't done whatever he'd done.

'Declan.' She moved her body against him and pushed one of her hands into his lovely thick hair and pulled his head back to hers. Maybe she could have sex with him. Remind him.

And then she froze. Because he was unbuttoning her bra. And, no, she couldn't. Her huge, milk-filled boobs. What if they *leaked*? What if he kissed her there and tasted milk and, no, eurgh, she just couldn't. And, actually, what was she thinking? She couldn't get naked in front of him. He'd be repulsed by all her new flab that she just couldn't get rid of. And what if the other woman had never had a baby and had a perfect body? What if he compared them? Well, he probably would.

'Declan. No. I...'

He trailed a line of kisses down her chest.

'Declan. Really. No.' She'd spoken very sharply, she realised, as he pulled away so fast that he almost scratched her.

'Pops, I love you and it's been seven months.' He tried to pull her back against him and... Oh, God, she'd suddenly registered the smell again. He did smell different. He smelled like he'd been... somewhere else.

'Sorry,' she said flatly. 'I can't.'

'Okay. Yep, great, no, of course. Sorry.' He let go of her completely and moved along the sofa, away from her.

Oh, God. She wished *so much* that she could say or do something to make everything better, make this whole situation go away. But the wisdom she'd need was so far from being available to her that it might as well have been locked inside Fort Knox.

So she said nothing.

'I love you.' Declan's voice had entirely lost any hint of amorousness. Perhaps he'd been pretending before. 'You must be tired. I know I am. Let's go to bed.'

'Great.'

* * *

When she was lying wide awake between her sleeping husband and her sleeping baby in his cot (she couldn't bear for him to move to his own room yet), wondering how long Declan and she would still be living together, her phone buzzed with a message.

It was Georgie. She'd found a yoga class in Cirencester and booked it for the two of them, and had messaged Beth and Ankita to see if they'd like to join too.

Poppy was definitely going to go, she resolved. She couldn't lose her girlfriends as well as her husband.

7

GEORGIE

'Grapes. Got to do the hospital visit cliché.' Georgie placed a large punnet of mixed green and black seedless on the side table next to Raf's hospital bed. 'Also...' She checked over both shoulders for nurses or doctors and then pulled a little envelope out of her handbag. 'Noah sent a little present to make your hospital coffee Irish. And he's going to come in to see you tomorrow once he's got cover.'

'Nice.' Raf grinned at her and pulled out the tiny bottle of whiskey Noah had sent.

'He looked *so* longingly at it when he gave it to me,' Georgie told him. 'And then I saw that he'd been posting photos of zero-alcohol beer in the "Resolutions" chat.'

'Ha. Maybe he's hoping to live vicariously through me.'

Georgie picked up the little bottle and studied its label to distract herself from how ridiculously sexy Raf was managing to look despite being in a hospital bed. Maybe it was the way his hair was tousled and how his jaw was darkened by a day of no shaving. Or maybe it was his very seductive smile. And beautiful eyes and... She pulled her attention back to the whiskey. 'It's so cute. And it would make you so ill if you took it before an anaesthetic.'

'Anaesthetics are all done,' he said. 'And the very nice nurse explicitly told me that it would be fine to have a little bit of alcohol while I'm on the antibiotics. So I genuinely might Irish-up my coffee.'

'Okay, good,' Georgie said, relieved. 'I would not feel happy if I inadvertently helped to kill you.'

'Other than sending me up the ladder?'

'Okay, I don't want to nearly kill you twice in two days.' She sat down on the chair at the side of his bed and gestured at the white-pole-hung TV above him. 'What were you watching?'

'Darts. There aren't a lot of channels available and that was my best option.'

Georgie stared at the TV for a moment. 'Wow. It's quite...'

'Yeah, boring, unless you're big into darts. I am therefore very pleased to see you and your grapes and whiskey.'

'I'm going to pretend that's a compliment.'

'Not joking,' Raf said generously, 'I'd even be pleased to see you if I'd had some snooker to watch.'

'Wow, thank you. I'm truly flattered. So how's your hand feeling?'

'It's just starting to throb a bit as the anaesthetic wears off. How's yours?'

'Average. I still can't believe how much pain one small cat can inflict. But at least I didn't get an enforced hospital stay. How long are you in for?'

'They want to observe me for a while and keep cleaning the wound, but I think I've negotiated them down to two more nights.'

'Wow,' Georgie repeated.

'I know.'

'Okay, so I also brought—' she rummaged in her bag '—Bananagrams.'

'What?' Raf stared at the yellow bag she'd brought out.

'It's a word game. I thought you'd be bored.'

It was Raf's turn to say, 'Wow.'

'You look unimpressed but you'll be grateful. I made Max play it with me when I realised that he was developing a bit of a Minecraft addiction and he got really into it, and he is *not* a word game boy. And right now you're watching darts and—' she peered at the TV '—it isn't even *live*.'

'It's from three years ago. A *huge* match, though.'

'Sounds incredibly exciting.' Georgie accompanied her sarcasm with a big eyebrow raise.

'Yeah, no. Okay. Let's do this. Tell me the Bananagram rules. I'm just going to say now that if I lose it will be *entirely* because of my post-anaesthetic state, not because I am very bad at word games.'

* * *

'Okay,' said Georgie about forty minutes later. 'That *very bad at word games* thing was a total lie.'

'I know.' Raf beamed at her and she laughed. 'That was surprisingly fun.'

'Exactly. It's *so* much better than watching a screen.' Especially if you got to play with someone who made you laugh as much as Raf did. She looked at her watch. 'One more round?'

'I think I can squeeze that in around my three-years-out-of-date-darts-watching.'

They were a few minutes into the next round when a woman spoke from behind Georgie.

'Hello Rafael. Sorry to interrupt. I'm relieved to see you looking very well. I brought you some of your favourite food.' She stepped forward and dropped a kiss on his forehead.

'Mum.' Raf smiled at her.

There was something very endearing about a small woman treating her large, well-into-his-thirties son like a small boy.

'Let me introduce you,' Raf said. 'This is Georgie, a friend of Noah's from Melting. She's the one who also got bitten. And this is my mum, Manuela.'

'Oh, yes, I can see from the bandages. Are you alright?' Manuela had a very charming Spanish accent and lovely warm eyes, dark like her son's.

'Yes, thank you. Raf's injury was much worse. I should get going.' Georgie began to gather the game up.

'Oh, no, please don't let me interrupt you.' Manuela sat down on the chair on the other side of the bed. 'We could all play.'

'Okay, now you're freaking me out,' Raf said. 'You hate games like this. I am honestly fine.'

'I'd love to play with you both,' his mum said, laughing.

'I really do need to get going. I should get back to my son.' Georgie stood up. 'It was lovely to meet you.'

'Oh.' A tiny frown creased Manuela's otherwise perfect brow. 'How old is he? Is your husband looking after him at the moment?'

Georgie laughed as Raf shook his head. 'He's eleven,' she said, 'and I'm a single mum. He's with a friend.'

'How long have you been single?' asked Manuela.

'Mum! Seriously!'

The insane thing was that Manuela's smile was so inviting that Georgie almost told her that she'd been single since Max's conception, until she realised that she'd probably have sounded as though she was telling her that for Raf's benefit, not to mention the fact that not many people were single for their entire adult lives and it was far too much personal information to impart.

'Ha. Hope you get a good night's sleep, Raf.' She picked up her bag. 'Bye.'

As Georgie walked out, she reflected that either Raf was very good company or she should really make an effort to improve her social life because she'd enjoyed this hospital visit *hugely*.

* * *

'This really wasn't necessary, but I'm very grateful.'

Late the next afternoon, Raf folded his legs into the front passenger seat of Georgie's car.

'I did not enjoy that,' he continued. 'I shouldn't moan, because a lot of people in there had much bigger problems, but I didn't love the beeping monitors all night. I'm very glad that I talked them into letting me out today. And I have to admit that getting a lift from you is so much nicer than waiting for a cab. So thank you very much.'

He'd been discharged a day earlier than expected, and at such short notice that no one had been there to pick him up. Noah had put a message on their 'Resolutions' chat asking if anyone was free to go and get him, and Georgie had leapt in, insisting she should go because the whole injury was her fault. Which was true, and also it was ideal for spending more time with him and trying to work out how to get her secret back.

'The least I could do.' Georgie jumped as their fingers brushed as they did their seat belts up at the same time. Raf was large and her car was not. He looked quite ridiculous – and also very sexy – filling the entire half of his side of the front of the car. She was going to have to be careful when she changed gear or she'd end up touching his – very nicely solid-looking – thigh. 'Given that it was all my fault.'

'You are so right. If you hadn't been there I'd just have ignored the cat and left it up there to die. Or let a drunk elderly person take his chances up the ladder.'

She smiled at him and then put the car into first, very gingerly, keeping her fingers strictly away from his leg, and began to roll forward out of the parking space.

'Exactly. All my fault.'

'So how's your finger today?' He shifted towards her to reach into his pocket on the other side and their shoulders touched for a second and Georgie nearly crashed into the car ahead of them. 'Oops, sorry.'

'Ha, my car's too small.' It really was. If she didn't get used to being this close to him soon, she'd be hyperventilating by the time they got back to Melting. 'My finger's much better. Yours?'

'Also much better. I still can't believe that one cat can do so much damage.'

'I know.' Georgie shook her head. 'Such sharp teeth. Total vampire material.'

As she stopped at some lights, she reflected that the journey back to Melting would be about half an hour, and then she and Raf would say goodbye and sometime soon Raf would go back to New York and would be in possession of her secret letter. How was she going to get it back? How would she stay in touch with him so that she could even *hope* to get her hands on it?

'So when are you planning to go back to New York?' she asked as nonchalantly as possible, as they headed past converted Georgian villas towards grander ones on the outskirts of Cheltenham. This was the second time she'd tried to ask him this; he was going to think she was obsessed with his whereabouts.

'Quite soon, I think. But I'll probably be backwards and forwards.'

Hmm.

Maybe she could go on holiday to New York and steal it. If she went with Beth, say, it wouldn't be too weird to visit him. They could take him Marmite or brown sauce. British people abroad always missed those.

They'd want to make sure he was home, though, if he was travelling back and forth.

'So where've you been going on holiday since you've been living in New York?' Honestly, she was becoming so devious.

'I've been travelling within the US and South America.'

He had some very interesting stories about his travels and Georgie gave up for the time being on trying to work out how to get the letter back, and they didn't stop talking and laughing until she pulled up outside the Duck.

'Thanks again.' He hefted his overnight bag (Noah had taken it to the hospital for him) over his shoulder and held a hand up. 'See you on the thirty-first of December, if not before.'

Hopefully they'd be seeing each other way before the end of the year, Georgie thought, for her secret retrieval.

'Yep. Have a good year.'

And that was that. He'd gone.

The car seemed very... empty now. Odd.

She shook her head at herself as she drove round the corner to Poppy's parents' house, which was where she and Max were now staying (as it turned out, her mother and stepfather had indeed not wanted the pleasure of their company any longer, which had made her sad for Max and, frankly, relieved for herself).

How could you get used to a large man in your passenger seat in the space of half an hour?

* * *

The next morning, Georgie hauled herself out of bed early after a one-too-many evening with Beth (neither of them had included alcohol consumption in their resolutions) and took herself for a run.

Twenty-seven minutes later, she'd finished and was leaning against the side wall of the pub, breathing in huge chunks of nice, cold air. This was her third run of the new year and she was absolutely certain she was never going to become one of those people who swore by it. She'd run for this one year – or however long it took her to get her letter back – and that would be *it*.

Or, of course, she might find out that the secret was true, in which case she wouldn't need to get the envelope back *or* keep her resolutions. She did need to work out a way to find out very soon.

Ooh, eurgh, no. Everything felt very far away and swimmy very suddenly and she had to sit down. She saw stars for a moment or two and then felt someone's hand on the back of her head, encouraging her to push it between her knees.

She blinked a couple of times and then everything felt a lot clearer. She wiggled her head and the hand moved away.

The first thing she focused on properly was the feet in front of her. Or what was on the feet. Raf's trainers. There was no way they'd been vomited on and put in a washing machine. They were pristine.

She sat up straight, really fast, and bumped her head on the wall behind her. 'Ow,' she moaned, before looking up at him. 'You bought yourself new trainers!'

'Yep,' said Raf. 'Had them delivered while I was in hospital. I really liked that style and the other ones were kind of the worse for wear after our run, and also it felt like they were half a size too small anyway, so it all worked out for the best.'

'But I bought you new ones to replace the others. They're being delivered this morning. I was going to drop them in at the pub on my way back to Bristol. *And*, due to some amazing detective work from me, they're the same bloody size as your original pair.'

Raf's lips twitched. 'Sorry.'

Georgie heaved a sigh. 'I should never have got drunk and vomited.'

'You looked like you were going to vomit just now. Are you okay?'

'Yes, thank you. Fine. It's just that running really does not agree with me.'

'It'll get better.'

'Yeah, I don't think so.'

Raf held his hand out and hauled her up to her feet.

'Sure you're okay?' he said, still holding on to her. Their hands fitted very well together. His was exactly the right size and not too hot and not too cold. Of course.

'Yes, thank you. Honestly, I am.' She looked up at him and saw that he was gazing down at her face, his eyes doing their crinkle-at-the-corner thing again. Just the right amount, naturally.

He was smiling at her and she couldn't help smiling back and, gulp, his eyes were on hers, and now they were on her lips and, oh wow oh wow oh wow, he was going to...

Something banged against her legs and she screamed. *Really* screamed. Right below Raf's ear. He winced and looked down.

'Dog,' he observed.

'Oh. Sorry about the scream.'

They smiled at each other again and then Georgie decided that the moment – whatever it had been – was very definitely over.

'Bye, then,' she said. 'Have a good flight. *Sans* the half-a-size-too-small trainers.'

'Noah's feet are a little bit smaller than mine, I think. If you can't return them.'

'Good to know.'

'Yeah.'

'Bye, then.' And off she walked and oh fuck now he was going to see her bottom in these hideous leggings. Oh well, she was going to walk tall and pretend she was cool about it, and *ow*, she'd tripped.

Walking tall obviously did not work for her.

She looked round and Raf was standing there looking gorgeous and not at all accident prone, and *really* sniggering.

She screwed her face up at him and walked off again.

* * *

'*Buon giorno,*' Georgie repeated in response to the Duolingo prompt, as she and Max drove along the Fosse Way on their way home to Bristol that afternoon. Max was pressing the buttons on the app for her. (Obviously she'd screenshotted the app and added the photo to the 'Resolutions' chat.)

'Mum, can we stop with the Italian for a bit?' Max asked. '*Por favor*?'

'That's Spanish. *Per favore.*'

'Please?'

'Okay, let's just get to the end of this bit.' It felt like it was going to be a lot harder than she'd drunk-thought to reach GCSE standard in Italian by the end of the year, but she couldn't torment Max too much. It wasn't his fault that she was a complete idiot.

'*Ti amo,*' the Duolingo woman told her to say. *I love you.*

Hmm.

How was she going to keep in touch with Raf? And how was she going to work out whether her suspicions were correct? If they were, maybe it would be okay to have the secret read out. No, it wouldn't. Or, actually, yes, it would. Or would it? Gaaah, it was making her head hurt trying to figure it out. She needed to forget about it for now and just focus on sticking to her resolutions and getting the secret back until she'd found out the truth.

Her phone suddenly pinged about thirteen times in quick succession.

'Can you check to see who that was?' she asked Max.

'It's your "Girls" chat,' he told her, the girls obviously being Poppy, Beth and Ankita.

'Thank you,' she said. Then she automatically added, 'Don't read them.' While she was driving she often got Max to read certain messages out loud for her but never ones from the 'Girls' chat because you never knew when Ankita would write something really inappropriate for eleven-year-old eyes.

She shivered. She loved her friends so much. They really were her and Max's family. She had to do whatever she could to protect that. She could not lose them. So she had to get the secret back.

So she was staying in touch with Raf. End of.

The obvious thing to do was send him some friendly messages to check how he was recovering from his op. Plus there might be some banter on the 'Resolutions' chat.

Could she persuade a friend to go on a trip to New York with her and engineer a visit to his apartment? Not really, and it would probably cost a fortune.

Maybe she should just tell him the (partial) truth and ask him to send the letter back. But then – dreadful thought – what if Max opened it for some reason? It was unlikely, but like most kids of his age he didn't have the *best* privacy instincts and it was possible that he would.

Okay. First things first: she had to work out whether the secret was even true.

Maybe she should just *ask*? She'd need to be careful, though, that no one overheard.

God. If she was *right*, the repercussions would be just… well, mind-blowing.

8

POPPY

Poppy – standing in their little garden just outside the kitchen while Daniel sat in his chair just inside the open door – gave one final hip jerk and laughed at Daniel's giggling and clapping. He was *loving* his mother's completely failed attempts at hula-ing. She stepped out of the hoop, picked it up and leaned it against the back wall of the house before going back through the open kitchen door to join Daniel.

'I am *not* good at that.' She made a face at him and he clapped again. 'Okay.'

She unstrapped him and lifted him out of the chair and put him down on the floor where he immediately started rolling. He *loved* rolling at the moment, and as long as she kept doors closed it was perfect for both of them: he rolled and she could get some chores done.

'We're cooking a new meal,' she said. 'That's *right*, a new meal.'

While she chopped and sliced and danced to her favourite playlist, Daniel rolled and gurgled and did his best to beat the anti-opening devices she had on the drawers and cupboards.

This was *good*. She and Daniel were both having fun, she was making a Moroccan dish that she'd never made before, she was managing to put Declan out of her mind today *and* she had her three best friends coming over this evening to sample her tagine and share some wine.

She was having a really nice afternoon and she could do this any day. If she ended up single she would be *fine*.

* * *

Half an hour later, as she was finishing the made-from-scratch pomegranate jus for her exotic fruit salad – she wasn't having *dessert* dessert, but no one could call fruit salad unhealthy and she couldn't *not* serve her friends pudding – her phone pinged.

She had a message from Beth and there was another one from Ankita from an hour ago that she'd missed, probably while she'd been busy trying to hula.

Beth had written:

I'm so sorry, darling Pops, Dominic's insisting that I go to dinner with a client who's just arrived unexpectedly. I told him about dinner with you but he's getting really angry so I have to go. I'm so sorry about this evening but am free tomorrow – could I come over then instead?

And Ankita had written:

Poppy I'm so sorry but I'm caught up at work finishing something off and couldn't finish at lunchtime after all.

Poppy knew Ankita had a long weekend in the Cotswolds planned and had booked an afternoon off work.

So won't make it for dinner BUT I'll be a lot freer soon – will tell you everything when I see you – tomorrow??

Oh-kay, that was a little bit disappointing, but Poppy could still have a really nice evening with Georgie and maybe see the others over the week-end. And it would be good to have more one-on-one time with Georgie in case she'd seemed a little bit miserable before; she didn't want her friends to pity her or worry about her, so it would be good timing to be able to prove that she was actually very happy.

Twenty minutes later, after a quick walk, she and Daniel were back inside, Poppy's teeth still chattering as she unwrapped a much warmer Daniel from his snowsuit.

'Right,' she told him as he amused himself a *lot* by pulling her hair as hard as he could. 'We need to get you fed and bathed fast so that I can get everything ready for Georgie.'

She took her phone out to check the time and... there was a message from Georgie.

Poppy, I'm so sorry but Max has a friend here for a sleepover and the babysitter just cancelled and I can't leave them so I'm not going to make it for dinner now. I'm so disappointed not to see you all and eat your lovely food!!! Sooooo annoying. Have fun though with Beth and Ankita! Could Max and I come over and see you tomorrow or Sunday for a walk instead? And maybe sample some delicious leftovers??

Oh.

Poppy sat down on the bottom stair with Daniel in her arms and hugged him tightly into her. At least *he* always wanted to see her.

No. It wasn't that her friends didn't want to see her, it was just that they had other stuff going on. And of course they did. They had their own lives.

It didn't feel good, though, having a whole Moroccan-themed meal pretty much ready and just waiting to be served to... no one.

She heaved another enormous – pathetic, if she was honest – sigh, and carried Daniel into the kitchen and put him in his highchair. Again. There was a *lot* of in-and-out of the highchair when you had a baby. There was a lot of repetition, full stop.

She looked over at the fridge. She'd made him a turkey, potato, broccoli, carrot and cranberry mush earlier. And right now all of a sudden it felt like it was too much effort just to walk over to the fridge and get it out and get it ready for him, let alone feed it to him and – yet again – dodge all the mess. She was just so *bored*. Hmm. Maybe Georgie was right to think she needed cheering up.

Daniel wrenched his bib off with a massive effort and threw it at her and laughed and laughed.

His gorgeous little double chin was wobbling away as he chortled. Poppy couldn't help laughing too.

And, okay, she was not going to give in to a little bit of unhappiness about *all* three of her best friends cancelling on her one after the other. She was a mother. She shouldn't be giving in to misery, she should be a grown-up. She did *not* need to be cheered up, actually; she was *fine*.

There had to be someone else she could share the meal with.

As she manoeuvred the pureed turkey into Daniel's mouth with her right hand, she typed out a message to her mum with her left. She'd almost phoned her but had worried that an actual call might seem a bit desperate.

Just suddenly decided to cook some Moroccan food and wondered if you'd like to come over and try it??

That was good. Nonchalant. Not remotely humiliated and let down.

Her mum replied immediately.

Can I come tomorrow? On my way to a party now. Iona from Little Bishop. Her sixtieth. Big black-tie affair.

Okay, yep, good, nice that her mother had a good social life, but also – her mother had a *much* better social life than she did. Was it supposed to be that way round?

Okay, never mind. It did at least look like she'd be seeing people tomorrow.

Okay. Declan. They'd barely seen each other since her abortive be-nice-to-him-with-breakfast attempt. Maybe she should have another go at reminding him what he was missing. He liked her cooking. He was watching a rugby match on TV with friends this evening – that was his story anyway – and, assuming he actually was doing that, he obviously wouldn't want to miss the game but maybe he'd like to have dinner with her afterwards.

Maybe she'd call him to ask.

He picked up on about the seventh ring, just as she was about to put the phone down.

'Hello?' He sounded oddly terse.

'Hi. Just wondered what sort of time you thought you'd be home.' She could hear a voice in the background. A woman's voice. Was Declan watching rugby with a *woman*? 'Oh. Who's that?'

'Oh, just, that's... that's Sally. Rory's wife.'

If he was with Rory's wife, why could Poppy also hear loud traffic? Why would he be outside next to a road with Sally? Why wouldn't he just be inside Rory's house?

'Where are you?' she couldn't help asking.

'At Rory's, as I said.' Still sounding terse, and blatantly lying, unless Rory had huge lorries rumbling through his living room.

Right.

No. Poppy was not going to go mad with him now. And she was not going to put Daniel in his car seat and drive over to Rory's and *check*. She was... Well, she was... She was going to continue to think things through, for Daniel's sake if nothing else. Plus she wasn't going to humiliate herself in front of another woman. And, really, had anything changed if he *was* with the other woman now?

'Why did you call?' Declan asked.

'Oh, nothing major. It's just that I have a lot of extra food – I cooked a *lot* – and wondered if you'd like any when you get home.'

'Yes, great, or maybe tomorrow – I'd love some then – just going to be ordering a lot of pizza here I think and I doubt I'll be that hungry later.'

'Oh, of course. Yes, definitely leftovers tomorrow. Yum.' She sounded weird now but really, who cared. 'So, have a lovely evening. Hope Ireland win.' She was impressed at how polite she'd managed to be.

'You too. Say hi to your friends. Enjoy your dinner. Love you.'

'Thank you. See you later.'

She was crying, she realised, as she ended the call.

She placed her phone on the table face down so she wouldn't be tempted to go on any social media and see how perfect and busy and social everyone else's lives were, and sniffed back her tears.

'Just you and me,' she said to Daniel, smiling, which took a lot of effort, 'and we are going to have *fun* this evening.'

She could watch something good on TV after she'd put him to bed. It would be fine. When she was working she'd always wished she had more time to watch TV. She could totally pass this evening happily starting on a new box set. Something she hadn't watched with Declan or discussed watching with him, so that it was *hers*.

She might be doing a lot of solo television watching in the future.

Daniel beamed back at her and picked up his bowl and spoon and threw the whole lot at her head. She ducked sideways and it sailed behind her and splatted on the floor.

'Well,' she said, after she was sure that she wasn't going to swear. 'That. Is. A. Lot. Of. Clearing. Up.'

There was puree on the walls, on the kitchen units, everywhere. It was genuinely as bad as Declan's fire incident. She needed to get cleaning. But first she was going to have to get some more food for Daniel or he'd be hungry. Fucking yay.

* * *

'Morning.' Declan rolled into the kitchen at nine the next morning as Poppy was finishing the clearing up that she should very obviously have done last night – the puree would have been a *lot* less stuck on – but just hadn't been able to make herself do at the time.

'Morning.' She couldn't quite look at him after yesterday evening. She'd lain awake listening out for him last night, and had then pretended to be asleep while he slightly drunkenly tiptoed around the room shushing himself so that he wouldn't wake either her or Daniel. (It hadn't worked, obviously; shortly after Declan had sunk straight into a snory sleep, Daniel had woken up yelling.) And now she was very tired.

She *was* going to have a good day, though. She was going to ignore Declan until she'd had space to think more. Georgie and Max were coming over for lunch and a walk and she was seeing Beth and Ankita this evening.

She would be *fine*. As long as she could just pretend the Declan thing wasn't happening.

'How was your evening?' Declan turned the kettle on and settled himself at the table. The sheer *brazen-ness* of him.

'Great, thank you. How was the rugby?' She could hear her own voice sounding tight and bordering on angry.

'Ireland won so I'm not complaining, and I *might* have a sore head this morning.' How could he not be reacting to the way she was speaking?

She couldn't stomach this any more.

'Enjoy your breakfast, then.' She picked Daniel up and left the room.

Maybe she'd walk round with him to see her parents before Georgie and Max arrived. She didn't want to be around Declan this morning.

And while she was there she could focus on pretending that her life wasn't falling apart, and she would look online for tips on how to learn to do the splits. The *splits*. What an idiot. Stupid resolution. She was *not* flexible. YouTube would be able to help, though, she was sure, and you read stories all the time about ninety-three-year-olds with bodies like twenty-eight-year-olds who could win Iron Woman competitions, swim the Channel and *obviously* do the splits.

Oh. As she wrestled Daniel into his snowsuit she realised that it probably didn't matter what resolutions she'd put down; if she and Declan split up everyone would know her secret that he'd had an affair.

'Are you going out?' Declan had appeared at the door of the kitchen, chewing, a slice of toast in his hand.

'Yep.' And she whisked herself and Daniel out of the house.

* * *

Poppy had just finished doing Daniel's lunch and Declan had taken him to put him down for his afternoon sleep when Georgie and Max turned up.

When Declan came into the room a couple of minutes later, he hesitated for a moment, and then shook Max's hand before giving Georgie a very distant air kiss.

'How are you both doing? How's school, Max? I was thinking I might just nip out.'

'Oh, but it's lunchtime?' Poppy was sure he hadn't already eaten, and

Declan was not a man who ever missed a meal. Was he planning to eat with someone else?

'Yeah, no, not hugely hungry. I'll pick something up while I'm out.'

'But you wanted to try my Moroccan food?' Maybe Poppy would just keep on questioning him like this every time he behaved oddly until he cracked and told her the truth.

'Yes, I'd love to try it. Really love to. Later, though. I really need to go out now. See you later.'

'Bye. Good to see you.' Wow. Georgie sounded weird too. She must have noticed the oddness between Declan and Poppy and be feeling awkward. To be fair, she'd only known Declan in person for the few weeks since he and Poppy had got back from Australia and had met him on only a few occasions during that time, and it probably shouldn't be a surprise that sensing tension in the air between Poppy and a relative stranger might make her feel awkward.

Declan left and Georgie immediately went pretty much back to normal – clearly it *had* been the marital tension that had been making her feel awkward – and Poppy decided that she was going to have fun with her best friend and her godson and not think about her stupid husband.

* * *

When Declan got back, Georgie and Max had gone and Ankita had arrived.

He came up behind Poppy in the kitchen, pulled her against him, hard, and kissed the back of her neck, and said, 'I love you,' low and huskily into her ear.

Poppy didn't know what she'd have done if Ankita hadn't been there. Maybe she'd have allowed herself to press back against him just for a second... before asking why he was being so passionate all of a sudden, and was it guilt passion. Or maybe she'd have accidentally on purpose trodden hard on his foot. Or maybe she'd have turned round and walloped him and yelled a lot.

But Ankita *was* there.

So she moved sideways away from him and ignored his words and said,

'Ankita and I thought we might go to the pub for dinner. Are you happy to babysit Daniel?'

* * *

The following Tuesday, Poppy took Daniel shopping in Cheltenham. As she emerged from the supermarket, her buggy laden down by very full bags for life on the handles on each side, she heard someone calling her name and looked round.

'Sally!' she said in a strangled voice. She'd only met Declan's friend Rory's wife once, at the pub the night before New Year's Eve, but she recognised her immediately, possibly because she'd thought about her a *lot* since Declan had clearly been lying about being inside with her.

'How are you?' Sally squatted down in front of the buggy – managing to look graceful the entire time – and said, 'Hello, Daniel. I've heard a lot about you.'

Poppy raised her eyebrows and fought with herself not to speak until she'd calmed down. She felt almost shaky with anger; she didn't remember saying much about Daniel to Sally when they'd met, so she'd obviously heard about him from Declan. *Nice* to talk about your baby to your lover.

'He's *gorgeous*,' Sally said, turning her flawless, heart-shaped face up to Poppy.

'Thank you,' Poppy said, through extremely gritted teeth.

Well. Here was her opportunity to do some digging.

'Did you enjoy the rugby on Friday evening?' she asked.

'Rugby?' repeated Sally absently, cooing at Daniel.

Poppy *really* wanted to yell that she should move away from her baby.

'The rugby on Friday evening,' she repeated.

'Oh, the rugby. Oh, yes, Rory mentioned Declan was coming over. I went out with some girlfriends.'

'Did you see Declan?' Poppy's questioning probably sounded odd but she didn't care; she sensed that she was on the brink of catching him out in a tangible lie and she just wanted to get it over with.

'No, I left quite early.'

And there it was: the lie. Just like that. Either Sally was lying now – and there could only be one reason for that – or Declan had been lying on Friday when he'd said he was with her.

'He said he saw you,' Poppy said.

'Nope, definitely not me.' Sally's smile seemed entirely guileless.

'Oh. My mistake. Well, it was lovely to bump into you. I have to go.'

9

GEORGIE

Georgie would not have predicted that she'd have been able to talk all three of the others into joining her, but here they were the next evening, bottoms in the air in the middle of a yoga class in a hall in a fairly run-down leisure centre on the outskirts of Cirencester.

Beth had said yes immediately, because taking up yoga was one of her resolutions too.

Ankita had had big news on Saturday, which was that she'd resigned from her job and was undergoing a metamorphosis from seventy-hour-a-week banking superstar to laidback rural dweller, and she'd said she was totally up for switching her yoga classes from a swish Notting Hill studio to a less glamorous one much closer to Melting.

Poppy had said yes at first but had then predictably – at the last minute, when Ankita arrived to pick her up – said she couldn't come because of Daniel. Ankita (not entirely metamorphosed from scary kick-arse investment banker) had told her she would carry her to the car if she didn't walk to it, so Poppy had walked.

So here they all were.

Georgie wasn't loving the yoga experience. She was still not enjoying running, and it was already clear that she was not a yoga natural either. They were all in a row, rolled up on their shoulders with their arms bent, their hands supporting their waists and their legs in varying degrees of straightness with their toes pointed towards the ceiling, in a so-called 'very basic' Yoga Pose Shoulder Stand.

Georgie was alternating between being very grateful for her lovely new, comfortably waist-banded, large-size running tights, very pissed off that she'd been stupid enough to make her yoga resolution, and really worried that she might *fart*. She never did, ever – the last time had literally been during labour – but there was a first time for everything, and the way yoga was going for her so far it didn't seem unlikely that today would be that first time. Next time she came (dreadful thought), she'd remember not to eat curry the night before.

And then into the pain and heavy breathing-filled silence, Poppy blurted out a bombshell.

'I think Declan's having an affair.'

It took Georgie a little bit of time to grasp what she'd said. It was obviously taking Ankita and Beth some time to process her words too, because none of them said anything for a few moments.

Beth recovered her powers of speech first. 'Oh my goodness, Poppy, I'm so sorry. Are you sure?'

'Yes.' Poppy sniffed.

'Why do you think that?' asked Ankita. The rest of them had rolled down but she was still in her perfectly vertical shoulder stand.

'He's distracted. He smelled of someone else's perfume the other evening. He snapped at me when he thought I'd looked at his laptop screen last week. He snatched his phone out of my sight when he got a message recently. He's been over-nice at times, like *guilty* nice. Lots of small things like that. And *then*...'

It turned out Declan had been with a woman on Friday evening and had lied about it. Shit. That did sound very damning.

Georgie's mind whirred as the extraordinarily toned legs of the instructor, Mags, came into her eyeline. What Poppy had just said was so shocking and with so many ramifications that she really couldn't get her head round it. All she could think about was the very mundane, that Mags had to be well into her fifties but had a body that most teenagers would kill for.

Possibly because she took yoga, even beginner yoga for idiots, far too seriously.

'Ladies, we aren't here to chat. We're here to do yoga. You're disturbing everyone else. Please be quiet or I'll have to split you up.'

Mags was ridiculous. Yoga wasn't GCSE Maths. No one *needed* to do it (unless they'd made a stupid resolution that they had to keep).

'Poppy,' Georgie whispered.

'*Ladies*,' hissed Mags.

'Let's go for a coffee afterwards.' Ankita was *still* upside down on her shoulders. *How* was her head not throbbing? Unnatural.

'Can't,' Poppy said. 'I've got to get back to Daniel. Although I'd better not get back earlier than I said because I don't want to see Declan with the other woman.'

Georgie moved round behind Beth to give Poppy a hug. 'Poppy, maybe there's an innocent explanation,' she said, really hoping that was true. Poppy and Declan had had quite a whirlwind relationship and the rest of them didn't know Declan very well. They'd only met him a few weeks ago when he and Poppy had arrived back from Australia with Daniel. 'There's no way Declan's with another woman at this moment. He's a devoted father and husband. He'll be grappling with Daniel's bedtime and then he'll probably be kicking back with a beer or something.'

'I wish,' said Poppy.

This was terrible. Even Raf probably wouldn't be able to put a make-someone-smile spin on this.

'Ladies,' bawled Mags from the front. 'Final warning.'

Poppy made a weird gulpy, sniffy sound, like she was crying but trying not to.

Surprisingly, it was yoga queen Ankita who then said, 'Okay, let's leave right now. We can find a different class.'

Five minutes later, they were sitting with polystyrene cups of coffee, huddled round a stained Formica table in the unheated leisure centre café.

'Poppy, whatever happens, we're all here for you,' Georgie said, as they saw a tear dribble down Poppy's cheek.

Beth, who was closest, folded Poppy into her arms, and said, 'Yes, darling Poppy, always,' while Ankita said, 'Absolutely.'

'Poppy.' Ankita pushed her chair round the table and put her face right in front of Poppy's. 'Have you asked Declan about any of it? Given him a chance to explain in case it isn't true?'

'No.' Poppy sniffed again. 'I've been trying to work out what I should do. I want to tackle him, but I need to know what I want to do afterwards. Like, what if it's just been a short affair? Would I take him back for Daniel's sake? So I've been waiting. But now I feel as though I'm going mad.'

'I think you should probably discuss it with him as soon as possible,' Georgie said, horrified at the awfulness of this for Poppy, and mind-blown at the wider ramifications.

For example, what would happen with Daniel and custody if Poppy and Declan split up?

'I think you should too,' Beth said. 'Now that you're this upset you need to know for definite. The reality probably isn't going to be worse than what you're imagining and it *could* be better. There *could* be a rational explanation for all of it?'

'Really?' Poppy said. 'I don't think so.'

'Better to find out, though,' Ankita agreed. 'Would you like any moral support while you ask him?'

Georgie turned to stare at her. *Surely* it would be better for Poppy to have this conversation alone with her husband.

'That's very kind but I should do it by myself,' Poppy said miserably.

Beth put her arms round Poppy again. 'So you're definitely going to ask him outright? Very soon? I really do think he might be able to reassure you. And you know what?' She gestured very over-vigorously at Poppy and knocked over her coffee cup. They all stared as poo-brown-coloured liquid dribbled down Poppy's pale-blue top.

'I probably look about how I feel right now.' Poppy did a big circular air-motion around the stain with her right forefinger, with an accompanying head roll.

Georgie felt like her heart might break at the sadness of Poppy trying to claw back some of her usual humour.

'I'm so sorry.' Beth mopped ineffectually at the stain. 'I'll buy you some new kit.'

'Honestly, gym kit is right at the bottom of my list of worries at the moment.' Poppy gave a honking sniff and said, 'Okay, I can't talk about this any more. I want to be distracted. How's everyone else? Give me something interesting to think about.'

Georgie, Beth and Ankita all mumbled nothings.

'No, I mean it. I want to hear what's going on with you. When I'm lying awake tonight, wallowing in Declan misery, I want to have some gossip to think about too. Come on. You must have *something*.' Poppy was so brave. Georgie wanted to cry on her behalf. And, yes, she personally *did* quite possibly have 'something', and she certainly wasn't going to be sharing that right now.

'Erm, one of my Year Eights wrote really bad swear words all over the wall of a loo cubicle this morning, in full view of several other boys and had been suspended by lunch time,' she offered.

'Immediately suspended? How *bad* were the swear words?' Poppy said. 'You have to tell us.'

'Lean in,' Georgie said, and whispered what he'd written.

Gratifyingly, Poppy did join in with Beth and Ankita in saying, 'Noooo.'

'Okay, I need more to distract me.' Poppy looked at Ankita. 'You have to fill us in properly on the job thing. Your old and new boss. Alex. What's he like?'

'Very nice.' Ankita sounded odd. Georgie suddenly wondered whether she had a thing for Alex. She couldn't actually remember the last time Ankita had had a serious boyfriend.

'Nice?' asked Beth, her head on one side, like she always did when she was asking a question that she felt was a bit over-curious.

Georgie knew her friends *so* well. She could *not* lose them. What would *happen* if her secret was true? Or if it wasn't but someone read it? It might well blow their friendship group apart. She *had* to find out soon if it was true.

'He's very nice,' Ankita was saying, in a slightly strange, brisk kind of voice. 'Very decent. We went out for dinner with clients a couple of weeks ago and he stuck up for me when one of them was a complete letch, and he totally didn't have to. Not every boss would have done.'

'What did he say to them?' Poppy asked.

By the time Ankita had finished describing Alex's forthrightness to the client and the way she and Alex had then marched out of the dinner and gone and got a burger, Poppy seemed fully distracted, thank goodness.

'So, Alex?' Beth had her head to one side. 'And you?'

'You're such a romance junkie,' said Ankita. 'Seriously.'

Georgie looked at Ankita and then at Poppy, and then Ankita raised an eyebrow in Beth's direction. Yep, it was a shame that Beth – Mrs Romance – was in the most un-romantic engagement ever.

'No romance with Alex,' said Ankita.

'I think there's a *but*,' Poppy said.

Ankita screwed up her beautiful face (and still looked beautiful).

'*Ankita*,' Poppy said. 'Is there romance with someone else?'

'No?' Ankita said. 'Ish? Maybe.'

'Ankita, you have to tell us,' Poppy commanded. She spread her hands. 'I'm miserable so you have a duty tell me everything.'

'*Fine*,' Ankita said. 'Total emotional blackmail, *so* unfair. But okay. And to be fair you're my best friends and I might need some moral support if it all goes wrong.'

'And?' Poppy urged.

'Okay. I have a date lined up for next Sunday.'

'Who with?' asked Georgie. She was pretty sure that Ankita went on quite a lot of dates, but this one seemed like a big deal.

Ankita was screwing her face up again. 'I don't think I can actually get the words out.'

'Er, what?' said Georgie. 'You're *Ankita*. You're fearless.'

'Is it your lovely next-door neighbour in London?' asked Beth.

'Nope. He's gay. And even if he weren't, we're too good friends.'

'Your uni friend, Fred?' asked Poppy.

'No,' said Ankita. 'Also too good a friend.'

'Who?' said Georgie.

'Okay.' Ankita's smile was coy, there was no other word for it. Which was weird, because in the thirty years that they'd known her, she'd never done coyness. And now she was twisting her hair round her finger so much that her hair was literally in danger of looking messed up. 'It's Noah.'

Beth blinked. 'Noah who?'

'Noah Burton. Duck and Grapes.'

'No way,' Poppy breathed.

'I've basically had a crush on him since we were about fifteen.'

'Oh.' Beth's jaw was literally hanging open. Georgie gave her a little nudge. Obviously it *was* astonishing. Noah was gorgeous, but in a cuddly, rugby-playery, slightly dishevelled way. He was the perfect pub landlord. Always cheerful, always chatty, always nice. But not like a London banker. Not like Ankita. It was mind-boggling imagining them together. What would they have in common? But Ankita was obviously really excited, so they should be pleased for her.

'So did he ask you out?' said Georgie.

'I asked *him* out,' said Ankita.

'Wow,' said Poppy. 'Congratulations.'

'He didn't mention it,' said Beth.

The others all turned to stare at her.

'*Does* Noah mention a lot of stuff to you?' asked Ankita, frowning slightly.

'I've been doing his flowers at the pub twice-weekly since New Year,' said Beth, 'so four times now, and we've ended up chatting quite a lot. Speaking of which, he told me that Raf's moving back to England.'

Raf was moving back to England? Wow. Huge. *Huge.* Georgie really needed to find out where he'd be living; if it was anywhere nearby she might be able to engineer going to his home and getting the letter back. That would be *amazing.*

As Georgie opened her mouth to ask about Raf's move, Beth said, 'But I'll tell you about that in a minute. First tell us about the date with Noah. Where are you going? When did you ask him out? What happened?' She sounded almost accusatory. Honestly, absolutely everyone seemed to have gone a bit mad recently.

When they'd finished talking about the quite astonishing Ankita-and-Noah-date news, Georgie would have to manoeuvre the conversation back to Raf.

Apparently, Ankita had fancied the pants off Noah for nineteen years and had dated a lot less than everyone had always assumed.

It was funny how you could know people really well for most of your life and still not know everything about them. Well, not *that* funny. None of

Georgie's friends had a clue about her current predicament and it was not amusing.

'This is so exciting, Ankita,' Poppy said. 'I'm so impressed that you asked Noah out.'

'It'll be nice for Raf's family that he's moving back to England, won't it?' Beth hadn't said anything for a while. She really was giving the impression that she wasn't super happy about Ankita dating Noah.

'Raf's gorgeous, isn't he, Georgie?' Ankita clearly thought it would be nice to move the conversation away from her and Noah. 'Maybe something will happen between you and we could go on a double date.'

Georgie laughed. Frankly, if it would get her secret back, she'd go on any number of double dates.

'Assuming everything works out with you and Noah,' Beth said, not sounding at all jokey.

Georgie turned to stare at her. Beth never, ever said negative or mean things.

She looked at her three best friends: Beth sweet and mad-haired in pink, Ankita svelte in black, Poppy in her stained top, her ponytail lopsided from all the hugging earlier and her eyes and nose still a little bit red, but still looking beautiful, and doing *so* well to try to rise above the hideous Declan affair thing. Apart from Max, they meant more in the world to her than anyone else. This Noah thing was not good.

She did not want there to be strife amongst her best friends. Now or ever. She wished *so much* that she could just ignore her secret. She didn't have any choice though; she had to work out whether her suspicions were right.

'I wonder whether we should all get going,' she said. 'Can we all have a big hug first?'

She group-hugged them into her *hard*. She didn't want them to argue with each other and she didn't want any of them to hate her.

So she'd be back at yoga in two weeks' time, and she'd better learn some more Italian in the meantime and make a plan to get her secret back from Raf. And obviously work out soon whether or not the secret was *right*.

* * *

Georgie had ample time to reflect on all sorts on the very long drive home after yoga, including the fact that it didn't matter that they'd pissed off Mags so much; realistically it would not work for her to schlepp all the way to Cirencester for yoga every fortnight. She also thought a lot about Poppy and Declan, obviously, and about Raf. And her secret.

Once she was home and scrabbling around her kitchen to get things ready for work in the morning, her eye alit on the secret letter she'd received in the post a few days before.

She couldn't actually remember who'd put their secret in her envelope, but she had to admit she was curious about what was in there.

She wondered whether Raf was curious about what was in *her* envelope. He wouldn't dream of opening it, though, she was sure. She hoped.

* * *

Georgie was jogging slowly past her favourite café the next morning, the one that made her favourite carrot cake with butter icing (she *hated* her resolutions), when she had a brainwave.

Recent events had proved that she needed to be surreptitious, but there was a really easy way of doing that.

As soon as she got home, she took her laptop out. Nope, no good; there was nothing available online for ages. She was going to have to call.

Seventeen minutes later, after she'd listened to 'Bohemian Rhapsody' all the way through three times on hold, she finally got through.

'It's urgent,' she said. 'Could I get an appointment one evening this week?'

'You have to call on the day and book a daytime one if it's urgent.'

'Okay. Great.'

Dammit. Okay. Fine.

She went back online and booked the first one she could – for three weeks away – as a backstop for if she couldn't find another way.

10

GEORGIE

Shiiiiit. It was 10.58 p.m. Georgie dropped her tea towel and sprinted for her bedroom, leapt into bed, pulled the duvet right up to her chin, took a selfie of herself and posted it to the 'Resolutions' chat. It was already becoming difficult to remember to keep on proving that she was going to bed in good time four nights a week.

If only it was as easy as this to 'prove' that she was sticking to all her other resolutions. Bloody yoga. Bloody skating. Bloody Italian.

Back out of bed, because she had at least another hour of tidying and marking to do, she went back into the kitchen to finish the dishes.

As she was squeezing all her saucepans into an over-full cupboard a message pinged in from Raf.

So I'm back in Bristol. Having been away for so long, I don't have many running partners here so naturally you sprang to mind. You up for a run?

No. Actual torture. She was getting better at running and was heading towards the point where she might even post a picture of her 'map my run' time on the chat instead of herself in running kit, but she didn't want to run with actual fit people.

Although... Maybe, somehow, they might end up in his house and she could find the letter...

Running, though.

Oh. Brainwave.

You know what kind of partner I WOULD like? A skating one.

You Torvill, me Dean?

Exactly.

I think I might disappoint you. I can skate but I cannot perform Olympic ice dance routines.

Me neither but I need to learn. I need to be Torvill by the end of the year. Specifically, I need to be able to successfully perform a jump.

Resolution?

Yes.

No problem.

Okay.

Georgie's face was almost aching she was smiling so hard as she typed.

I'll research ice rinks and I'll be back...

Aren't you asleep right now, though?

What? Oh, she'd posted the early-to-bed selfie. Dammit. Raf was very annoying.

I'm in bed, NEARLY asleep. I'll be properly asleep in a minute.

They say you shouldn't use your phone in bed. Blue light.

You never use your phone in bed?

Ha yes of course I do.

Georgie took a moment to imagine Raf in bed – mmm – and then typed,

Ha hypocrite. Night.

Goodnight. Sleep well x

Funny how quickly they'd got to this comfortable messaging stage. After Beth had mentioned that Raf was returning to Bristol, Georgie had sent him a few messages asking how his finger was because she wanted to stay in touch because of the letter. But somehow here they were now, texting like buddies. She hadn't been friends like this with a man for a long time. Ever, really.

It was hopefully going to come in very handy for getting the secret back.

* * *

Georgie used her lunch break the next day to make hay while the sun shone and booked the two of them in for a skating lesson the following Friday evening. She messaged Raf.

Send me your address and I'll pick you up.

Honestly don't worry. I can cab it.

No, really, I'll be passing almost by your door.

You don't know where I live?

Quirk of geography: all other places are somewhere between me and the ice rink.

Oh right well in that case I'd love a lift.

And hey presto she had his address.

And inside his address – which was now in Bristol, not New York, hooray, hooray, hooray – would be her letter.

She dipped a carrot in houmous and thought about her position. She obviously needed to find out as soon as possible whether she was right about the secret, but either way it would be *much* better not to have it written down and out there, so it would be amazing to get the letter back. Or swap it, actually. She should swap in a different piece of paper with a tamer secret on it. Use her new steaming skills. She'd better remember to take some Pritt Stick.

She took another carrot stick. It was still two and a half weeks until her appointment. She wanted to find out the truth about the secret *now*. Maybe she should think about pulling a sickie and going during the day.

* * *

The second Georgie saw Raf emerge from his front door on Friday evening, all big and handsome in his navy tracksuit bottoms, grey hoodie and puffer, her heart rate stepped up. And when he opened the car door and squeezed himself inside, well... She could barely speak.

'Hello,' she managed.

'Hello.' He always sounded as though he was on the brink of laughter. She looked round at him and his eyes were crinkling again and now she wanted to laugh too. And all they'd done was say hello.

'I remember now,' he continued. 'This car was designed perfectly for me.'

'I moved the seat back for you.'

'Yeah, loads of room.' He laughed and stretched, whacking Georgie on the shoulder with his arm and his head on the car ceiling. 'Whoops. Sorry.'

'No worries. I think you've probably just broken my collarbone, nothing else.' She smiled and put the car into gear, keeping her fingers to herself, and pulled away, trying very hard not to think about where he'd touched her shoulder.

'So, how much skating experience do you have?' he asked. 'And how advanced do you need to be by the end of the year?'

'I've been quite a few times but I haven't ever really progressed beyond holding the penguin. And I need to do a successful jump as part of a routine.'

'Wow. What kind of a routine?'

'I did not specify that, so the routine will be basic. I'm also thinking that the routine and the jump could involve me holding on to something at all times. Like I could just hold on to the side of the rink and jump.' Georgie thought for a minute. 'That would actually be quite hard though, wouldn't it?'

'It'll be fine. It's all just a matter of confidence.'

'I mean, confidence and *some* ability.'

'You'll be *fine*.'

'How's your no caffeine resolution going?' Georgie asked. They didn't need to talk about ice skating any more. 'I'm seeing lots of virtuous decaf coffee photos on the chat.'

'I'm still on fire. Although if I'm honest, I don't even need to keep my resolutions anyway because my secret is not a big one. So I'm just laughing at the rest of you, basically.'

'Hmm, good to know. So is it weird to have moved back after so long?' Georgie regretted the question as soon as she'd asked it because they all knew that the reason he'd moved to New York in the first place had been to escape his grief after his wife had died. Noah had once, when he'd sunk a good five pints, said that he thought that Raf hadn't just wanted to escape his own grief but also that of his family and friends. So probably in moving back he couldn't help thinking about the past.

'You know, it felt like the right time. I mean...' He paused and Georgie stared at the road ahead, waiting. 'Yeah, so, basically, all good.'

Yep, fair enough; of course he hadn't been going to talk about his wife to her – they barely knew each other. A couple of weeks of text banter did not a deep and meaningful relationship make.

The rest of the journey passed quickly, and relatively safely apart from when Raf made Georgie laugh so much about a divorce client he'd had to turn down she nearly hit a bollard. By the time they arrived at the rink she wasn't even really too over-aware any more of his gorgeousness and proximity to her, she was just enjoying herself.

* * *

'Do you think you can tell a lot about someone from their socks?' Raf asked her when they were changing into their skating boots.

Georgie looked down at her *Minions* ones. 'I don't need to justify my footwear to you, but I could tell you that I haven't had time to do a lot of laundry this week—' the resolutions were making her even more ridiculously busy than usual '—and Beth very sweetly bought these for Max for Christmas and he didn't like them so I'm wearing them.'

'Or you could just admit that you're a huge *Minions* fan?'

Georgie nudged him hard in his (very lovely and firm) side and then wondered what she was doing.

She looked down at his feet (clad in nice, non-*Minion* socks) and opened her mouth to ask if he thought you could tell a lot about someone from their (large) foot size and then thought better of it. Nothing to do with her, anyway. Obviously. *Really* obviously.

'Georgie?'

'Mmm?' She bent down to hide her face under her hair while she did her boots up.

'Were you thinking something obscene?'

'No, I was not.' She totally had been.

'Ha ha ha.' He stood up in his large boots and held out a hand. 'Come on.'

Georgie took the hand, stood up, and swivelled really, really alarmingly.

'I'm going to die,' she said, when Raf had her vertical again. 'We aren't even on ice yet.'

'It's easier on the ice,' he told her. 'That's where skates are *meant* to be.'

'Oh please.' Georgie rolled her eyes as she began to inch forward towards the entrance to the rink.

* * *

'Hi, so I'm Billie and I'm your instructor for today.' Billie was a lot closer in age to Max than to Georgie and was wearing an all-in-one slinky orange skating outfit and had her black curls piled high on her head. She basically looked like a youthful goddess, who Georgie could never hope to emulate. 'What are your aims from this session?'

'I'd like to be able to perform a jump on ice,' Georgie said.

'Like this?' Billie skated off, did a simultaneous jump and turn in the air and then came back.

'I would *love* to do that,' Georgie said. 'How much training would that take?'

'Depends on your skill level and your commitment.'

'Skill level low. Commitment high,' Georgie said.

'Amazing.' Billie turned to Raf. 'And what about you?'

'No specific aims. Just to have fun.'

'Amazing,' Billie repeated. She looked at the two of them and smiled. 'You're cute together. I love teaching couples.'

'Oh, no, I...' Georgie said, but Billie was already skating off in goddess fashion.

Raf was laughing.

'Come on.' Billie turned and beckoned.

Raf pushed with one foot and off he went. Georgie stared at them both in horror and then set off walking along the side of the rink holding on to the side.

'Over here,' Billie called.

Georgie shook her head. 'I literally can't.'

'You literally *can*.' Billie was a positivity goddess too. Her encouragement wasn't going to work, though.

Maybe Georgie could do a jump holding on to a penguin.

* * *

Fifty minutes later, Billie had said, 'Amazing,' a lot of times and Raf seemed to have learnt a lot and was on his way to being able to do an unaided waltz jump, whereas Georgie had fallen over a lot of times and still couldn't skate by herself more than two feet away from the side.

'Okay, you've both been amazing,' Billie said. 'Now we're going to have some fun for the last ten minutes.'

'Fun?' Georgie was pretty sure she would be having no fun until she was out of her skates and well away from the rink.

'Yes, we're going to put some of your new skills together. With your chemistry, it's going to be amazing.'

'Chemistry?' Georgie queried.

'The two of you.' Billie drew a heart shape with her finger between them. 'It's amazing. Sizzling. Now.'

Nonsense. Obviously a *lot* of people would find Raf attractive, and yes Georgie might be one of those people, but she had definitely not been demonstrating that for the past hour while she'd been concentrating on avoiding breaking a bone.

Before Georgie could correct her, though, Billie took her arm and pulled her away from the side.

'Don't let go,' Georgie shrieked.

'Relax,' Billie said, and guided her over to Raf and stood her next to him, side to side. 'Okay, I'm going to show you some basic moves together. First, just link hands.'

Georgie did not want to link hands with Raf. It would just be a bit weird. You didn't link hands with people who, despite your better judgement, you couldn't help finding excruciatingly attractive.

'I...' she began. And then Billie let go – *let go* – of her, right there in the middle of the ice. 'Help!' she screamed.

And then Raf took her hand. The *relief*.

'I said "link",' Billie said, laughing, 'not hang on for dear life.'

'Doing my best,' Georgie said.

'Okay. So keeping your fingers linked, just stand there and relax, and roll your shoulders.'

Raf rolled his shoulders and his arm moved up a bit.

'Dooooon't,' Georgie warned.

'Yeah, okay, no shoulder rolling,' Billie said. 'You're obviously warmed up anyway. So. Amazing. Right. Turn so that you're facing each other and hold hands.'

No way could Georgie do any turning. And also: hold hands?

'Erm.'

She didn't have much time to worry before Raf moved his feet and reached for her other hand and pulled slightly so that they were standing facing each other on the ice.

And... gulp.

His hands were big and warm and enclosed hers perfectly. And her eyes were level with his nicely muscled chest, and when she looked up a little she could see his firm, very slightly stubbled chin, and his mouth and... he was looking at her, just like she was looking at him, as though they were drinking each other in with their eyes.

Georgie swallowed and then she saw Raf swallow too. She could see a hint of dark hair at the neck of his T-shirt again, and wondered whether he...

'I *said*—' Billie's face was suddenly almost between theirs '—Raf is now going to skate backwards and you're going to skate forwards, Georgie, so that you're skating together. And with all this *amazing* chemistry—' she indicated between them with her finger and nearly took Georgie's eye out '—your bodies are going to be so in sync you won't believe it.' She clapped. 'And off you go. Raf left foot and Georgie right foot.'

Raf started moving backwards and Georgie tried to move at the same time, but she already couldn't remember which foot to move and, help, her feet were going in opposite directions from each other and she was going to fall... and, no, it was okay, Raf was holding her up. She clung on to him, possibly screaming slightly, until he drew them to a stop and she was able to arrange her feet underneath herself.

'I'm not ready for this,' she said.

Raf was laughing so much he couldn't speak.

'Amazing.' Billie skated effortlessly over to them. 'This time, Georgie, why don't you keep your feet still and Raf can just guide you.'

'Drag me, you mean?'

'Guide you.'

Raf was still laughing.

'Shut up.'

'Okay. Georgie, stop holding Raf's arm so tightly,' Billie told her. Georgie looked down and, oh, right, she had both her hands clamped, knuckle-whiteningly hard, around Raf's left arm.

'Okay.' She transferred her hands into his and planted her feet beneath her. 'Ready to glide gracefully.'

Raf began to skate backwards slowly, pulling Georgie, and really, this was actually quite pleasant. She wasn't moving her feet at *all*, but it felt almost as though she was properly skating. It wasn't fast enough for exhilaration, but it was definitely mildly exciting.

As was being in such close proximity to Raf. They were just sliding around the ice, holding hands, standing really very close together, and she was struggling to look anywhere other than at his chest and face.

'I think we're ready for a twirl,' Billie said. 'Raf, lift one of Georgie's hands and turn her. Georgie: amazing. Don't move your feet at all, just let Raf guide you and you'll be dancing in no time. Don't move your feet, though.'

Raf lifted their hands and let go of her right one and began to twirl her. Georgie jerked her legs in horror and next thing all of her was spinning and she was definitely, definitely going to hit her head on the ground. This was all terrible and she *hated* her resolutions, and… and then Raf caught her round the waist with his left arm and pulled her against him and suddenly everything was alright and she was not going to hurt herself. They were pressed right up against each other and she could hear his heart beating where her face was against his chest, or maybe that was her own heart beating. When she looked up, she saw him moisten his lips a little and his eyes gazing down at her. She moistened her own lips and all she could think about was where their bodies and hands were touching, and whether he might actually kiss her.

And then Billie said, 'Gorgeous. You two have *so* much chemistry,' and Georgie realised that she'd been practically undressing Raf with her eyes. In that moment, if she hadn't been terrified to do so, she'd have leapt away from him.

'Apparently you slipping on ice and me catching you is our thing.' Raf's voice was a little hoarse.

* * *

'Well, that wasn't what I was expecting,' Raf said a few minutes later, when they were back in their lovely, lovely regular, non-bladed shoes.

'I know. It's like we mistakenly ended up in a couple's sex therapy session.'

'Hahaha,' Raf laughed, which was lucky because now Georgie thought about it she could have phrased that a lot less embarrassingly. 'I see a hot chocolate stand over there and I'm thinking we've earnt one?'

'We certainly have.' She kind of didn't want the evening to end.

* * *

Standing cradling beautifully warm cups of hot chocolate overlooking incomprehensibly expert skaters speeding and twirling around the ice, Georgie said, 'I love *watching* skaters.'

'Me too. But also actually skating. That was fun.'

'Fun?' Georgie rolled her eyes.

'Yes. Remember, these people have been skating for years. Rome wasn't built in a day.'

'Oh, please.' It would definitely take longer for Georgie to learn to skate well than for the whole of Rome to be built.

'You going to carry on, though?' he asked.

'I have to,' she said morosely.

'This ice jumping thing. Did you specify alone or in a pair?'

'No specification.'

'Well, there you go. Let's do it together. We can get Billie to video us and post it to the chat. A tiny bit of a spring from you, that's a jump, and then I can lift you for a tiny bit of assistance.'

'You're *right*.' Georgie felt her face spread into a beam. Oh, the relief of knowing she should be able to get one of her seemingly-impossible resolutions ticked off. 'Can you do the same time next week if Billie's free?'

'Not sure... I'm going to be spending quite a lot of time in Melting helping out in the pub, because Noah's broken his leg. But if we agree in advance I'm sure I can get cover.'

'Oh no! What happened?'

'Up a ladder trying to unblock a gutter, apparently. Beth found him and called an ambulance and went with him to A&E.'

'Oh dear.' Hmm. Beth and Noah seemed to be getting very close. But Beth was with Tosser-Dominic and Noah was about to be going on a date with Ankita. Georgie hoped things wouldn't get messy between them all. 'So when are you going?'

'Well, I'm just trying to sort cat feeding.'

'You have a cat?' Georgie had really not imagined Raf as a pet owner.

'Two. Inherited from my aunt who owns the house.'

'Oh.' Georgie could feel an idea coming to her. 'I could feed them,' she said.

'Oh no, that's far too much to ask.'

'It really isn't. I drive past most days on my way to—' she shouldn't lie about where she worked because he could just ask the name of the school '—Max's activities. And he *adores* cats. And I keep refusing to get one.' She could spend *so* much time looking for the letter. This was an amazing gift from heaven. 'Honestly, we'd love to. I really, really mean it. And I owe you because you're going to help me out with the skating.' She wouldn't even need to skate again if she got the letter. 'Please?'

'Er, you're literally begging me to allow you to feed my cats?'

'Yup.' Now was not the time to have any shame.

'Well, thank you very much indeed. I'd definitely be grateful if you did it for a day or two while I sort out something long-term.'

'Fab.' She was hopefully only going to need a day or two.

So easy. Who would have thought the envelope was literally going to fall into her lap like this?

11

POPPY

'He's gorgeous, isn't he?' Nancy, the village surgery receptionist, pointed at Declan on stage with one hand and clapped against her arm with the other.

Poppy considered him. Yes. He was gorgeous. No two ways about it. And compering a quiz night suited him.

Being a husband had *seemed* to suit him, but apparently no longer.

She still didn't know what she wanted to do about their situation, which was why, right now, she was sitting here with staff from Declan's surgery, putting on her best jolly, not-at-all-stressed-to-high-heaven-by-the-state-of-her-marriage front.

They were in the village hall of Little Bishop, the closest neighbouring village to Melting, and the biggest of the three Bishops, despite its name, taking part in the annual village quiz night.

'Now this next one—' Declan stared in mock confusion at the card he was holding '—I mean, I don't even understand the question, let alone the answer.' Everyone except Poppy laughed. Poppy produced a fake *Ha*, but she actually just wanted to scream.

It was like she was looking at a stranger. His exterior was so familiar to her – achingly familiar – so much so that she almost just wanted to run up to the stage and throw herself into his arms. His interior, though... Well, that had turned into a lying, philandering arse. And she still couldn't decide whether she'd ever be able to forgive what he'd done or whether she was definitely going to ask him to leave. She was pretty sure that, if she did ask him to leave, she wanted him to *regret* what he'd done and *miss* her, because she had her pride. And she also didn't want to tackle him about anything until she knew exactly what it was she was tackling him *about*. And that was why she was here this evening, pretending to be happily married.

'Poppy?' Nancy was staring at her as though *she* was the one who'd been behaving oddly recently. Which was particularly ridiculous given that they were very recent acquaintances, so what did Nancy even know.

'Sorry, Nancy, I didn't hear. I think I was miles away. Sleep deprivation.'

'Do you happen to know it?'

'It?'

'The answer? What's the capital of Turkmenistan?'

'Ashgabat.' Poppy knew a *lot* of world capitals because Max had had to learn them over Christmas for a sponsored test at school and she'd helped test him one day with Georgie and they'd stuck in her head.

* * *

'Space for a small one?' Declan asked two rounds later (world flags and kids' nineties TV), pulling up a chair and inserting himself between Poppy and Nancy. For a moment, his face was right next to Poppy's and their thighs were pressed together, and her heart and body went flippity flop as they always had done when he came near to her. Giving herself an internal slap at her weakmindedness, she took a close look at Declan. He was wearing the slightly glazed look that he often wore when they came together, and she suddenly realised that maybe – despite his affair – he was having a similar reaction to her. Which was satisfying. She shifted her chair a bit away from him and saw him almost flinch. Good.

Declan frowned slightly and then visibly straightened his shoulders, turned and looked her right in the eye and mouthed something that looked like, 'I love you.'

Really?

'What?' she asked.

'I... No.' He shook his head. 'Nothing.'

Then he smiled round the rest of the table and it was like he was a different person again.

All food for thought, though. If Poppy asked him in due course to choose between her and the other woman – *if* she decided she wanted to do that – maybe he *would* choose Poppy.

'Are we on track to win?' Declan asked.

'We're missing your OTT sports knowledge,' Hassan, one of the other GP partners said from the other side of the table. 'I know we've only known each other for a month but I've never met anyone who can trot out so much sports trivia at any given moment. Pretty sure you'd have got that dodgeball question.'

'I actually would,' Declan said. 'I was watching a dodgeball match on Sky Sports at around 4 a.m. literally only about three nights ago.'

'Four a.m.?' Hassan queried.

'Daniel couldn't sleep.'

'Aww, such a devoted father,' Nancy said. 'You're so lucky, Poppy.'

Poppy applied a superhuman effort and did not say *Sorry, what? That's the first time he's been up at night with Daniel for months, it's always me. Oh, and by the way, he's been unfaithful to me and all this niceness is due to guilt.*

After a couple of seconds, she heard herself say, 'I am very lucky, of course I am—' it was genuinely quite hard to get the words out without *choking* '—but Declan does *not* really get up at night with Daniel.'

'That's true.' Declan nodded vigorously, like a strangely eager puppy. 'I really don't. Poppy does it all. She's amazing.'

'Well, to be fair to you—' Nancy had already demonstrated a strong fondness for Declan and was blatantly always going to be more than fair to him '—you're working and Poppy isn't.'

To give everyone else their very big due, the rest of the table all began to contradict her at once, with Declan's voice winning the battle for prominence.

'No, that isn't being fair to Poppy,' he said. 'She's working really hard during the day with Daniel and then she's up at night with him a lot too because he isn't a great sleeper, so she has to do it all on not enough sleep. I should actually be helping a lot more than I do, it's just that we have this slight issue that he still feeds in the night because breastfed babies don't tend to sleep through the night as early as bottle-fed ones, and Poppy prefers not to express.'

Poppy couldn't decide whether he genuinely meant it or whether he was just saying the right thing to impress everyone else. 'Thank you, hun,' she said. Two could play at the saying-the-right-thing game.

'Why don't you think about expressing, then?' Nancy said.

'Just not for me,' Poppy said briskly. She did not wish to discuss the whole cow-udder-milking-machine feeling that she got when she expressed, not to mention the pain. And the fact that it just didn't work that well for her, and Daniel didn't like bottles that much so it just wasn't a goer.

'Maybe try harder?' Nancy suggested.

'Poppy tries *really* hard,' Declan said. Poppy couldn't work out whether it sounded lovely and supportive or staggeringly patronising.

'Thanks,' she said again.

'Look!' Hassan spoke very loudly, possibly (wisely) trying to change the subject. 'Profiteroles! We're spoilt!'

'So we are!' Rajula, the other partner in the practice, was also being very change-the-subject exclamatory. 'So much chocolate and cream! Yum!'

Poppy looked at them. She *loved* profiteroles. And then she looked down at her tummy, which was slightly bursting out of her dress. And then she remembered her resolutions. She couldn't break them in public. Dammit.

'No, thank you,' she said. She'd just have to have a secret Tunnock's Caramel later to make up for this.

'Poppy, I...' Declan slid his arm round her. She did her best to relax into him for a moment, because now was not the place to make a scene, and nearly sighed out loud. They'd always fitted so well together, in all ways. His warmth permeated through to her and she could feel the strength in his arm and body. It was... It was the kind of hug he probably gave the other woman. She pulled away slightly, and Declan immediately dropped his arm.

'I'm just going to pop to the loo.' She stood up quickly because she didn't want anyone to see that her eyes had filled, and pushed her chair back.

'Me too, actually.' Declan stood up too. 'Got to be on top form for the second half.'

They walked across the room together, Poppy very conscious of Declan behind her, and hoping that he wasn't looking at her bum and thinking how big it was now.

'Poppy,' he said, as soon as they were through the double doors into the entrance hall outside the main room.

'I need the loo.' She wrapped her arms round herself, and didn't bother to smile at all. This was not the moment for the talk that they were obviously going to have to have soon. Also, it was *freezing* out here.

'I love you, Poppy.' His voice was really different from normal, and his eyes were searching her face, his smile tentative, almost as though his words were entirely sincere. Maybe they were sincere; maybe he was just a weak man who liked to have his cake and also eat it.

He held out his hands.

She'd always loved his hands. He had very square fingers, always with very clean, perfectly trimmed nails. They were capable hands, perfect for a doctor. Perfect for a lover, too.

She could just take them, let him draw her against him – if he wanted to – and hug him and, just, be held by him. She could even pretend that she didn't know about the other woman and hope that the whole situation fizzled out. She was *so* tired. That would be the easiest thing. Except it wouldn't. She would never trust him again if they never spoke about it, and it would eat away at her and at their marriage.

'I love you so much,' he said. He took a step forwards, with his hands still held out.

Poppy just stood there as he placed his hands on her upper arms and then very gently lowered his head to hers and kissed her on the lips. She felt her idiot, stupid, traitorous mouth respond to his, and he deepened the kiss, with an urgency that felt almost animal. She found herself responding and winding her arms round his neck as the sane part of her brain yelled at her that this was surely *stupid*. Maybe it wasn't, though. She didn't know; she couldn't think any more.

Declan groaned deep inside his throat and Poppy felt her legs go jelly-like, and then someone cleared their throat behind Declan and they jumped apart as though they were doing something extremely illicit, rather than a married couple sharing a kiss.

Poppy opened her eyes properly and discovered that Ned Fox-Houghton, their way-past-retirement-age local MP, was tapping his watch. 'Time to restart, Declan.'

Declan cleared his throat. 'Of course. Just give us a moment?'

'Alright. See you in a minute.'

'Bloody politicians,' Declan said after he'd left.

Poppy tried to smile but it turned out, horrifyingly, because she was *not* a pathetic person, that she was crying.

'Oh, Pops, no, don't cry. Look, why don't I get someone else to finish the compering? It *really* isn't as skilled a job as I like to pretend it is. You literally just have to hold a mic and read questions out and make a few weak jokes.' He was great at acting the caring husband, she had to give him that.

'No, it's fine.' She dried her eyes with her fingers and walked past him and into the ladies.

She waited until she could hear his voice booming out across the hall and then went outside and got in the car to drive herself home. All sorts of people would offer Declan a lift, so he'd be fine.

And right now she was not going to carry on crying. She was going to sort her life out.

She needed details about the other woman now. She needed a name. She needed to find out what secret he'd written down on New Year's Eve.

12

GEORGIE

A couple of days later, Georgie – by now wondering whether she should just pick up the phone and *ask* straight out whether her secret was actually true – was slipping into detective mode. She was gathering gloves (you never knew) and a balaclava Max had worn for a fancy dress party (again, you never knew) into a large bag for life (for burglar-style anonymity), ready to go to Raf's to feed the cats and find her envelope, when Max opened the front door.

'Gaaah,' she screamed.

'Mum? Are you okay? You look surprised? I live here?' Honestly. Eleven-year-olds could be such smartarses at times.

'I thought you were going to Josh's after school. Obviously I'm pleased to see you.' Eek, what if she sounded as if she wasn't? 'Love you. How was your day? And are you not, in fact, going to Josh's?'

'He vomited in Geography and had to go home. It went everywhere, including in Ella White's pencil case. It was really funny. Like when you vomited on New Year's Day.' He took his coat off.

'Hilarious,' Georgie said. 'Soooo, you're home now for the evening?'

'Yes?'

'Great. Um, I'm going out, though.'

'To do what?'

'Feed someone's cats.'

'Another one? You should say no sometimes.' Max had a point. Georgie was the go-to pet-feeder for half the households on their street, and all her pet-owning friends when they went on holiday. 'Whose?'

'Just Raf. You know, Noah from the pub in Melting's cousin.'

'Oh yes, the one you vomited on. Is he on holiday?'

'No, Noah broke his leg and Raf's gone to help him out in the pub.'

'Does he live nearby?'

'Not really. But, yes, in Bristol.'

'Oh. Are you trying to make up to him for vomiting on him?'

'Exactly.' Georgie rolled her eyes and then smiled because, well, just because he was her gorgeous on-the-brink-of-becoming-a-nightmare pre-teen – she could see it now – but she adored him.

'Okay, cool. I like cats.' He put his coat back on. 'Are we going now?'

'Yep. Let's go.' She'd just have to be surreptitious and get him to play with the cats while she searched.

* * *

Forty minutes later they were inside the house, having successfully negotiated the Ring alarm.

Georgie looked around the hall appraisingly and then began to open doors. Where would Raf keep the envelope? Kitchen drawer? Bedroom? No. Study, if he had one?

'Why are there video cameras everywhere?' Max asked from behind her.

'Oh, ha ha ha,' Georgie said sarcastically, as she poked her head into a sitting room and spotted a bookcase with drawers in it. Maybe it would be in there.

'Why is that funny?' he asked.

Oh yes. Max didn't know that video cameras everywhere would be her worst nightmare.

Which meant... *Fuuuuuuck.*

'Are there actually?' she said, whipping her head back out of the sitting room.

'Yes, look.' He pointed towards lots of little, white-boxed cameras in ceiling corners.

'*Oh.*' Georgie had seen a panic button inside the first door she'd opened, a walk-in cupboard near the front door. 'This is Raf's aunt's house. She's quite elderly and has recently had to move into a nursing home. Maybe her relatives had the cameras installed for her safety in case she had a fall. One of my friends at work did that for his elderly father.'

So lucky that Max had mentioned it. It wasn't like Raf would watch the videos – presumably – but at the same time, what if he did? She'd have to find out somehow whether there was any chance of that before she searched properly.

So frustrating.

The envelope had for a while been on a different continent, but now it was in the same *house* as her and she couldn't look for it.

You could barely get a more classic case of so near and yet so far.

While she grappled with cat food – the tin was quite difficult to open – she thought through her options.

Maybe she could disable the video system.

No, she could not possibly do that.

Maybe she could... Well, her mind was blank.

'Mum, would you like some help with that?'

She looked down. She'd been holding the tin and basically doing nothing with it for ages. 'I think I'm okay, thank you.' She gave the ring pull a yank and it came open.

* * *

Fifteen minutes later they were back in the car, and Georgie could barely sit still at the wheel, she was so annoyed.

The journey home was also very annoying. What was *wrong* with other road users? Why couldn't they drive remotely competently?

'Mum, are you okay?' Max asked, as she pulled into a parking space about three houses along from their flat and beeped at the idiot behind her who apparently could not understand that a left indicator and reverse lights obviously meant that she had been about to park.

'No, I am not.' She beeped again. 'Why can't other people drive properly?'

'Do you hate cats?'

'No?' She beeped for a third time.

'You've been a bit angry ever since we were in Raf's house.'

'Oh. Sorry. No. Just tired.' And *deeply* disappointed about not having got the letter. 'Sorry. Bad example for you. I am going to be friendly to other drivers now.' She did a big smile to demonstrate that she was honestly no longer feeling tetchy.

And *oh*...

Why hadn't she just looked for the letter anyway? What was the worst that could have happened if she'd got it? Raf was highly unlikely to have been spying on her and Max, but if he had and he'd seen her take it, so what? She'd have got it and disposed of it by then.

Actually, the worst that would have happened was that she *wouldn't* have found it and he'd have spotted her rummaging through all his stuff. That definitely wouldn't have been good. But probably worth the risk, because if she didn't find it, she was going to have to ask for it, and really it would just lead naturally into that conversation.

Yep, when she fed the cats tomorrow, she was going to do that.

* * *

She messaged Raf when they got inside.

Fed the cats. All good.

Great. Thanks so much. Found a local cat feeder so might call on you for help again when they can't make it but other than that won't need to call on you again – way above the call of duty. Thanks again. I owe you a huge drink.

Damn. It.

* * *

The following evening, they were back in the Cotswolds. Max was hanging out with Georgie's mother's cleaner again, because her mother and stepfather were at another family party that they hadn't told Georgie about (to celebrate Georgie's half-sister Lottie getting a new job) and Georgie was with her friends in the pub for Beth's birthday. Noah was sitting in state next to the fire, with his plastered leg up on a stool, laughing with Beth. Raf was behind the bar, doing the landlord thing, ably assisted by Mick, the new barman, and Mick's boyfriend, Leo.

'Have you thought any more about speaking to Declan?' Georgie asked Poppy, when she was sure that no one could overhear them.

'I keep thinking about it and then I can't decide what I want so then I bottle it. And I don't want to have any kind of shouting match in the house with Daniel there, because even though he obviously can't understand the words he might get the emotion, and I don't want to do that to him.'

'Oh, Poppy.' This was so sad. Georgie hugged her friend, and tried to think what the best advice might be.

She was still wracking her brain when Raf plonked himself down next to them.

'Hey,' he said. 'How's it going?'

He gave Georgie a companionable little nudge in her side and to her shame, because she really should be focusing on Poppy and her problems, and also slightly to her horror, because she wasn't spending time with Raf for *romantic* reasons, was she, she felt her entire body heat up.

'Good, thanks,' Poppy said. 'Great, actually. Yep.'

Georgie's heart broke again at Poppy's bravery.

'I might get going, though.' Poppy looked at her watch. 'Yep, it's half eleven.'

They carried on talking after Poppy left, and were still going at midnight, when Raf kicked everyone else out of the pub and they all moved on to one table together. Georgie could feel herself beaming as she and Raf had to squish up next to each other.

'Last week I had *far* too much to drink,' he said, gesturing to the pint of water he'd just got himself. 'Seriously. It's a huge occupational hazard, being a landlord. I'd never thought about it before. So I'm on water this week.'

'Same as you,' said Beth, nudging Noah in a very companionable way. They seemed to have become very good friends recently.

'Yes, although it took me about seven years to realise and act on it rather than seven days,' said Noah. 'Raf was always the clever one.'

'I think you're very clever.' Beth smiled at him. Now Noah was smiling back at her in a way that Georgie would have had to have described as love-struck in other circumstances. It was such a shame that they both seemed to be with the wrong people.

Georgie looked up and caught Raf looking at her looking at them. He raised one eyebrow very slightly, and she nodded, knowing that he was thinking exactly the same thing as her. Maybe they could discuss it later. Raf wasn't going to want Noah to get hurt either.

'Another drink?' Raf asked everyone.

'Maybe just one,' said Beth, like she had the last three times she and Georgie had had another glass of wine. She looked at her watch. 'Oh my goodness, it's so late. I should go home.'

'How are you going to get home?' asked Georgie. 'A taxi would cost an absolute fortune from here to Bath. And you're *way* over the limit.'

'You'll have to drive back in the morning,' said Raf.

'My parents are away, though,' Beth said. 'And your mum won't want me to stay, will she, Georgie?'

'I mean, no.' Georgie didn't need to pretend to her best friends about her family. 'But we could just turn up and what can she do?'

'Why don't you stay here?' Noah's neck was reddening.

'Are you sure?' Beth said.

'Definitely.' Noah was absolutely scarlet now.

'Let me help you carry the drinks, Raf.' Georgie stood up.

'I'm fine,' Raf told her. 'Been honing my landlord drink-carrying skills.'

Honestly. Georgie swivelled her eyes in the direction of Noah and Beth, and Raf finally caught on and said, 'However, I *would* like some help with *these* drinks.'

'Not to be too pantomime-obvious or anything,' Georgie grumbled to him as they moved over to the bar together.

'Speak for yourself.'

'Shh,' Georgie admonished. 'Let's focus on the *point* here. We have to make sure nothing happens between Noah and Beth before it *should* because we don't want them to start their relationship off on a bad footing.'

'Are they *having* a relationship?'

'Well, I think they will. But first Beth has to split up with Dominic and Noah has to realise that Ankita isn't the one for him. And if both those things don't happen, they can't get together.'

'True. And we're whispering about this now because...?'

'Because obviously you have to be on it tonight. I'm just reminding you. You need to make sure nothing happens between them.'

'Oh, okay. Yep, I'll be on it. Well reminded.' He grinned at her and Georgie looked up at his mouth, barely able to take her eyes from the cuteness of his smile. 'What?'

'I like...' Whoops, no, what was wrong with her? She'd literally nearly said out loud that she liked his mouth. 'I like... this... pub,' she improvised.

Raf laughed, his breath tickling her neck. 'Good to know. Come on, let's get water for everyone. A bit of sobering-up wouldn't hurt for a start.'

* * *

Once they'd drunk their water, they all decided it was time to head off towards their beds.

Raf insisted on accompanying Georgie across the green back to her mum's.

'You're supposed to be in the flat with Noah and Beth, though.' Georgie was feeling ridiculously pleased that he wanted to walk with her.

'I should.' Raf nodded. 'Although I think we're okay for a few minutes. I reckon that at the moment they're still both feeling awkward and saying nothing.'

'What if they *aren't*, though? What if they've both lost all their inhibitions?'

'Okay. Once I've made sure you're safely home I'll sprint back and make sure they aren't having rampant sex.'

Georgie took a moment to imagine Raf sprinting. If he was wearing running kit when he did it, she was fairly sure he'd look very good. Of course, he wasn't wearing running kit at the moment; he was wearing old jeans and a rugby shirt. Which he didn't look bad in either. She sighed out loud.

'What?' said Raf.

'Nothing. Just... looking at the lovely stars.'

'Wow, you have X-ray vision.'

Georgie looked up. Oh, okay, there were no stars visible.

'Oh,' she said. 'It must suddenly have got really cloudy.'

Raf laughed and put his arm round her shoulders and Georgie felt the most incredible thrill.

They walked across the green like that, not really saying much, and it was *lovely*.

'Right.' Georgie was disappointed that they'd got to her parents' front door so quickly. 'We're here. Thank you so much.'

She had her key out. It was a good job she knew he wouldn't come in for coffee if she asked him, given that he had to get back to Beth and Noah, and that the babysitter was inside and there was every chance that Max was still up. Otherwise...

Raf was standing close to her and his eyes were on her face and her mouth and...

She really couldn't work the key.

'This is tricky.' She fumbled around the lock some more.

'Like some help?' Raf's eyes were twinkling *again*. And they were fully focused now on Georgie's lips. He was totally going to kiss her. Which would be so bad. Also probably very good. His gaze moved away, back to her eyes.

She finally managed some finger dexterity and inserted the key into its hole.

'I'm good, thank you.' She turned the key and dragged huge willpower from somewhere and said, 'So, goodnight. You should get back to your chaperone duties.'

'I should,' said Raf, not moving. Georgie had to make a really big effort not to close her eyes in anticipation of A Kiss.

Okay, this was ridiculous. Her mind should not be going in this direction.

And then Raf leaned a little bit towards her. She could see his stubble, the little lines at the corners of his eyes, a muscle moving in his jaw. Her hand was practically twitching to reach up and touch his cheek. Her whole body was doing a massive *zing* and they hadn't even touched. Although they would if she just leaned in a tiny bit. Raf was just gazing at her.

She moistened her lips – she couldn't help it – and he leaned even closer. He lifted his hand up and brushed a strand of her hair away from her eyes. She could feel – really, really feel – where his finger touched the side of her face. She couldn't breathe. He was going to kiss her. He was definitely going to. What if she was a bad kisser? She'd kissed literally no one since she got pregnant with Max.

Max! What if they *did* kiss and he saw? She needed to go inside.

'Goodnight,' she said. 'Thank you. That was lovely.' She knew it was embarrassing even before the word *lovely* came out, but her mouth still said it.

Raf didn't limit himself to a bit of eye twinkling. He laughed out loud.

'It was indeed lovely,' he said.

Georgie just dived inside the door. Sometimes it was better to know when saying something else wasn't going to help.

13

POPPY

Poppy peeled a banana with a dramatic flourish while Daniel laughed and tried to grab it, and then she mashed it with a fork in a little bowl for him, before peeling a second one, equally flourishingly, for herself. She'd had a goodish night's sleep for once, and today she was determined to have a good day, involving at the bare minimum some proper food and a walk, and also hopefully some actual enjoyable social interaction with another adult, plus maybe she'd have a little look online about how she might get a part-time job in a few months' time. She was also going to look into joining some carer-and-baby classes. She missed her ante-natal class from Australia; maybe she could meet some people locally who had similar-aged babies.

Yep, she could totally make a plan. And if Declan *was* having an affair, she could totally cope. She could. Really.

Today was going to be a good day.

* * *

Ten minutes later, there was slimy, greyish-yellow banana splatted all over the place and Daniel was delighted. Poppy was not.

'You know what,' she told him, going for maximum facial expression exaggeration, because he loved that, 'I *know* I'm supposed to be giving you the spoon so that you learn but my sanity is important for you too, and I'm sorry but I'm just going to be feeding you myself for the foreseeable.'

Daniel laughed in delight and lunged for her face with his sticky fingers.

'Eurgh.' Poppy put her phone down on his highchair tray for a moment to wipe banana off her cheek. Daniel picked the phone up and threw it at the wall.

'Noooo.' Poppy leapt over to it. 'Oh, thank goodness. It's working.' She turned back to Daniel and said, '*No*. That was naughty.'

He laughed even more. Yep, he was probably a good two or three years too young to understand the concept of naughtiness.

She smiled at him and then looked around at the kitchen and sighed. She *really* didn't want to clean it up yet again.

Maybe she'd just have a sneaky little Tunnock's Caramel to give her a bit of energy for the task.

She stood up to go over to the cupboard where she'd put her stash (slightly hidden, if she was honest) and then looked at Daniel, who pointed at it.

Hmm. This wasn't great, actually. She didn't want to set him a bad example. She *really* wanted some chocolate, though.

Really wanted it. Quite a lot of it.

Okay, no, she was better than this.

She was going to take Daniel for a walk instead and then plan her chocolate-free day.

When they got back, it was still only ten-fifteen. There were a lot of hours to fill between now and Daniel's bath-time.

She could justify having a Caramel now. She'd just done some exercise, after all.

No. She was going to manage *one day* without lying on the 'Resolutions' chat.

The truth was that, wonderful as Daniel was, she was a little bit bored

without much adult conversation. She needed to arrange to see some
people.

She messaged Georgie, Beth and Ankita separately to say hello and
does anyone fancy getting together in the next week to do something fun.

Then, before she lost the impetus, she emailed an address for a baby
music class in Little Bishop saying she'd like to join immediately.

And then she messaged the vicar's wife. She'd noticed as she walked
past the village church this morning that they wanted someone to start
helping with flowers once a month when their church hosted the rotating
service. Helping with flowers had to be a pleasant thing to do and she could
take Daniel.

Right.

Okay. And now... Hmm. Okay, she was going to take Daniel for another
walk and then maybe she'd do some batch baking.

* * *

Poppy was so bored by all the solitary walking (because yes the countryside
was lovely blah blah blah but trees and wildlife didn't *talk* to you, did they?)
that when Beth sent a message saying that one of her resolutions was to do
go-karting and it would be a lot more fun in a group, Poppy had replied
within about twenty seconds.

Yes meeeee, I'd love to.

Ankita replied about two minutes after that.

Yasssss seeing you all more is one of my resolutions!!! Thank you Beth for
organising and I am THERE. And I will smash you all.

Georgie replied about ten minutes later.

Yes!!!!! And no you won't – no one is more of a demon at the wheel than a single
mother with a full-time job.

Raf, Noah and Declan all said yes not long after that.

Beth replied:

Perfect. With Dominic that's eight of us – I'll book it now.

* * *

The next day was such a big rush to get home with Daniel from the (genuinely enjoyable) baby gym class in Cheltenham that Poppy had suddenly decided to take him to, get him fed, bathed and into bed, and dash out of the house with Declan to get to the go-karting place, that she had no time to worry about leaving Daniel with her mum. She also had no time to talk to Declan in the car because she was busy texting her mum about what to do if and when Daniel woke up and then emailing the gym people to say that she and Daniel had loved the taster class and would love to carry on with it, and then paying online for the classes.

'How was your day?' she asked Declan, as they entered the building. She could *totally* be entirely normal and civil to him for the time being.

'Good. Busy. I was going to ask you whether you thought you might like to locum for us one day a week starting soon?' He was looking straight ahead as he spoke. Poppy couldn't detect anything from his profile. Did he *want* her to go and work at his surgery, or was he offering her the job out of politeness before advertising?

'Um,' she said. 'I think...'

She stopped, to try to work out what she did think – she was beginning to feel that one day a week at work would be an extremely good thing for her and it would be very convenient to be in the village and therefore close to Daniel just in case. She was pretty sure that her mum would be happy to babysit him regularly if she only did one day a week, because she'd offered a *lot* of times. Maybe she should. Although also maybe she shouldn't, because there was every chance it would be awful working with Declan, given what had happened. But it might give her the perfect opportunity to work out exactly what had been going on. And also it would be on her CV and make it easier for her to find another job. Maybe she *would* go for it.

She turned towards Declan, to begin a reply, except she didn't have time to speak.

'I mean, obviously not if you don't want to. Forget I mentioned it.' Declan was still focusing over-hard on the door in front of them.

Oh. *Oh.*

He'd just asked out of politeness.

Well, fine then. *Fine.* If she decided to look for a job, there'd be other options.

* * *

Inside, it was big and noisy and petrolly, and, oh Gawd, everyone was wearing padded boiler suits which clearly weren't that flattering.

When she had hers on, she turned round and bumped straight into Declan. He smiled at her, that lopsided, just-for-her smile that she'd always loved.

'You are *cute* in that,' he whispered in her ear. Honestly, he was such a good actor. He really did sound as though he meant it.

She caught a glimpse of herself in the mirror looking honestly like a Michelin man. Yeah, no, clearly he did not mean it.

'Great acting,' she told him.

He shook his head, his smile gone. 'Not acting.' Yeah, whatever.

Poppy said nothing further, instead whisking herself away to talk to her lovely godson Max, who Beth had suggested Georgie bring to replace Dominic, who predictably was busy with work this evening.

When, a couple of minutes later, one of the people who worked there did a loud hand-clap and asked them to go into the briefing room, Poppy happened to look over at Georgie and Raf. They were sitting at a table, just the two of them, Georgie clearly telling some kind of story, and Raf with his elbow on the table and his chin in his hand, eyes focused fully on Georgie, just *gazing* at her, and smiling a big, lazy smile, like he was just *enjoying* her.

It was gorgeous. It was the kind of moment that Poppy used to share with Declan, in what now felt like the dim and distant past.

* * *

The pre go-karting briefing was an excellent opportunity for observing everyone else, especially Declan.

Raf and Georgie ended up next to each other again, with Max this time, and honestly the three of them almost looked like a unit. Poppy really hoped for Georgie that she and Raf would end up in a relationship; they just looked right together.

Beth was being a teensy bit gormless about the whole thing, and as Noah was explaining matters to her he looked secretly adoring.

Declan was standing by himself, shooting slightly odd looks around the room. You'd actually have to use the word *shifty* to describe his demeanour. Why was he being shifty *now*? Did he think someone else here knew about his affair?

'You got everything I said?' the go-karting man asked, interrupting her thoughts.

'Yes, definitely,' she lied.

How hard could it be? Although, eek, now she was looking at the go-karts she was thinking she should maybe have listened. Like, how did you even get them started?

She felt an arm – Declan's, obviously – slide round her Michelin-man-like waist, and stiffened.

'Good to go?' he asked.

'Yes, thanks.' She couldn't carry on pretending for much longer and she did not want a cosy little conversation now where she smiled while he summed up the instructions. She'd rather just not be able to work the kart.

* * *

She stalled three times during her first lap and accidentally drove hard into the tyres by the side of the track, and by the end she was definitely in last position time-wise. Hmm. She screwed her face up inside her helmet. It kind of felt like she was a bit rubbish at everything at the moment.

And then Max shot past her on her inside. And *what*? Eleven-year-olds were overtaking her now?

No.

They were not. No way.

Poppy shoved her foot down as hard as she could and she and her kart flew forwards.

And it was *amazing*. She'd already crashed hard and knew that it did not hurt, so now she had no fear, which was an excellent position to be in.

She skidded round the next corner, fought with the wheel and stayed in command of her kart, squeezing past Raf on the inside.

'No way,' he shouted.

'Loser,' she yelled back, and kept her foot down.

* * *

'That was so much fun,' she said to Beth afterwards, as she peeled herself out of the boiler suit.

'You were insane.' Beth's eyes were round. 'You beat us all! How did you drive that fast?'

'Just channelled all my immense life frustrations and anger into it.' Poppy laughed with Beth as she spoke, but as she looked at Declan out of the corner of her eye, she realised that she wasn't totally joking.

They ate pizza and drank bright blue slushies afterwards, and Poppy sat at the other end of the table from Declan and did pretty much enjoy herself as long as she didn't look at him. When she *did* look at him, she couldn't stop wondering why he wasn't speaking to anyone else and was looking weird again.

As she and Beth chatted to Max about Formula 1, his new obsession, she realised that she could hear Raf and Noah talking on her other side, and it sounded as though they were maybe talking about Raf's love life. She shouldn't eavesdrop, except... Georgie's face kind of lit up every time Raf got anywhere near her, and Poppy's heart clenched at the thought of lovely, sunny, always-kind Georgie getting hurt.

'How are you feeling now?' Noah had just asked. It was cute; he obviously found talking about emotional things awkward. 'About Anna.'

Raf didn't speak.

'Asking because I care about you, mate,' said Noah, after some silence.

'Thanks. I know you do. Thank you,' Raf said. 'You get used to it.'

'Five years is quite a long time.' Noah was still sounding like he'd rather stick pins in his eyes than have this conversation. So sweet of him to press on anyway.

'Yep.'

'And you're young still. I mean, nearly forty, but young. You know. You have the rest of your life ahead of you.'

'Yep.'

'I care about you, mate,' said Noah again.

Aww.

'Thank you.'

'You know,' Noah persisted, 'Anna was amazing and we all loved her. I mean, not like you did obviously, but what I mean is even though obviously we haven't been through it ourselves, we all get how devastated you are, but she wouldn't have wanted you to mourn forever. You could maybe meet someone else. Have kids. You have the rest of your life to live. The future. Sorry, mate, sorry if this is intrusive, but you know.'

He sounded so awkward and so sincere; Poppy just wanted to *hug* him. Anyone with Noah in their life was very lucky.

'No, it's okay, and thank you for caring.' Raf's tone matched the seriousness of Noah's. 'I do have the rest of my life ahead of me, and I've recovered to the extent that I can actually be happy in the moment. And I would now genuinely like to have a long life ahead of me if I'm lucky enough for that, and, yeah, maybe one day I might be ready for a relationship again.' Oh, wow. Maybe he and Georgie *might* get together.

'That sounds like brilliant progress. You didn't seem happy at all for a long time.'

There was a pause from Raf and then he said, 'No, I wasn't. I went to New York because I couldn't be here. I couldn't stand being around people who knew her, going to the places we went together, people who I know care about me looking at me pityingly. I had to get away.' Heartbreaking. He hesitated again and then said, 'I worked very hard and I partied very hard and I managed to focus so much on other stuff that I started to enjoy myself sometimes. And now I'm doing well. I'm home because I'm ready to see family and friends again. It's a relief to have got to where I am now. Because everything was shit, really shit, for a very long time.' So tragic. Poor, poor Raf.

'Yeah, mate, I see that.' Noah's voice sounded thick with emotion. 'You're doing fucking fantastically.' Aww again.

'Thank you. Really, thank you. When Anna died, I knew how much you all cared and I couldn't deal with it. Like your grief for me made my own even worse. Now I'm grateful. Thank you.'

'And?'

Raf laughed. 'You want to ask me about something, don't you?'

'No.'

'Like Georgie, you're a terrible liar.'

'And how do you feel about her?' Noah asked.

Poppy held her breath.

'She's great. She's funny. She's very nice. She's beautiful. She's a terrible liar, like I said.'

'And so do you think you might, you know?'

Raf said nothing, for ages, before eventually saying, 'Maybe.' Then he said, 'What about you?'

'It didn't work out with Ankita,' Noah said.

Okay, no, Poppy should not eavesdrop about this. Ankita had been a bit tight-lipped about what had apparently been a disastrous date, plus she was fairly sure Noah liked Beth but Beth was with Dominic and it was all messy and she didn't have a good reason for listening.

She stood up and said, 'Declan, I think we ought to get back to Daniel now.'

'Of course,' he said immediately.

'That was fun, wasn't it?' Declan said, as he reversed the car out of its space when they set off for home. He could have been talking to anyone, a complete stranger, even. In the past, they'd have immediately been dissecting the whole evening.

'Yes, great,' she said, equally distantly.

They drove along, neither of them speaking, for a few minutes, and then very suddenly, like a volcano that had been rumbling for a while and then erupted, words just burst out of Poppy. Volcanic words.

'Are you having an affair?' she asked.

'What?' Declan turned to look at her, the car swerved a bit and Poppy screamed.

'Look at the *road*. We can't die together in a car crash. Think of Daniel.'

'Sorry, yes, but sorry *what*? What did you just say?'

'I said, are you having an affair?' Now she'd started she wasn't stopping.

'No! I mean, no! Why would you ask that?'

'Why would I ask that? Are you joking?' Poppy could hear her voice shaking with anger. She did not want to be gaslit.

'No.' Declan indicated left and pulled into a layby, and twisted in his seat to face her. 'What makes you ask that?' he repeated.

'*Everything*. The way you've been behaving. All the evidence.'

'What?' He was such a good actor. He sounded genuinely confused and horrified.

It wasn't just Poppy's voice that was shaking now, it was her whole body. 'Okay,' she said. And then she began. She ran through all the times he'd acted distantly or weirdly or suspiciously, the things with his laptop and his phone, the way he *smelled* different, and then got to the Sally thing. By the end of it her voice was hoarse and she was crying.

'No, Poppy, no, no, no,' Declan said, when she'd finally finished.

He reached towards her and she jerked backwards and banged her head on the car window.

'Don't touch me.'

'Poppy, you have to let me explain.'

She looked at him. He was right. She did. She wanted to know everything now. 'Okay.'

'Firstly, I am *not* having an affair. I love you and I have never looked at another woman in that way since I met you. There are no words to describe how much I love you.' He *couldn't* be this good an actor, surely. But...

'I see now that I probably have been acting oddly,' he continued, pausing between words as though he was considering carefully what he should say. 'I've been... worried about things since we got back to the UK. I've been thinking a lot about various things. And I am so, so sorry if that's made me seem distant and made you think that I might be having an affair. Please believe me, Poppy, I would never do that. And the new smell is literally just a different aftershave because they don't sell my Oz one here.'

Poppy wanted to believe him *so* much. But no. She shook her head.

'But what was it on your laptop and on your phone that you didn't want me to see? And why did you lie about Sally?'

'I'd been googling and I'd asked a couple of people for advice and I was...' He paused and visibly swallowed 'I just didn't know what to do. I have something I do need to talk to you about...'

'What?'

Declan closed his eyes and then said, 'I know that this sounds utterly ridiculous, and that you have every right not to believe me given that I've been behaving oddly, but could you just give me a few days? It's a very strange thing. I just want to make sure of my facts. I *did* lie to you about Sally and I am so deeply ashamed of that. It's the only thing I've ever lied to you about. I was speaking to someone else and I just panicked because I wasn't ready to explain to you because I'd like to have my facts straight first. But just to be very clear: I have not been unfaithful. I wouldn't be.'

And now that they were talking properly for the first time for a while, the weird thing was that Poppy *did* believe him, despite the incredibly frustrating mystery behind his words.

His voice broke and she looked at him.

'Poppy, I love you.' Declan's voice broke as he spoke. 'I am not having an affair.'

'I'm sorry for suspecting you,' she said.

'No, no, no. No apologies. I *have* been acting oddly. And I will talk to you properly very soon.'

'Okay.'

'Are you sure?'

Poppy nodded.

'Come here?' Declan tentatively held his arms out towards her and she smiled at him and reached out for him.

It was difficult and not that comfortable to hug while wearing seatbelts, but it was a wonderful hug.

14

GEORGIE

'You *are* Torvill-esque,' Raf told Georgie, as they handed their skates back after their lesson. They'd squeezed another session in at short notice because Raf was home from Melting for a night after a late afternoon meeting.

Georgie rolled her eyes. 'Yep, I'm short like her.'

'And a natural on ice, as it turns out.'

'Natural is obviously stretching it, but oh my goodness the *satisfaction* when I binned the penguin.' Georgie had skated across the ice all by herself a few times, not fast but not that slowly either. 'A couple of times I felt like an actual skater.'

'You were brilliant. You could get the resolution done next time if I lift you.'

Georgie realised with a jolt that she didn't want her skating resolution to be finished that soon because she was *loving* seeing Raf.

Oh, no. She could feel her skin heating.

'Did I put the photo on the chat?' she asked, to divert attention from her now probably tomato-coloured face.

'Yes, think so.' Raf checked his phone. 'Yep, you did. Skates very visible.'

'Good. Okay, hot chocolates on me? I owe you for skating with me again.'

'No.' Raf shook his head. 'I owe *you* for feeding the cat the other evening and for any future cat feeding I might have to beg you for. There's a nice Italian round the corner from me where I might have provisionally booked a table in the hope that you'd join me?' He paused for a second and then his eyes widened. 'I've just heard what I said. I feel like you could now feel very pressured into having dinner with me. Please don't feel pressured into it. You might want to go home. You might have other plans. You might have no plans but can't imagine anything worse than sitting opposite me watching me splatter spaghetti sauce all over my chin. Please feel extremely free to say no. I have a neighbour who is *always* up for an Italian, so the restaurant owner won't suffer.'

'What's the neighbour's name?'

'Clive.'

'I don't want to deprive Clive of watching you with your spaghetti sauce.'

'Clive's very easy. He loves eating with me, he loves eating without me. Clive will roll with however the evening pans out. Don't feel bad about Clive either way. Also: I'm not trying to pressure you or anything, but I can actually eat spaghetti without making *that* big a mess.'

Georgie laughed. 'Well, in that case, I'd love to eat Italian with you.'

His smile in response got her somewhere deep, deep inside, with some very serious melting and butterflies. Which was ridiculous, wasn't it? She was basically hanging out with him to get her secret back. And he was basically hanging out with her because he'd been away for years and didn't know that many people. And of course he was just being kind-hearted by helping her with skating. And had time on his hands between jobs. That was all it was.

* * *

'I haven't asked how you got on with the cats.' Raf moved his shoulders around against the back of the too-small-for-him front passenger seat as Georgie pulled out of her parking space and tried not to get all *eek* about the fact that they were going for dinner together.

'They were adorable,' Georgie lied. One of them had been; the other had been very hissy and spitty. 'I've just remembered something I forgot to ask: their names.' She'd been focusing entirely on the letter retrieval. Max had been astonished that she didn't know what they were called because usually she knew the names, ages, habits, you name it, of the friends' and neighbours' pets that she fed.

'Clive and Molly.'

'Wow. Two Clives cannot be a coincidence. Is Clive the cat named after the neighbour?'

'Erm. That is a good question. I'll have to ask my aunt.'

'Do you also have a neighbour called Molly?'

'Also a good question.'

Georgie looked at him out of the corner of her eye and gulped. He was looking at her and smiling, and suddenly it felt like they were having a really important conversation. What had they been talking about, though? Oh! Nothing important at all. Cat and neighbour names.

She slowed the car right down while she caught her breath; it couldn't be safe to drive, even on a quiet side road, when you were feeling this, well, *flustered*.

Okay, so she was going to de-fluster herself. Get some conversation going again.

'What would you call a cat if you got a new one?' she asked, changing gear very deliberately (and also very nerve-wrackingly, because his thigh really was very close to the gear stick).

'Hmm. I really don't know because I've never thought about it, but now you ask I definitely prefer human names for cats. I don't like your Fluffy or Tiddles type names.'

'Me neither,' said Georgie approvingly.

'Your top two names for a cat?'

'I mean, Horace and Peggy, obviously,' Georgie told him.

'Of course.' He grinned at her as she glanced at him as they stopped at some traffic lights.

They were still talking about animal names when they parked on Raf's road.

'No horse should ever be called Humphrey,' he insisted, as they walked round the corner and came to a halt in front of the restaurant.

'You're wrong, but agree to disagree.' Georgie stepped inside and looked around. 'Oh, wow. This is lovely.'

It was the quintessential British neighbourhood Italian with red-and-white-checked tablecloths, dripping candles in wicker holders, mellow music, black and white photos of Sophia Loren on the walls, the works, all done in a very, very nice way; there was something about the ambience that just drew you straight in.

'I can immediately see myself with a heaped bowl of pasta and a glass of red here as often as I could afford it.'

'Yes, I've been spending a *lot* of time in here. Pretty sure I know the menu off by heart.'

'Raf.' A smiling, bearded man wearing a black shirt and black trousers moved towards them with his arms out, and the two of them exchanged a hug.

Raf introduced the man as the owner, Antonio, and Antonio hugged Georgie too, and then told them to follow him to one of his best tables.

'How many times have you *been* here since you got back?' Georgie asked.

'Ha, not that many. We go way back. I used to come here before I moved to New York.' With his wife presumably, although he didn't say so.

Georgie waited a second in case he wanted to mention her, and then opened her menu and said, 'Wow, it all looks *delicious*,' and started talking very animatedly about the listed options to put the thinking-of-Raf's-wife moment behind them.

They chose a sharing platter of olives, hams, sun-dried tomatoes and focaccia to start off with and Georgie chose penne carbonara and Raf a beef and polenta dish.

'I don't want to go down the spaghetti-sauce-on-chin route,' Raf said, twinkling at her.

'Same.' When she'd been choosing, Raf's comments about spaghetti had been right at the top of her mind.

'Wine?' Antonio asked.

'Just one small glass for me. I'm driving.' Which was a very good thing or the way she was feeling right now she might just end up *chucking* herself at Raf.

'I will also have just one glass,' Raf said.

Their conversation wound all over the place until during their main courses they were talking about skiing. Georgie and Max had skied for a week once, a couple of years before.

'Max loved it, obviously,' Georgie said. 'Whereas if I'm honest I loved the après-ski a lot more than the getting-terrified-and-also-cold-and-falling-over-a-lot-often-quite-painfully daytime skiing.'

Raf laughed. 'You sound like my... my late wife. Anna.' He looked down at his hands for a moment and then back up at Georgie, right into her eyes.

Georgie felt as though she'd been punched in the stomach by his words; they'd brought her right back down to earth with an unpleasant bump. Clearly, and understandably, Anna was never far from his thoughts. Georgie should very much bear that in mind and not even begin to think that she could or should have any kind of romance with him.

'You must miss her terribly,' she said. 'I'm so, so sorry.'

'Yeah, but... Well, yes. But... also... I have to keep living. In the present. I can be happy now.'

'I'm glad,' Georgie said round the enormous lump now in her throat. 'That you can be happy, I mean.'

'Thank you.' Raf cleared his own throat and then said, 'Okay, so tell me your most embarrassing ski incident.'

Georgie laughed and launched into the story of when she'd mistakenly turned onto a black run from a green run and had to crawl back up because going down did not feel like an option.

Some time later – Georgie had no idea how long because, once the moment where Raf had mentioned Anna had passed, the time had sped by while they talked and laughed about everything and nothing – they were sharing a large bowl of tiramisu.

'That is *divine*.' Georgie might just have groaned out loud but she didn't care. 'The best tiramisu I've ever tasted, I think.' She put her spoon down. 'I can't eat any more, though. I might have to open the top button on my jeans as it is.'

Raf stuck his spoon back in and took another mouthful.

'I am very fortunately greedier than you.'

Georgie couldn't answer because her eyes, and mind, and whole body, seemed to be fixated on the way he was holding his spoon and putting it into his mouth. His fingers were long and strong, and his lips were just... perfect.

Oh, crikey. He was looking at her looking at him. He finished his mouthful and smiled at her, very slowly. His eyes went to her lips and then to her hands on the table and then back to her lips, and he smiled some more.

'This is... delicious.' He very deliberately took another spoonful and then put it in his mouth.

Georgie couldn't stop looking at him. She could hardly breathe.

'Shall we get the bill?' He put his spoon down and she found herself staring at his hands again.

'Great!' she said eventually. They should definitely get the bill, actually; they were the only two people left in what had been a very busy restaurant earlier on. A *lot* of time must have passed very quickly.

* * *

The cold air outside hit hard after the just-right warmth of the interior.

'You're shivering. Let me give you my coat.'

'No, honestly, I'm fine.' Georgie clamped her teeth together to stop them chattering.

'Liar.' Raf nudged her and then shrugged out of his jacket and put it round her shoulders.

'You shouldn't have,' she told him, 'but that *is* lovely and toasty warm.' And *his*. She snuggled into it and had to try very hard not to breathe in his scent very deeply, in case he saw her do it. 'You're going to be cold, though.'

'Nope. I am a very warm person. In a good way, naturally.'

Georgie laughed. 'Naturally.'

They wandered along the road, their arms bumping a little, not really talking, in a nice, companionable, eaten-a-lot-of-food kind of way.

Then Raf said, 'I have a secret to tell you.'

Georgie nearly gasped out loud and did a massive eye swivel in the darkness. Did he mean... Had he... *Please* let him not have opened her secret. Please let it be something else.

'What?' she managed to ask.

'I invented Clive.'

'Clive?' She had no idea what he was talking about. Oh, yes she did. *Clive.* 'Which one? Or both?'

'The neighbour. Because I'd booked the table for us and then worried that I'd been very overbearing and presumptuous, and didn't want you to feel that you *had* to go. So I came up with Clive.'

'Is the cat at least called Clive?'

'Yes. I would never lie twice about a Clive in one evening.'

Georgie laughed. 'Of course you wouldn't. That would be ridiculous.'

'Exactly.' They'd reached her car and as they came to a halt he turned to face her. 'I'm glad I invented Clive. I wanted you to want to have dinner with me.'

Oh! Georgie bit her lip to try to stop herself from just *beaming*.

'The food was amazing and the company wasn't too bad, either,' she said. 'Thank you.'

'My pleasure.' He'd insisted on paying. He looked into her face for a long time and then reached down and took her hands and drew her closer to him. 'I really enjoyed it.'

'Me too,' Georgie breathed. His gaze was *so* intense.

Very slowly, Raf drew her even closer until it was only their hands between their bodies that was stopping their chests from touching. He was going to kiss her, he definitely was, and if she was being honest, she really, really wanted him to. So much that if he didn't do it soon she might just reach up and kiss him herself.

Oh wow, oh goodness, he was lowering his head to hers now.

Georgie turned her face right up to his and parted her lips and just *sighed* into his gorgeous, *gorgeous* kiss when it finally came.

Raf's lips were warm and firm and almost *demanding*, in a wonderfully exciting way. Georgie hadn't experienced a kiss as good as this *ever*.

Raf's hands left hers and reached around her waist and shoulders, and she pressed her hands up his solid chest and around his neck and into his hair.

They kissed for who knew how long until they stumbled off the kerb together and against her car.

'Oops,' Georgie said.

They were still holding each other.

'Oops indeed.' Raf tugged gently on her hair with the hand that he had on the back of her neck and placed another kiss on her lips before saying, 'Would you like to come in for coffee?'

Georgie opened her mouth to say yes reflexively, and then paused, without speaking.

Because of course she'd *like* to do more with him – if that's what was on the cards; she hadn't dated as an adult at *all* so she really wasn't sure what she should expect to happen if she went inside – but that feeling was mingling with a little bit of 'ooh I could maybe get my secret back but dammit I don't have a replacement one; why didn't I come prepared; hmm that's weird because most people regret not bringing a condom, not not-bringing a replacement secret' and awareness that soon she'd be finding out whether or not the secret was actually true and also just worry that it would feel *huge* to do stuff with him plus he was famously a serial one-dater since he'd lost his wife – for whom he was clearly still grieving – and she didn't want to get hurt and basically it was all just too scary, and she'd definitely rather find out whether – if this *had* totally been a date – there would be any more before she went any further.

'It's late.' She took a little step backwards, away from him. 'I should get back. I mean, I'd love to have coffee, definitely, but I should get back now.'

'Of course.' Raf studied her face for a moment and she smiled at him, because it was hard not to smile at Raf, and he smiled too and then kissed her quickly on the lips again.

Which turned into quite a long kiss. Raf slid his hands inside her jumper and she put hers under his shirt, and when he kissed her lower and lower down her neck and chest, her legs went almost entirely to jelly, and her resolve not to go inside with him nearly did too.

But no. She was not going inside.

'I really should go.' She hoped she didn't sound as though she was panting (even though she was pretty sure she was).

'Of course.' He let go of her immediately.

She got straight into her car before she could be tempted any more.

As she pulled away, she could see in her rear-view mirror that he stood looking after her car the whole time until she turned the corner, his face inscrutable.

What was he thinking?

What had *she* been thinking? She'd only been hanging out with Raf to get her secret back. Hadn't she?

15

GEORGIE

The next morning, Georgie arrived bright and early at her new yoga studio.

She'd decided that she would not have time to run, learn Italian and ice jumping, look after Max *and* do her job properly if she had a two-hour round trip yoga commute, so she'd joined the studio on the next road over from her flat in Bristol.

She'd better take a quick selfie to post to the chat. She pasted a smile onto her face for the photo before allowing her features to settle back into a non-smile. The worry about the secret was weighing more and more heavily on her shoulders now. Plus, this morning, in the cold light of day, she was wondering what she'd been *thinking* kissing Raf like that.

After her lesson, she pushed open the door to the studio and exited onto the street, and immediately shivered. She pulled her coat more tightly around herself. It was *freezing*.

As she took her gloves out of her bag, she saw that Declan had posted a photo of what looked like pie and chips to the 'Resolutions' chat. As usual now, when she thought of either Declan or Poppy, she felt a wave of guilt spread over her. She was *desperate* to find out whether her secret was true, so that if it was – fuuuuuck – she could act. The appointment she'd booked was still nearly a fortnight away; maybe she should just phone later today instead.

* * *

A couple of hours later, she'd dropped Max at a friend's house so that she could go to Raf's house alone (his cat feeder couldn't do today), and she was on her way to find the envelope.

She'd decided that Raf seeing her on Ring rummaging through his belongings was a hazard she was going to have to accept; she'd cross that bridge if it happened. The main thing was to get the envelope.

She piled straight into the house, did the alarm, got the cat food out at the speed of light (the tins were a lot easier to open once you knew what you were doing) and got searching.

She was kneeling down, on her fourth drawer in the pedestal desk in the study, when there was a sound behind her and a woman's voice said, 'What are you *doing*?' Shiiiiiiit.

She closed the drawer and swivelled round on her knees very slowly.

And, oh God.

Raf's mum was standing in front of her, immaculate with her steel-grey, very sleek bob and olive skin, and dressed in a camel jumper, slim navy trousers and navy suede pumps, her eyebrows raised.

Georgie stood up, attempting a confident I-totally-have-good-reason-to-be-here smile, but her face felt wobbly.

'Hello.'

'What were you doing?' Raf's mum repeated. She looked a lot less friendly than she had in the hospital.

'I'm feeding the cats.'

Yes, convincing, Georgie.

'What?'

Georgie screwed her face up. 'I'm so sorry. Obviously, no one tries to feed cats by going through drawers. I'm looking for something.'

'What?' Raf's mum said again.

Why, why, why hadn't Georgie just told Raf the truth immediately? Well, not the *truth* truth, but the I-need-my-envelope-back truth.

'On New Year's Eve a group of us wrote secrets down and posted them to each other to make ourselves stick to our resolutions. I posted mine to

Raf. It's huge and nothing to do with him and I need it back. I was looking for it.'

'What?'

'If we don't keep our resolutions, our envelope will be opened next New Year's Eve and everyone will hear our secrets.'

'Oh. Why didn't you just ask Raf for it?'

'Yes.' Georgie nodded earnestly. 'Yes, absolutely. Yes. I *should* have asked him. Obviously. Yes. And now, I *would*. I mean, I didn't. Obviously. But I absolutely should have done. And I really don't know why I didn't, except I just, well, the secret is *huge*. I can't really describe how huge it is. Or might be. I just felt like I couldn't even tell him how big it was, I just needed – need – it back without discussing it and without any danger of another person ever seeing it.'

The woman was just staring at her as though she was *mad*. Fair enough.

'The thing is,' Georgie continued, 'I *really* do understand that it is *outrageous* to go through people's drawers. Properly outrageous. Terrible behaviour. I *know* that. But my secret is just... I just, it can't be uncovered. It just can't. I'm so sorry.'

'Obviously it's Raf you should be apologising to.'

'Absolutely, and I certainly will.' Georgie pressed her lips together. Maybe this was a blessing in disguise. She would now *have* to tell Raf and he could just give her the envelope and all would be well. Apart from him probably never wanting to speak to her again, which, she realised, would be really sad, because it felt like they'd become good friends recently, maybe *more* than good friends.

'Great.'

'I'm going to call him. I'll put him on speaker.'

'Okay. Thank you.'

'Hi, Mum,' Raf said.

'Hello. You're on speaker. I'm in the house with your friend Georgie.'

'Oh, hi, Georgie.'

'I just found Georgie rifling through the drawers in your study looking for an envelope containing a secret?' Raf's mum sounded a lot more relaxed now it was obvious to her that Raf really wasn't surprised that Georgie was in his house.

'What?' he said.

'Hi, Raf,' Georgie said. 'Basically I'm desperate to get my New Year's secret back because it's truly awful and no one must ever see it, and I didn't dare tell you that just in case so basically yes, your mum's right, I've been going through your stuff this evening and I'm so, so sorry.'

There was a long silence and then he said, 'Right,' his voice completely flat.

'I know that I should just have asked you for it,' she rushed on. 'But it's such a big secret that I was kind of too scared to say.'

'Right.' Still flat.

'I'm sure you would have given her the envelope, wouldn't you?' Raf's mum asked.

'Yep.'

'So this was all very silly,' his mum continued.

'Yep,' Raf said.

'Yes,' Georgie agreed. 'Again, I'm incredibly sorry.' Excruciatingly, she was now going to *have* to ask for it. She couldn't not. She just wanted the earth to swallow her whole, right now. 'Erm...'

'You want to know where the envelope actually is?' He sounded almost impatient now.

'Yes, please.'

'I brought it with me here. It was in my admin in-tray and I just bundled it all up and brought it.'

'Oh.' She was *such* an idiot. 'Again, I'm really sorry.'

'I'll post it to you, if you like.'

'That's very kind, thank you, but could I get it from you in person?' The thought of it arriving in the post at their flat and for some reason Max opening it was hideous. And oh, of course, she was supposed to be going to Melting this evening because Raf had organised drinks for Noah to cheer him up because he wasn't enjoying having to be inactive due to his broken leg. Her brain was working slowly from the shock of being caught. 'I'll see you this evening in the pub anyway? We could do the handover at the end of the evening maybe?' That would definitely be when it would be easiest to make sure no one else noticed; she could just stay behind after the others left.

'Of course.' His lack of enthusiasm was in stark contrast to how he'd been speaking to her only last night.

And oh, of course. When he'd suggested he could post it, he'd probably meant that he didn't want to see her any more after this. *Because* of this. She really shouldn't feel as gutted about that as she did now feel. Ridiculous. The main thing had been to get the secret back, not to become close to him.

'Thank you.'

Raf didn't answer.

'I'll call you later,' his mum told him.

'Great. Bye, Mum.'

'I am *so* sorry,' Georgie told Raf's mum again when they'd finished the call.

'I think Raf's the one you should be apologising to the most,' she said.

'Yes, totally, absolutely,' Georgie grovelled. 'So, would you prefer me to lock up or you?'

'I'll do it. I came to collect some things for my aunt and it will take a bit of time. And, frankly, I don't really trust you now.'

'No, of course not. Huge apologies again. Bye.' Georgie backed herself out of the room, across the hall and out of the house as fast as she could.

So. Embarrassing.

At least she was going to get the secret back, though, which was a huge relief. And then maybe tomorrow she'd make her call, and then think about next steps.

And she would just have to not think about the fact that she might have lost Raf's friendship, because it wasn't like it was going to have been going anywhere.

* * *

Ankita was already in the pub when Georgie arrived that evening. She was wearing black wide-legged jeans and a really nice, simple cream top. Her classic style was similar to that of Raf's mum. Georgie shuddered slightly just at the thought.

'You okay?' Ankita was staring at her.

'Yep, totally.' Georgie didn't even know why the thought of Raf's mum had made her shudder. It didn't *matter* that obviously Raf and his mum were both going to despise her forever. It did not matter at all. It did not matter that Raf probably wouldn't want to speak to her again. All that mattered was getting the secret back. And it wasn't like that kiss had really meant anything because everyone knew that Raf was really not up for proper dating. And she didn't want to date a grieving widower. So, *really*, it did not matter. As long as she hadn't upset him; she really wouldn't want to have done that because he was very nice.

It *didn't* matter.

It still felt awkward being here in the same room as him, though.

Beth arrived as Ankita got back to their table with a bottle of Prosecco and four glasses. Served by Raf. Mortifying.

Georgie poured for everyone and then clinked her glass hard against the others in a big *Cheers*. She was going to get her secret back and she'd made an appointment to hopefully get to the bottom of whether the secret was right, and she was pushing Raf out of her mind.

'Are you sure everything's okay?' Ankita asked her, as she practically downed her glass in one. 'You seem a bit antsy.'

'Yes, definitely.' She coughed as the bubbles caught in her throat.

'Okay. Great, then.'

'How are things with Noah?' Georgie asked, because she did want to know, and also to divert the attention away from herself.

Their conversation wandered along, punctuated by smiles and some cackles of real hilarity when Ankita was talking about the details of her (disastrous) second-and-final date with Noah.

And then Poppy and Declan turned up.

Poppy led Declan over to them, holding his hand, and then said, 'Actually, Dec, would you mind getting us all some crisps from the bar?'

'Course.' Declan dropped a kiss on top of her head and then tucked some of her hair behind her ear in the most gorgeous way.

'Poppy!' Georgie, Beth and Ankita exclaimed as one.

'Yes.' Poppy beamed. 'I was just being a paranoid idiot. It was all a huge misunderstanding.'

Thank goodness for that.

The relief that her friend was happy again.

Although...

Yes, Georgie needed to find out asap.

16

POPPY

An hour later, Poppy, talking to her girlfriends, looked over for a moment at Declan, who was chatting to a couple of Noah's friends at the bar. He looked gorgeous, dressed in a purple shirt and jeans, his hair a little bit mussed. Her heart expanded just at the sight of him. Thank *goodness* she'd been wrong about the affair.

As she listened to Georgie describe how terrible she'd been at skating while Ankita and Beth laughed and assured her that she'd probably in reality been an ice dance genius, she thought again how much she loved her friends.

Honestly, she was *so* lucky. Gorgeous son, amazing husband, wonderful friends.

The only fly in the ointment was that Declan still hadn't told her what he'd been worrying about. She knew he was going to – she trusted him fully again – but she did just want to know sooner rather than later so she didn't have that niggle of worry. Was it something about his parents? Was it a worry about work? Their finances? She just wanted to know so that whatever the problem was they could tackle it together, now.

Also, she had one of her tiredness-headaches coming on.

She wouldn't mind some paracetamol and a few minutes of silence while the pain relief worked.

She made her way over to Noah.

After a quick chat about his leg, she said, 'Noah, I've got a small headache. Would you mind if I popped through to your kitchen and took some paracetamol and just had a moment of quiet while it takes effect?'

'Of course. They're in the cupboard to the right of the sink. Are you okay?'

'Yes, absolutely fine, just a bit over-tired.'

'Oh, glad it's nothing serious. Of course, go ahead.'

* * *

A couple of minutes later, she was in Noah's kitchen and absentmindedly looking for the paracetamol. She realised that she'd switched off when he told her where it was. She always did that; it was like asking for directions and then having no idea afterwards what the answer had been. Had he said they were in a cupboard? A drawer?

She couldn't just randomly open cupboard doors and drawers; it was rude. Maybe she should go back and ask him again and this time *focus*.

As she turned to go, her eye alit on a pile of papers stacked on the side. They were clearly Raf's. His name was all over them. And the top one was an envelope addressed to him in New York. Which she was pretty sure was the one from New Year's Eve.

Declan had put his secret in the one addressed to Raf, she was certain. It hadn't really occurred to her until now that she might have the opportunity to read it, because how could she possibly have got hold of it?

But here she was. Standing in a room all by herself right next to the letter.

Obviously, she should not read it. She certainly shouldn't. She *really* shouldn't.

Presumably his secret was the thing that he was going to tell her soon.

She should wait for him to tell her.

She should not open it.

She *really* wanted to, though.

And would it really hurt?

Suddenly, she took the two steps required to move across to the counter, and picked up the envelope and stuck it in her cross-body bag. Declan had bought the bag for her for Christmas the year before last and she *loved* it.

And now it contained Declan's secret.

She couldn't open it now, just in case someone came in.

Okay, so she was going to go to the loos in the pub and open it in there.

A minute later, she was perched on top of the toilet inside a cubicle, and pulling the letter out of her bag.

She knew *as* she did it that she really shouldn't, but having come this far...

She eased the envelope open, so that no one would notice when she put it back, and then slid the piece of paper out from inside.

And... What?

It wasn't Declan's handwriting; it was Georgie's.

She closed her eyes for a second and thought back. She *had* been quite drunk that evening and maybe she'd misremembered.

Hmm.

She should definitely put the letter back. She actually didn't know what had come over her. She should *not* have decided to read Declan's secret. And she shouldn't be reading anyone else's secret, either.

She opened her eyes and then froze.

There was only one sentence on the page and Declan's name had leapt out at her.

She couldn't help reading it.

And no. *No.* No way. *No way.*

No no no no no.

It was so much worse than she'd imagined.

She couldn't even...

She leaned her head on the side of the cubicle for a moment and then opened her eyes and stared at the *weird* wallpaper lining the three walls of it – tiny women in pornographic sapphic poses. Strange thing to be looking at when you'd just discovered that your husband and your lifelong best friend had betrayed you in the worst way possible.

Fuck them both.

Fucking fucking fucking fuck them.

She put the letter back in the envelope and stood up, accidentally scraping her fingers hard against the toilet roll dispenser on the side of the cubicle, and stumbled her way out. She walked blindly out of the loos and stared into the main body of the pub.

Georgie and Declan were both there together, in the same group, laughing and having fun.

Just. *What*? Unbelievable.

How. Fucking. Pathetic they must think she was.

Were they laughing at her now? Did they laugh at her behind her back? Fuck them. *Fuck* them.

17

POPPY

Poppy pushed her way blindly through everyone and stumbled out of the front door of the pub.

She was crying so hard that it felt as though she was going to be sick. She could barely breathe.

The *pain* of it.

She now realised that the whole time she'd suspected Declan of having an affair she'd never fully, fully believed it, she'd always felt some hope, because she'd never felt like this: hurt, *injured* right the way through, body and soul.

'Poppy.' Someone was calling her name from the pub doorway. Declan.

She turned in his direction. 'Fuck off.'

'Sorry, what?' He was staring at her as though she had no reason to be angry, as though she'd lost her mind.

She hadn't lost her mind, though; she'd lost her fucking husband. And best friend. All in one go.

'I said, *fuck off*,' she stated very clearly.

Declan shook his head. 'Why?'

'Because I know. I read Georgie's secret.'

'You...' He took a step closer to her. 'What did the secret say?'

'What, like you don't know?'

'No.'

'Really? You really don't know? Don't be so ridiculous. How could you not know?'

'What did it say?'

'Really? We're doing this? You're going to make me say it?'

'Please?'

'Fine,' she said. 'Fine. It said "Declan is probably Max's father".' Poppy didn't think she'd ever forget the sight of that piece of paper for as long as she lived.

'What? No. Oh my God. Oh my God. It must be true then. It must be her. I mean, there can't be any reason for her to suspect I'm the person if she isn't the person. But oh my God, Max. Poppy, I'm so sorry that you had to find out like this.' Declan moved right next to her and tried to put his arms round her. 'Poppy. Poppy, I'm so sorry. Poppy, I didn't know.'

She pulled herself out of his arms and stepped away from him.

'You didn't *know*? You didn't *know* that you impregnated my best friend? You didn't know that? How could you not know that?' She could hear herself shrieking like a banshee.

'Oh no, Poppy, Poppy, I love you. Poppy, it was *once*. Poppy, you have to listen. It was *once*. We were strangers. We didn't know each other. We had sex once. And then we never saw each other again until that night just before Christmas when you introduced us. And I wasn't sure whether it was her or not. I *wondered*. That's why I was so distracted. I've been trying to find out, ask around, people who were there, find out.'

Poppy's mind wasn't working. It was like someone had punched her in the head and she was too stunned to think. Deeply painful realisations were filtering very slowly through to her.

'This was the thing that you were trying to confirm and you were going to tell me about? Not something about work or your mum and dad or holidays or anything nice or just okay? But the fact that you were sleeping with Georgie?'

'Slept with. Once.'

'You lied *so* much. You should have said *then*. After go-karting.'

'I wasn't sure, though.'

'I don't believe you. I can't believe anything you say now.' Poppy was suddenly just far, far too tired to talk any more. She turned away from Declan and began to walk in the direction of the house.

'Poppy, please, please listen.' He was following her.

'I can't. Please just stop.'

'I... Okay.' Declan carried on walking next to her, but in silence now.

'I don't want you to come with me.' No way could she spend tonight under the same roof as him.

Declan didn't speak but didn't stop walking. Fine. He wasn't coming inside, though.

When they got to the house and she was opening the door, he said, 'Please, please can we discuss this now?'

'I have nothing to say tonight. Goodnight.' Poppy went inside and left him standing on the doorstep.

She went into the kitchen. 'Hi, Mum.' Her mum had been babysitting while they went to the pub. 'Thank you so much for babysitting.'

'No problem. Where's Declan? How was the evening?'

'He's coming back later. It was a great evening, thanks, but I have a headache and really need to go to bed now.' She really couldn't bear to talk about it now.

'Oh no.' Her mum came over and put her arms round her. 'Can I help at all?'

'No, honestly, I'll be fine after a good night's sleep.' She just wanted her mum to leave now so that she could cry and cry alone. She'd tell her in the next few days that she and Declan had split up, as they were obviously going to do.

'Night, then.' Her mum left and then Poppy heard her saying, 'Oh, hello, Declan.'

Poppy waited for a couple of moments and then went and closed the front door that her mum had left ajar, presumably thinking Declan would be coming inside, and put all the locks on as loudly as she could so that he would know he was locked out.

And then she slumped down to the hall floor and just sobbed.

18

GEORGIE

Georgie was exclaiming at some London gossip that Ankita had just told her, but her heart really wasn't in it. She couldn't help glancing a lot at Raf, taking note of how he was clearly just avoiding her, plus of course there was the constant worry about Declan and Poppy.

She was going to get the letter back from Raf this evening and then she was going to speak to Declan tomorrow somehow, even if it meant knocking on his and Poppy's front door and just *asking*.

She and the man who she thought was Declan had met at a huge New Year's Eve Glasgow University medics ball that Poppy had invited Georgie to as her plus one. Georgie had been doing her teacher training that year and didn't know a lot of people where she was living and was very pleased to go. She'd met Declan (assuming it was him), had sex with him outside, under a bush – *what* had either of them been thinking – and that had been that.

In the morning she hadn't felt good about having sex with someone who she'd known for approximately two hours in total – she hadn't even found out his name – and she'd decided that one-night-stands weren't for her, and then she'd put it behind her until she'd discovered that she was pregnant. And then, despite much effort, she'd never managed to find him.

And she still wasn't *certain* it was Declan, despite all the googling of his life and oblique questioning and observing she'd been doing. So tomorrow she was going to ask him if he remembered going to a fancy dress New Year's Eve party at Glasgow Uni in 2012 dressed as a ghostbuster and having a one-night stand with a stranger dressed as a witch (she hadn't had much money, so she'd doubled up from Halloween).

'Also...' The end of Ankita's story was interrupted by Declan.

'Sorry, Ankita. Georgie, please could I speak to you outside? Immediately.'

Georgie stared at him. He looked, just, odd. His eyes were doing a really strange, twitchy thing and he had his lips pressed together in a weird way.

She began to go very cold with dread.

'Okay,' she said.

He nodded, and turned round, and she followed him outside.

As soon as the pub door was closed, he asked, 'Is it true that I'm Max's father?'

Oh. Wow. It *was* him, then. He'd obviously suspected it too.

'Yes, if you're the person I slept with in Glasgow one New Year's Eve. The ghostbuster.'

'Yes, I am.'

'Oh my goodness.' She was standing next to Max's father, after all the time she'd spent searching in vain for him.

'Are you certain that he's mine?'

'Yes. No question.'

'How do you know?'

'You were the only person I slept with that whole year. That was why I had the one-night stand. I'd made a resolution at the beginning of the year that I'd have a better love life, or at least sex life, by the end of the year, and by New Year's Eve I was feeling desperate.' She shook her head. That was all so irrelevant. 'Yes, he is definitely yours.' They were going to have to tell Poppy as soon as possible. Georgie hoped beyond hope that she wouldn't take the news too badly.

Declan frowned. 'Did you try to find me?'

'Of course. Poppy spent a lot of time trying to help me. But because I was drunk and I've always been bad with accents I thought you were South African and I couldn't really remember what you looked like and I thought you were a current Glasgow student, and we just couldn't find you. I think there were about two thousand people at that party.' It had been in a huge nightclub.

He nodded. 'I'd already graduated and was just back visiting friends who were still in Glasgow. Fuck me. Max is my son. Wow.'

'Can I ask?' Georgie had always wondered whether – hoped that – Max's father would be interested in getting to know him properly if she ever found him. 'Max. Would you...? Do you...?'

'I would like to be in his life, yes, if that's your question. He's my son. He's Daniel's half-brother. But right now you have to come and speak to Poppy. She's unbelievably upset. She thinks I've been lying to her. That's my biggest concern at this minute.'

'So you've already told her?'

'No. She read your secret.'

'She...' No. Raf must have shown it to her. Wow. Obviously he'd been angry that she'd gone through his stuff, but she hadn't expected him to do that. Irrelevant, though; this was all about Poppy. And Max. And Declan, his father, his actual father.

'Where is she?'

'At the house. She's locked me out. I need you to explain, corroborate my story. I think it read to her as though we'd had an ongoing affair and she's devastated.'

'Oh, no, I'm so sorry. Oh my goodness, what a nightmare. I'm so, so sorry that I wrote it down and that she found out like that.'

Georgie couldn't even begin to sort through the emotions crashing around her head as she and Declan walked fast across the cobbles. She'd found Max's father and he was a lovely man who wanted to be in Max's life. Unbelievable and wonderful. But Poppy had read her secret and taken it very badly, which was awful, and maybe Poppy would refuse to speak to her again. And, worse, it sounded as though she was very angry with Declan.

And Raf was apparently out of her life almost before he'd entered it.

Max and Declan, though: that felt wonderful.

But Poppy, though. Awful.

19

POPPY

'Go away,' Poppy said through the front door. She wanted to *yell* but waking Daniel right now would not help her.

Bang. The door was going to fall off its eighteenth-century hinges if Declan and Georgie carried on like this. They'd been calling and hammering on the door for several minutes.

'Please, please open the door, Poppy,' Georgie said through the letterbox.

Oh, for fuck's sake. *Fine.*

She opened the front door and Georgie and Declan both came inside.

'We'll have to go into the kitchen,' Poppy said. She really did not want to be sitting down in there with the two of them – it felt like the experience would *contaminate* the room and she practically lived in there when she was at home – but they'd wake Daniel up otherwise.

Georgie was talking almost before the kitchen door was closed behind them.

'Pops, I know that what I wrote sounds truly awful, but it isn't like it sounds. It happened just once, way before Declan met you and neither of us had a clue until you introduced us just before Christmas. And even then neither of us was sure until now. We both wanted to find out for certain and then tell you immediately. I love you, Poppy. Please, please don't be mad. Or at least not at Declan. He didn't know a thing, and even when he thought I was the woman from then, he didn't know that he was Max's father.'

'"We, we, we" all sounds very couply. Have you been discussing me behind my back?' Poppy was aware that her words sounded horrible and bitter and, oh, as it turned out, she didn't care, so what the fuck ever.

'No, we haven't,' Georgie said.

'I just filled Georgie in,' Declan said.

'Right.' Poppy just felt so unbearably sad, right to her bones.

They were all still standing. She sat down at the table because it was suddenly like her legs wouldn't hold her up any more.

'Poppy, drink this.' Declan had got her a glass of water. 'Let me make you a cup of sugary tea as well.'

Poppy drank some of the water, which did help clear the faintness she'd just experienced, and said, 'Thank you, but no tea.' Weird, to use the phrase *thank you* in any context with Declan right now.

'Poppy,' Georgie began again. 'I would never ever want to hurt you because I love you. But I know that I have. I should have mentioned my suspicions as soon as I had them, but I thought it would be better to wait and find out for certain. And obviously I intended to tell you myself, not for you to find out by reading the secret. And I'm so, so sorry that it's all happened like this. But honestly, Declan knew nothing about Max until literally just now.'

Poppy shook her head. She had so much to work through in her mind. She had no idea what she thought.

Daniel had a half-brother.

Georgie was Daniel's half-brother's mother.

Max. He was actually a lot more similar to Declan than he was to Georgie. Thinking about it now, she felt like she should have *noticed*.

Georgie. She'd had these suspicions for several weeks now but hadn't told her. But she'd known Georgie since they were both five and she knew that Georgie was a kind person and that she genuinely wouldn't have wanted to hurt Poppy. She *had* hurt her, though. Maybe with good intentions, but...

And then Declan. So much to unpick.

Suddenly, she needed all the facts.

'Why did you write it as your secret, Georgie? Why would you do that? Why didn't you just say?'

'I know, that was really stupid. I'm an idiot. I didn't say because I wasn't sure and I couldn't get my head round it, and I thought I should find out for definite, as soon as possible, before telling you and Declan, and it was on my mind and then on New Year's Eve I was really drunk and because I was aware the whole time that I potentially had this huge fact that I needed to share with you it felt like I had this gigantic secret and because I was so stupidly drunk I wrote it down.'

'I see.' Poppy still didn't know what she thought about that, but she could see how it had happened. Now she needed to speak to Declan. 'Georgie, would you mind leaving so that I can discuss this in private with Declan?'

'Of course. Again, I'm so, so sorry. I love you, Pops.'

Poppy didn't have the words to reply because she just couldn't work out how she felt about Georgie at the moment, so she said, 'Thank you. Good-bye,' and stared straight ahead until she heard the front door close behind her.

Then she looked up at Declan.

'Could you just give me all the facts straight, please.'

'Yes.' He cleared his throat.

'And maybe sit down?'

'Yes, of course, sorry.' He sat down exactly opposite her and cleared his throat again. 'What happened was that one New Year's Eve after I graduated I was back in Glasgow seeing some friends, and basically I had a one-night stand with a girl whose name I didn't even find out. And that was that, I never saw her again. Until you introduced me to Georgie and something rang a bell with me. I couldn't work out what it was at first and then I began to wonder, and then when I worked the dates out I wondered about Max and I had to know. That was when I started trying to find out and was distracted. But, Poppy, the whole thing is a coincidence. Because we were all in Glasgow that one weekend.'

'I see that it was a coincidence,' Poppy said slowly, 'but...' There were various things catching at the edges of her thought processes.

'Poppy, I love you,' Declan said into the silence she left.

She looked at him. He was tall, he was sturdy, he was dependable, he had boy-next-door classic good looks, he'd always made her laugh, he had an adorable Irish accent, he was nice, and since they'd met he'd always been *hers*, her rock.

And he'd also never lied to her, she'd always believed.

And now it felt like, while he hadn't outright lied, he also hadn't been totally honest with her.

A memory suddenly came to her. 'We talked once about that New Year's Eve. When we were trying to work out if we ever met when we were both in Glasgow.'

Declan nodded.

'And you didn't mention then that you'd shagged someone that evening.' Even as she spoke, she realised that it was a silly point to make. It had been about their third date and very few people would mention a previous one-night stand in that scenario.

'That is true. It was like our third date when we had that conversation, and it had happened nine years before. And I didn't feel like it was a great thing to mention at that point. I was with a girl who I knew from the moment I met her I wanted to spend the rest of my life with. And it was nothing. A drunken one-off that I could barely remember. It didn't seem relevant. Obviously it's turned out that it *was* relevant, and I'm so sorry that this has all come as such a difficult surprise.'

'I realise now that it was just a coincidence.' Poppy couldn't help wondering whether he'd seen both Poppy and Georgie at the party and chosen Georgie over her. But, actually, that was ridiculous. Maybe he had. Maybe he hadn't. But it didn't mean anything, did it? It had been a long time ago and they'd been in fancy dress, and, yes, it just really didn't mean anything.

But the one-night stand thing. She'd just realised what else had been niggling at her.

'You and I waited,' she said. 'We waited two months even though we both said afterwards that we'd known almost immediately that we were falling in love with each other and we were spending every day together. *You* didn't want to jump into bed quickly, you said.' That *hurt*. Obviously, relationships were about personalities and it was shallow to care about your husband finding you sexually attractive, except physical attraction *did* matter. Why had he wanted to have one-night stands with other people but not with her?

'That... is... true.' He was choosing his words carefully, like he had in the car after go-karting. 'But it was because I realised that I was in *love* with you. One-night stands mean nothing. I didn't want it to mean nothing with you. I wanted a long-term relationship with you and I wanted it to be special and at the right time. I wanted to get to know you really well before-hand. The day I met you, I knew you were the woman I wanted to spend the rest of my life with. I just *knew*.' He stopped and ran his hands through his hair, and then continued, 'I'd never... never felt like that with anyone before. It's... it's always been only you, Poppy.'

And *that* was what had been on the edge of her thoughts. His searching for the right words had reminded her.

'Declan. In the car, after go-karting, this was what you were talking about then. And, I mean, you gave me a very different impression. Who was the woman you were with?'

He hesitated and then said, 'Your friend, Anya.'

'You were with my friend Anya?' Poppy was stunned. How did he even know Anya? And why? And he'd met her behind her back?

'I was trying to find out about Georgie and Max from her.'

'You were...' Poppy could barely find the words to express her thoughts. 'Did you tell Anya about your suspicions?'

'Only in a very roundabout way.'

'What?' She stared at him. 'How could you possibly think it was okay to tell her *anything* that you hadn't told me?' Something else occurred to her. 'How did you get in touch with her?'

'I found her number in your phone.'

'What?'

'Poppy, I know, I know it sounds *terrible*, and I am so truly sorry, but I had the best of intentions. I didn't want to upset you and that's why I did all of this. I am so, so sorry.'

He reached his hands out to her across the table and she just looked at them. She physically couldn't make herself take them right now. She was just so *hurt*.

'Declan, I cannot believe that you would confide in a woman you don't even *know* instead of in me.'

'I know.' He shook his head. 'I'm a complete idiot. But you'd been seeming quite... low, I suppose... and I didn't want to add to your misery.'

'Patronising, would you say?'

'I... Yes... Probably. Poppy, I love you. I have no other words. I am so incredibly sorry.'

Poppy looked into the face that she loved so much.

She felt so, so hurt and betrayed.

'I think I need to be alone,' she said.

'Poppy...' Declan's voice broke. 'I love you so much. I'm so sorry for hurting you.'

She shook her head. 'I think you need to go now.'

She looked at him. Tears were tracing down his cheeks. She'd never seen him cry before.

'I'm sorry,' she said. She realised that she was crying too.

She stood up and walked to the front door and Declan followed her.

'I love you,' he repeated.

She wanted to tell him that she loved him too but the words stuck in her throat. Because he didn't feel entirely like the Declan she loved any more. She hadn't believed that the Declan she loved would lie to her or go behind her back.

'Goodnight.' She opened the front door.

'Okay,' he said. He stepped outside onto the porch and then said, 'Could we speak tomorrow? Please?'

'Maybe.' She didn't know how she'd be feeling when she'd had time to think.

After she closed the door behind him, she went back into the kitchen and plonked herself down at the table with a full packet of eight Tunnock's Caramels and began to unwrap the first one.

She couldn't remember the last time she'd felt so utterly, utterly bereft. It was like her entire world had been pulled from under her this evening and she didn't know whether she'd ever be able to get over it.

20

GEORGIE

Georgie didn't know how long she'd been sitting on the bench in the middle of the green, worrying about Poppy and thinking through the implications of finally having identified Max's father, when she heard someone say, 'Georgie.' Oh. It was Raf.

'Hi.'

'Are you okay? I think you've been sitting here for a while.' His words were pleasant, but his tone was distant rather than friendly; the warmth and laughter usually in his voice were completely missing.

'Yes, great, thanks.' Frankly, she didn't feel that warm towards him, either. She really did fully, fully understand that he'd been upset about her going through his things – she'd been so wrong and stupid to do that – but two wrongs did not make a right, and he should certainly not then have shown her secret to Poppy. That had been an *awful* thing for him to do.

'Are you sure?' He peered at her. 'You really don't look alright. Are you crying?'

'I don't know.'

'Georgie, I...' He hesitated and then said, 'You really don't look okay. Come into the pub and sit down for a minute?'

Georgie shook her head. 'I can't go back to the drinks.' And she had no desire to speak to him either.

'They've finished. We're just tidying up.'

'No, honestly, thank you, I'm fine.'

'Georgie, your teeth are literally chattering. If not the pub, go home? Where are you staying?'

'With my mother.'

'Let me walk you over there now, then?'

'Honestly, I'm fine on my own. I might just sit here for a little longer.'

'Right.' Raf gave an audible sigh. 'You know, I really don't want to stand out here. But I really don't feel like I can leave you here alone in the middle of the night.'

'Really, I'm fine.' Georgie did not want to go back to her mother's until she was certain that she and her stepfather were in bed. The moonlight allowed her to just about make out the house in the distance, and she could see that there were still lights on in most of the downstairs windows.

'Okay, then.' Raf sat down at the extreme opposite end of the bench from her.

And then they sat in complete silence.

It wasn't companionable.

A couple of minutes in, Georgie thought about apologising again. She should do so but he should also apologise to her.

The silence continued.

A couple of minutes later, Georgie had come to the conclusion that sitting here with Raf was actually worse than encountering her mother would be. Her mother didn't notice much about her so she could probably just escape straight upstairs to bed, and she didn't want to be with someone who'd done such a horrible thing in response to the horrible thing that she herself had done. They'd both behaved badly and clearly things – such as they had been – were over between them, and she'd rather not have to be around him any more.

She should apologise one final time, though, because she really hadn't behaved well.

'I'm really sorry about this morning. I shouldn't have gone through your papers. Because the secret was so huge, I couldn't think straight and I was worried you wouldn't give it to me or would look at it or something.'

'Yeah, kind of pissed off that you would think I would do that.'

'Sorry, what? You gave it to Poppy! And, okay, I'd clearly made you really angry first, but I don't think there's any justification for what you did. So if I'm honest, I think I was right to assume you might look at it.'

'I did not give it to Poppy.'

'What?'

'I think she saw it herself. She went into Noah's kitchen to get paracetamol and it was on the side where I'd got it out to give it to you.'

'Oh. Oh my goodness.' What a terrible conclusion she'd leapt to. 'Raf, I'm so, so sorry for accusing you of that.'

'Yeah. Kind of just more of the same really. You thought I might look at it. And then you thought that I might, in anger, show it to Poppy. Which would have been truly dreadful behaviour.'

'Yes. I'm so, so sorry. The secret was so huge that it was clouding my judgement on everything.'

'You know, I actually thought we had something. You're the first woman I... since Anna... the first one I've wondered whether...' His voice croaked a little and he stopped speaking. 'And apparently you were only spending time with me in order to get the secret back, *and* you had no respect for my integrity.'

'No,' Georgie said. 'I mean, yes, initially that's why I was spending time with you, but then I grew to like you. So much. I loved skating with you.'

'And you grew to trust me so much that you confided in me that you needed the secret back? Oh, wait, no, you tried to steal it from me instead. And then accused me of giving it to Poppy.'

Thank goodness the moon seemed to have been obscured by clouds so Raf wouldn't see the tears travelling down Georgie's cheeks.

'I am so, so sorry,' she whispered. She'd become friends with him on false pretences and then she'd misjudged him *so* spectacularly.

'Let me walk you to your mother's now.'

'Thank you.'

They walked a good metre apart and Raf said, 'Goodbye, then,' the second she had the door about an inch open, and immediately began to stride off back across the green.

Way to go, Georgie.

With her total lack of judgement she'd managed to do terrible damage to her relationship with her lifelong best friend and – worse – she'd apparently damaged Poppy and Declan's relationship, and she had also ruined whatever fledgling relationship she'd had with Raf.

Idiot didn't begin to describe her.

* * *

The next morning, after very little sleep, she went to call on Poppy. Poppy didn't answer the door.

Georgie called on her at nine, ten and eleven. There was no answer each time. She was sure that Poppy was home, but she apparently she didn't want to speak to Georgie.

Understandable and, oh God, Georgie might be making things worse; Poppy might feel that she was harassing her now.

Plus she needed to get home because she had to pick Max up from his sleepover and tell him about his father, given that Declan now knew.

In the end, she sent Poppy a message.

Poppy, I'm so sorry again. I love you and I never intended to hurt you – I was trying NOT to hurt you but of course failed spectacularly – if I could go back in time I would do things so very, very differently. I would just have told you and Declan immediately of my suspicions. I have to go back to Bristol now to pick Max up. I'm going to tell him about Declan, because I have to, and I want you to know that because, if I'm lucky enough for you to want to continue our friendship, I don't ever want to hide anything from you again. If you'd like to talk any time please just tell me and I'll come to Melting as soon as I can.

Then she sent one to Raf.

I'm so sorry again. For everything. I was just desperate not to hurt my friend and in so doing I treated you badly. I'm so sorry. I really enjoyed our time together. Thank you for everything.

Neither of them opened the messages.

21

GEORGIE

After an insanely busy week – which she'd needed like a hole in the head – Georgie set off for Melting with Max as soon as she could the next Saturday.

Her first stop was meeting Declan with Max at an adventure playground in Little Melting. Max, as it turned out, was the perfect age and temperament for a surprise reveal of his father's identity; he'd taken it entirely in his stride and was just keen to meet up and play some football with him in the field next to the playground. And Declan had been very keen to spend some time with Max as soon as possible.

When they arrived, Declan strode towards Max and gave him a big handshake and shoulder clasp, while Max did his standing-taller thing, grinning ear to ear. And then they were off with the ball, Declan leaning down to speak to Max and Max looking like he was already hanging on Declan's every word, and Georgie was blinking back tears of happiness and relief and taking some photos of her gorgeous boy *and his father*.

And then she got back in the car to head over to see Poppy. Apparently she'd refused to see or speak to Declan all week other than for him to see Daniel each day for half an hour, which did not sound good. It would be terrible if Poppy and Declan split permanently because of this.

Having, she now realised, drunk far too much water in the car, she was desperate for the loo by the time she arrived in Melting.

This was really not a time when she wanted to see her mother, so she couldn't go to the loo there.

She also couldn't knock on anyone else's door and ask to use their loo, because they'd wonder why she wasn't using her mother's. And she wanted to go before she saw Poppy, because saying, 'Please can I use the loo,' was not the first part of the speech she'd been rehearsing in her head all the way here.

She should really, really not have had those three bottles of water.

There was no other option – she was going to have to use the pub's loo, even though Raf was probably still landlording and he still hadn't read her message from last weekend. Up to last Saturday they'd been messaging each other a lot. And there'd been the kiss. Obviously it was a silly thing to think because of course what they'd been doing had been *far* from actual dating, but it still kind of felt as though they'd gone through a break-up.

She was going to try to speak to Raf again, because it was horrifying to think that she'd hurt his feelings, especially after he'd told her that she was the first person he'd thought about dating since he lost his wife, but she needed to speak to Poppy first, because she was worried about her, and she didn't want to just go casually into the pub until she'd spoken to Raf properly.

Needs must, though.

Raf was bending down doing something with barrels at the end of the bar when she sidled in through the door. His T-shirt was stretched across his shoulders and you could see the muscles in his legs through his jeans. Georgie was torn between wanting to feast her eyes on him and wanting to run away before he saw her.

'Hi,' she said eventually. 'I'm just going to use the loo. Hope you don't mind.'

Raf jumped quite convulsively and there was a big clunk and then a thud. 'Fuck.'

'What?' She moved closer to see what had happened.

'It's nothing.' He stood up, his thumb dripping blood. 'You surprised me. I dropped the barrel.'

'Oh my goodness. That looks bad. I can't believe you've got *another* hand injury. Let me get you a plaster. Where do you keep them?'

'Honestly, don't worry. It's fine.'

It couldn't be; there was blood *everywhere*. Who knew that a thumb could bleed that much? Shit, what if it was a really serious injury? That would be unlucky to say the least, coming on top of his recent finger surgery.

'You should put it above your head. What if you've hit an artery?'

'It would be spurting out. I'm absolutely fine, really.'

'Can I get you a napkin or something to bandage it?'

'I'm just going to wash it and stick a plaster on.'

'Let me get the plaster.'

'It is *seriously* fine. Although I'd be grateful if you'd keep an eye on the bar for a couple of minutes while I go into the house and sort it out.'

'Of course, no problem.' Now didn't seem like the right time to mention that she was *bursting* to go to the loo; she'd have to keep on crossing her legs.

If it hadn't been for Raf and the leg-crossing, she'd have enjoyed being behind the bar for a few minutes. It brought back happy memories of working in the pub in the summer holidays when she was at university.

While Raf was gone, Barry the builder and a couple of other locals came in for a pre-lunch pint. They all seemed to think that she and Raf had had a bit of a fling and had then split up. Barry, with the air of a man expressing great intellectual discovery, asked if she'd come this morning to try to patch things up with Raf.

'No,' she told them.

'Pity.' Delphine, one of Barry's drinking friends, who had to be eighty if she was a day, had already downed two whiskeys. 'You make a lovely couple.'

Raf walked back in, his thumb in a blue plaster.

'We were just saying that it's a pity that you and Georgina aren't getting back together,' said Delphine.

Georgie glared at her.

'And *I* was just saying,' she said, 'that we were never together.'

'Indeed.' Raf looked spectacularly unamused. Clearly he was still upset about Georgie having started their friendship on effectively false pretences. She should try to convince him somehow that she *hadn't* just been using him, so that he wouldn't continue to feel hurt, but her biggest priority today had to be Poppy.

'So it's been lovely to see you all,' Georgie said, squeezing past Raf to get out from behind the bar. He was very large and her boobs and tummy weren't exactly small – running hadn't made any discernible difference to them – and the space was narrow, so she ended up squeezed right up against him for a moment, really embarrassing at any time but especially now, given the current conversation. She was *desperate* for the loo too, so she couldn't escape the pub yet.

When she came out of the toilets, feeling a *lot* better – physically, anyway – Barry said, 'Here's your never-been-girlfriend, Raf.'

When Delphine had stopped cackling, she said, 'Have you heard that the doctor's wife's kicked him out? Now that's sad.'

Raf looked at Georgie and raised his eyebrows. She gave him a tiny nod. She wasn't really sure what she was confirming, if she was honest. Yes, Poppy's kicked Declan out? Yes, she knew all about it? Yes, it was a very bad thing and if there was anything Raf could think of to say to Poppy that would help it would be fantastic? Although, no, she wasn't going to tell Raf any details right now.

'I'll see you,' she said, and left the pub to a resounding no-reply from Raf.

She walked along the road and banged the door knocker on Poppy's house.

When she opened her front door, Poppy just shook her head.

'Hi, Poppy,' Georgie ventured.

'I'm sorry, I'm really not in the mood.' Poppy's voice was expressionless. Georgie was horrified; she'd known her for twenty-nine years and she'd never seen her like this before.

The way she looked was no less horrifying. Her hair was glisteningly greasy. Her eyes were red around the edges with grey, puffy bags underneath. She was wearing very baggy tracksuit trousers and a weird jumper, maybe hand-knitted. Poppy's natural beauty was still visible but it was like she was doing her very best to hide it.

Georgie had goosebumps, in a really bad way. It was her fault that Poppy was so miserable. She had to do something to help.

Poppy began to close the door and Georgie reflexively stuck her foot in it.

'What are you doing?' Poppy said.

'Please, please let me come in?' Georgie was desperate not to leave her like this.

'Oh, whatever.' Poppy let go of the door and retreated inside.

Georgie followed her into the kitchen.

She only just managed not to gasp out loud at the state it was in. Usually, Poppy was very house proud; today the work surface was covered in empty food packaging and dirty dishes, there was dried-on food splatted on the floor and up the side of one of the pale-green-painted Shaker cupboards, and there was a big pile of what looked like dirty laundry on the kitchen table. The only thing that was clean was Daniel's high chair.

Georgie put her hand over her mouth, wondering whether or not the best approach would be to mention the mess.

She looked at Poppy, who was standing on the other side of the table basically glaring at her, and decided that a messy kitchen was the least of her worries.

'I'm so sorry, Poppy,' she began. 'I know that the second I suspected that Declan was the person from that New Year's Eve, and therefore Max's father, I should have told you. I was always going to tell you, obviously, if it was true, but I didn't want to say anything if it wasn't.'

'If it hadn't been for Max, would you have told me?'

'Um. I don't know. I've never thought about that because it's always been about Max.'

'Oh, yes, I see.'

'Why?' Georgie asked. 'Are you wondering whether Declan would or should have told you, given that he wasn't certain about Max?' This rift between Poppy and Declan was *awful*.

'Yep.' Poppy looked at her for a long moment through her red-rimmed eyes and then said, 'What do *you* think Declan should have done?'

Oh God. What a terrible question to have to answer. The responsibility.

Georgie was going to have to reply and she was going to have to choose her words extremely carefully.

'I have never been in a serious relationship, as you know,' she began. 'I'm really sure that Declan would never have wanted to hurt you and that I suppose he would want to weigh up what would be best for you.'

'And what do you think would have been best for me? If Max hadn't been involved?'

'I...' Shit. This was so difficult to answer. 'Obviously everyone's different and has different views, but I feel that Declan having had an anonymous, utterly meaningless shag under a bush nine years before he met you should have no bearing on your relationship with him, even if the person he shagged is someone you know. Because it was so, so far before he met you.'

'And so you're saying that he should have told me immediately because I wouldn't have minded?' Oh fuck. *Did* Georgie mean that?

'I... I don't know. He wouldn't have wanted to upset you. Or hurt your feelings.'

Poppy said nothing and just looked at Georgie with raised eyebrows.

'I just don't know.' Georgie spread her hands. 'He wouldn't have wanted to hurt you, but then maybe he would have thought you would want to know.'

'I'll tell you one thing I'm pretty sure he would have known, and you would too if you'd thought about it. You would both have known that I wouldn't want to be lied to. Lies and secrets between spouses and best friends are toxic. And Declan did lie to me. He should have told me immediately that he suspected and then just asked you.'

'I'm so, so sorry, Poppy. I should have done too. I think we were both just panicking because it seemed so huge.'

'You want to know another reason that I think Declan might have been panicking?'

'Mmm?' Georgie very much did not want to know – this was one of the worst conversations she'd ever had – but if Poppy needed to talk she needed to listen.

'Because.' Somewhere in the last minute or two Poppy had started crying. She gave a big, honking sniff and wiped her face with the backs of her hands. 'Because when he met *you* – and yes I accept that you weren't actually *you*, you were just a random stranger in a witch's costume – he shagged you right then and there. But when he met *me*, we waited two months even though we immediately started spending a lot of time together, and we waited because *he* wanted to.' Her voice rose into a wail as she choked out the words, 'And that hurts.'

'Oh, Poppy.' Georgie moved round the table to try to put her arms round her friend, but Poppy moved out of her way. It was heart-breaking seeing her like this. 'Poppy, I'm sure that must have been because he wanted things to be special with you. Different. He had no interest in getting to know the girl dressed as a witch on New Year's Eve. That must be why.'

Poppy sat down. 'He also went behind my back and found my friend Anya's details and met up with her and lied about that when I heard her with him. I can't trust him.'

'Oh, no, Poppy you *can.*'

'Really, Georgie? Really? Do you know my relationship with my husband better than I do?'

'I... No, no, of course I don't. But the facts...'

'The facts are that he didn't want to sleep with me as much as he wanted to sleep with a random stranger, and that he lied to me.'

'Could you maybe talk to him about this, though?'

'No. I can't.' Poppy's voice was wobbling into tears. 'It hurts too much. And I haven't slept properly for a really long time and I've been finding things difficult since Daniel was born, and sometimes I'm okay and sometimes I'm not and now I don't think I have the strength to talk to Declan.'

The baby monitor in the corner of the room started vibrating and then Daniel started to yell.

'Oh no,' said Poppy. 'I think he's beginning to drop his morning sleep. Such as it is. But I just want a break.' Tears started dribbling out of her eyes. Like she didn't even have the energy to cry properly. Daniel stepped up the yelling.

'No,' Poppy moaned.

'Okay. I'm going to look after Daniel while you take a shower and get some sleep.'

'No.'

'Then I will call Declan to come and help. Or one of your neighbours. Or Beth or Ankita. Or I'll call your parents on their cruise.'

Poppy slumped in her chair, shoulders drooping, tears still dribbling, while Daniel carried on yelling.

'I feel like a really bad mother,' she whispered, 'but sometimes I just want a *break*.'

'You are not a terrible mother. You're a great one. Everyone needs a break. Kids are exhausting. How much sleep did you have last night?'

'Four hours, maybe. In forty-minute chunks. He keeps waking up.'

'No wonder you feel rough. That's not enough. Let me get Daniel out of his cot and look after him so that you can have a sleep.'

'I don't think so.'

'Okay, I'll have to call Declan.' Georgie didn't want to sound mean but Poppy clearly really needed some help today.

Five minutes later Poppy was in bed and Georgie and Daniel were downstairs in the sitting room, and Georgie had agreed by text with Declan that he would hang out with Max for the next few hours while Georgie stayed with Poppy.

She decided that three hours would be a good length of time for Poppy to sleep in the middle of the day without stopping her from getting to sleep that evening. She gave Daniel some lunch and played with him. She also cleaned the whole kitchen and downstairs loo very thoroughly, with him on her hip. Daniel was exhausted by the end of the three hours. So was Georgie. Looking after a baby really was hard work. You forgot as your own child got older.

'Right,' she said to Poppy, once Georgie had woken her up and she'd come downstairs. 'Why don't you have a shower now? And I'll put Daniel down for a sleep just before I leave. Hopefully he'll sleep for a while. He's knackered now. I've gone for some major over-stimulation.'

Poppy almost smiled.

Half an hour later, as Daniel began a very loud demonstration of how tired he was, Poppy finally came downstairs in some different trackie bottoms, that fitted slightly better, with clean hair and her eyes less out on tiredness stalks than they had been before.

'I should thank you,' she said.

'No, you really shouldn't.' Georgie picked Daniel up. 'I'll be back down in a minute.'

Daniel took more time to settle than Georgie would have expected; it was easy to see how Poppy would be frazzled now, irrespective of everything that had happened with Declan and Georgie and Max. No one would be at their best in Poppy's position, and now she had so much to work through in her mind.

When Georgie got back downstairs, she found Poppy at the kitchen table, with her laptop open.

'I'm going to catch up on some admin while I have the functioning brain cells,' she told Georgie.

'Good plan.' It was a relief to see Poppy recovered enough to show a tiny bit of her usual humour. Georgie should try to strike while the iron was hot. 'I wondered whether you thought it might be a good idea to talk to Declan soon.'

'I can't right now. I appreciate that he is probably feeling miserable too, but I just... can't. It still hurts too much.'

'Okay. Of course.' Georgie felt *so* guilty about her contribution to the situation between Poppy and Declan. She'd have to try to help in some other way. 'I have to go now and pick up Max.' Oh God, oh God. Had Declan told Poppy he was meeting Max? Georgie hadn't, she realised. What a stupid oversight. 'He's with Declan. They met today.'

'That's nice,' said Poppy, in suddenly freezing tones.

Georgie pressed her lips together, not sure what to say next.

'Oh, Georgie,' Poppy said a moment later. 'It *is* nice for the two of them, obviously. But. It hurts. Thank you for coming. I'm really sorry, but I think I need some space from you too for a while.'

'Of course.' Georgie ignored the misery she felt and looked at Poppy for a long moment and then said, 'Okay, well, bye, then.'

'Bye.'

Georgie let herself out of the house, walked to her car and sat staring at the steering wheel trying very hard not to cry.

She was going to miss Poppy so much. And it was so sad that Poppy couldn't speak to Declan right now. How was Poppy going to cope if Daniel carried on not sleeping?

She needed to find someone to keep an eye on Poppy, because she really had to go back to Bristol.

It was obvious who she should ask. Clearly not Declan. Poppy's parents had just left for a month-long cruise. Beth was in Bath. Ankita was back in London at the moment. Poppy would be hugely embarrassed if Georgie told any of the villagers about this.

She got back out of the car and went into the pub to look for Raf. He didn't know the details of the secret but he did know that Poppy had read it and that there'd been a huge fallout, and he was a very kind person so he'd never say no to keeping an eye on Poppy.

Only Noah and, oh joy, Barry, Delphine and a couple of their cronies were still there. Georgie nearly bottled asking for Raf but then she thought about Poppy.

'Is Raf around?' she asked.

She actually couldn't hear Noah's answer at first, over all the 'Looking for your boyfriend?' chat. Eventually she heard him. And excellent. Raf was playing tennis and probably wouldn't be back for about an hour. So she could sit in the pub and endure more chat. Or she could visit her mother. Or she could go for a walk in the drizzle.

In the end, she decided to sit in her car and 'catch up on some admin' on her phone. Or, in reality, pointlessly surf the internet. She also called Ankita for a quick chat, and, without telling her the details, asked if she could maybe stay with Poppy for a couple of nights because Declan was away. Ankita said she'd do her best to get there soon.

Hopefully Raf could keep an eye on Poppy until then.

Within about fifteen minutes Georgie was cold. Within another fifteen minutes she was unbelievably freezing and caught between not wanting to switch the car heating on and contributing to global warming or pollution but also not wanting to develop frostbite.

She didn't want to go for a walk and maybe miss Raf's return, so in the end she heaved a sigh, got out of the car and went back to the pub and asked for a cup of coffee before sitting down in a corner.

Barry and Delphine gave up on hassling her after about five minutes and she did manage to go through her inbox, genuinely becoming quite engrossed in the task.

So when Raf did arrive back she only noticed him because Delphine called, 'Lover Boy's here, my darling.' And then, to Raf, 'She's been waiting for you. I think she wants to get back together.'

Lover Boy, who Georgie couldn't help noticing was looking very good in his tennis kit, smiled at Delphine but the smile didn't make his eyes go crinkly like his real smiles did.

'Hello, Georgie,' he said, with blatant reluctance.

Georgie jumped at the sound of his voice and up-ended her still half-full coffee cup.

'Napkins?' He managed to say it with only the merest hint of *FFS.*

'Yes, please.' The dregs of a cup could make a surprisingly large puddle on your lap.

As he handed them to her, she said quietly, to avoid anyone else hearing, 'I really need to talk to you.'

'I'm a bit busy.'

'You should listen to what she has to say,' said Delphine. She had super-human hearing for a woman of her age. 'What if she's pregnant or she wants to propose?'

'Unlikely,' Raf said.

'Please,' whispered Georgie.

'You have to,' said Barry. 'She's literally begging you.'

Seriously. Was there some weird sound-magnifying effect in this pub?

'Why don't you go and have a cup of tea in the barn?' said Noah. 'This lot'll just have to wait if they want anything that I can't manage.'

'Okay, thanks,' said Raf, looking extremely ungrateful. 'We won't be long.'

'I need your help with Poppy,' said Georgie as soon as they were through the pub door into Noah's house.

'Has something happened?'

'She's really sleep deprived and a bit lonely while Declan's... away—' she couldn't be the one to tell anyone else what had happened '—so I wondered whether you'd be able to pop in just to keep her company for a bit? Ankita's aiming to come to stay soon and I'm sure she'll be fine once she's arrived.'

'Yep, no problem. I'll go and see her in a couple of hours' time and Noah can hobble over too.'

'Thank you *so* much.'

'Not a problem,' Raf said, unsmilingly.

'I also wondered if... if I could buy you a drink sometime?' Georgie asked hesitantly.

Raf looked at her for an uncomfortably long time during which she had to fight with herself not to wriggle under his gaze, and then he said, 'That's really kind, thank you, but I'm quite busy.'

'Okay, yes, of course. Bye, then.' As Georgie walked out of the front door of Noah's barn and wondered whether she'd ever see Raf properly again, she had to blink a lot to stop tears coming.

22

POPPY

Quite bizarrely, for a woman who had a very busy life in London, Ankita turned up unannounced at Poppy's that evening and said, 'Hello! Can I come in?'

Coming on top of the fact that Raf had come over late afternoon within half an hour of Georgie leaving and had dragged Poppy and Daniel out for a walk, and had stayed and chatted to her all the way through Daniel's tea and then insisted on helping with the washing up, it was obvious that Georgie had gone all-out to make sure that Poppy had company.

Poppy couldn't decide whether she was pleased that people cared or embarrassed that people thought she was a charity case.

'Did Georgie suggest you come?'

'Yes.' Ankita walked straight in, pretty much through her, and into the kitchen. 'Coffee?'

'Oh.' Poppy wasn't one hundred per cent sure whether she'd rather have Ankita to stay or be left alone to think. Or just wallow. It didn't look like she was going to have the choice, though; it was difficult to say no to Ankita when she was in a determined mood.

'You know what?' Ankita took the lid off the kettle and put it under the tap. 'I've always wanted babies. That's part of the reason I asked Noah out. But I've always thought it would be piss-boring looking after them. No adults to talk to. Constant crap household chores to do. I'd have to carry on working, at least part-time. I don't think I could cope otherwise. I'm not sure how anyone does.'

'It can be difficult,' Poppy acknowledged. 'But also amazing. At times.' Soooo lonely, though, if she was honest. 'But *you*, you'd cope with anything.' There was no way Ankita would end up in the kind of situation Poppy was in now.

'Are you joking? I can cope with being *me*. That's completely different. I think it would be very hard to cope with being a stay-at-mum not seeing a lot of adults. And if I'm honest, I'm not sure you're coping brilliantly. You've got to do something about this, Pops. You need to go back to being the old Poppy. Yourself. Yourself plus Daniel. Not the miserable-as-fuck woman that you sometimes are.'

'I'm sorry?' Poppy frowned.

'Miserable as fuck. Like you were on New Year's Eve. And you aren't looking *too* happy now. It can't be good for Daniel. I think you should go back to work a couple of days a week, get yourself a non-Declan-related social life, and just get yourself back, basically.' Ankita turned round and looked at her, her hands spread. 'I know that I might sound mean but *are* you happy right now?'

Poppy just stood and stared at her.

'I love you, Pops,' Ankita said eventually. 'And I feel you aren't happy. I know that something big happened with you, Georgie and Declan at Noah's drinks, and I don't know what that was, and maybe that's contributing, but I feel as though you haven't been totally yourself for a while.'

And suddenly Poppy found herself howling, really, really howling, and Ankita pulled her down onto the sofa with her and curled her up into a gigantic hug.

As she sniffled and hiccupped in her friend's arms, Poppy wasn't even sure what she was crying about. Well, probably just everything. The sleep deprivation and loneliness-induced low-level misery she'd had going on for months now, and the fact that it felt like her marriage was over. Or that maybe it didn't have to be over but the way she felt at the moment she was powerless to make herself overcome her sadness at Declan's behaviour.

After a few minutes, she managed to speak. 'Your lovely jumper.'

She pointed at where she'd been sobbing all over Ankita's cashmere-clad shoulder.

'It's fine. Tears are just water and salt. They'll totally dry-clean out.' Ankita gave her another big squeeze. 'Good job you aren't wearing mascara.'

Soon, Daniel started crying along with Poppy. Ankita picked him up and they all had a big hug together. Hopefully his snot would dry-clean out, too.

'You know what?' Ankita tickled Daniel under the chin and he roared with laughter. 'Perfect solution. My flat's just gone under offer. I need to be based in the Cotswolds most of the time as of pretty much now because we're doing more and more planning for the new business.' She'd agreed to join her ex-colleague Alex in setting up a new venture. 'I love my parents but I can't *stand* living with them. I'm moving in.'

'What? Here? Now?' Poppy wasn't sure how she felt about that.

'Yep. Right now.'

'But do you have any stuff?'

'I just happen to have an overnight bag in the car,' Ankita said airily. She'd *clearly* planned this.

'But the spare room's a tip.'

'Not a problem. We can box up any stuff that's in there and I'll clean it.' Ankita hated cleaning; Poppy knew that for a fact. In fact, she was sure she hadn't actually cleaned anything herself at all since she started her hotshot job straight out of uni.

'The bed linen needs to be changed,' Poppy continued.

'I'll change it.'

'I'm not really on top of the laundry. I don't think we've got any clean sheets.'

'I'll buy some, then, or borrow some.'

'Are you sure?' Now the suggestion was sinking in, Poppy was beginning to think that it might be quite nice having Ankita to stay. The company would be lovely.

'Of course I'm sure. Right, first things first. What are we doing for dinner?'

'I'm a bit low on food,' Poppy said. It was an understatement, really. The only fruit or vegetables of any kind in the kitchen were puréed and in baby-sized ice cubes. The only protein was cheese. Both the recycling and regular kitchen bins were full of E-number-flavoured pasta 'n' sauce, Pot Noodle and weird microwave burger packets. If she was honest, the closest Poppy had got to a vitamin since she'd last put the bins out was the tomato sauce on a frozen margherita pizza.

'Wow,' Ankita said, when she'd finished looking through the fridge, freezer and cupboards. 'Okay. So we're going to the Duck for food,' she commanded. 'I'll pay. After you've got changed and put some make-up on.'

'I don't have time for make-up.'

'You do now, because I'll look after Daniel while you get ready.'

'I need to give him his tea first.'

'I'll do it while you're getting ready.'

'You have snot and tears on your jumper,' Poppy said as a last attempt.

'I'll live with it.' Ankita *never* lived with looking less than perfect. She was clearly making a big effort right now.

By the time Poppy made it back downstairs, Ankita had got quite a lot of butternut squash, beetroot and beef stew with green beans inside Daniel, but also quite a lot on her sleeve. Poppy was pretty sure the dry cleaners would have to be miracle workers to get rid of that.

'Whoops,' Poppy said. 'Sorry.'

'It's fine. I just need to dress differently when I'm doing childcare.' Ankita didn't look like she *loved* the idea of more childcare, but Poppy had realised while she was getting changed that she was just going to accept any offer of help she got – as long as it wasn't from Declan or Georgie. She wasn't ready for that yet. 'Can I just say...?'

'Mmm?'

'Daniel's eating *way* more healthily than you are. It's brilliant that you're looking after him so fantastically, but I think you need to look after yourself too. For his sake.'

Hmm. Maybe Ankita had a point.

* * *

'That's it.' Ankita, busy chopping fruit at the table, looked up as Poppy staggered bleary-eyed into the room the next morning, holding Daniel. 'Things have to change.' She pointed an orange at Daniel. 'All the screaming last night. I mean *I'm* going to be a wreck soon if he carries on like this. We need to get strict.'

That evening, Ankita insisted on starting sleep-training, and for the first two hours it worked.

'Maybe I should write a parenting book,' Ankita said. 'Apparently it's *easy*.'

'Oh my God,' she said the next morning. 'I have the headache from hell and obviously we have no paracetamol and oh my *God* that child has phenomenal willpower.'

Eventually, after nine nights – Ankita was not a quitter – Daniel was sleeping through the night.

* * *

During that time, Poppy didn't really see Declan, because he'd been away for a conference, and when he came to visit Daniel at the weekend she made herself scarce, because she still felt too hurt to talk to him.

Georgie messaged a couple of times and Poppy promised herself she'd reply... later... and couldn't find the words.

So that wasn't so good, but having Ankita there and the sleep thing – that was *amazing*.

The morning after the second night Daniel had slept properly, a back-to-her-svelte-well-slept-self Ankita said that she'd organised for her business partner Alex to babysit that evening and the two of them were going *out*, and Poppy didn't panic or worry or think she was too tired, she just thought that would be nice. And it was.

And on her way home, arm in arm with Ankita, dancing across the green like they were fifteen again, not about to turn thirty-five, gasping with laughter, she suddenly remembered a time when they'd done this with Georgie and Beth too, and she realised that she had *so* much history with Georgie and she *knew* her and she *knew* that Georgie hadn't wanted to hurt her, she'd just been *stupid* not telling her immediately.

And she knew that Declan had never wanted to hurt her, either.

The big question was, she realised as she crept into bed next to Daniel sound-asleep in his cot – she was going to move him into his own bedroom tomorrow – whether she could get over the fact that Declan *had* hurt her with the lie about meeting Anya and the fear that he just hadn't found her that attractive to begin with and that's why he'd wanted to wait to sleep together.

* * *

A couple of days later, Daniel started crawling. One minute he was on his tummy staring at a plastic train, and the next he'd got himself onto all fours and crawled across the room.

Poppy and Ankita were both busy telling him how clever he was and grinning at each other, when Poppy suddenly began to cry. She couldn't help it. She just sat on the edge of the sofa and tears rolled down her cheeks.

'Poppy?' Ankita asked. 'I want to believe that those are happy tears, but...'

'I feel terrible that Declan isn't here.' She sniffed.

'Realistically—' Ankita was always realistic '—even if he hadn't moved out, he probably wouldn't have been here, because it's four-thirty on a Wednesday afternoon so presumably he'd be at work.'

'That's true.' Poppy managed to stop crying. 'I should tell him, though.'

'That is true. So... tell him?'

'It feels awkward?'

'Just send the video you just took.'

'Okay, yes, you're right. Okay.' Before she could change her mind, Poppy took her phone and forwarded the video to Declan.

She and Ankita were still crawling round the floor with Daniel when the doorbell went a few minutes later.

'I'll go,' said Ankita.

'Hi, Declan,' she said from the hall a few moments later. And then, 'I'm just popping out.'

Ten seconds later, the front door banged shut and Declan said, 'So, hi,' from the door of the sitting room. 'Thank you for the video. I thought it would be okay to come over?'

Poppy stood up and then sat down again because her heart was suddenly beating incredibly fast and she just felt odd. 'Yes, of course,' she said.

'Thank you.' Declan beamed at his son as he crawled across to his father as fast as he could. He bent down and swung him up into his arms. 'Hey, genius boy. You're amazing.'

'Dadada.' Daniel took hold of Declan's cheeks and pulled them both hard, laughing uproariously, which made both Declan and Poppy laugh too.

Declan put Daniel back down and then said, 'Mind if I sit down?'

'Of course not.' This was so weird. And really sad; Declan had just asked her if he could sit down in his own home.

He perched on the opposite end of the (quite small) sofa from Poppy, which meant that there was no chance of them touching each other by mistake. And that was sad, too.

'Thank you again for sending the video,' he said after a moment, looking at Daniel, not at Poppy.

'Yep, no, I mean, of course.' Oh, this was awful. Poppy knew that Declan was a wonderful father and that Daniel and he needed to see each other in a more meaningful way. 'You should spend more time with Daniel,' she said.

'I'd love that.' Declan turned to look at her and the expression on his face was just heartrending; it was like love was just *shining* out of his eyes. 'I'd very much—' he paused, as though he was selecting words very carefully '—like to spend some time with you, too.'

Poppy just... She just...

'I...' She shook her head. It was too much to think about. 'I don't know.'

'Of course.' Declan picked Daniel up again and buried his face against his shoulder for a long moment, which made Poppy scared that he might be crying.

When he put Daniel down, he said, 'So I'm actually between patients in the surgery so I'm going to have to go back, but thank you again, and I'd love to come over again.'

'Of course, I mean definitely, yes of *course*,' Poppy said, not over-emphasising anything at *all*.

And then he left and Poppy felt very, very flat.

* * *

'Did you get Beth's text asking us all to meet on Friday?' Ankita asked when she'd returned to the house. 'Don't worry. Georgie called and she and Max can't do that weekend anyway. Also, Declan phoned me after he left and asked if I could tell you that he loves you.'

Poppy twisted her hands together.

It felt awful that her inability to be in the same room as Georgie meant that their group had broken up. And Georgie had been her best friend forever. But it was just so *hard* and it still felt like she had things to think through.

And Declan. She just... She was just *hurt*.

In the end, she said, 'Thank you,' in response to the questioning look on Ankita's face.

Ankita's silence was loud.

Yep.

Maybe Poppy should think hard about Declan and Georgie sooner rather than later.

* * *

Poppy made a butter bean, tomato and endive salad for a light dinner, only realising as she placed caramelised onions on top that she didn't need to keep making new meals any more because she wasn't sticking to her resolutions – it really didn't matter now if everyone knew that she'd written that she suspected that Declan was having an affair since he'd moved out anyway. And obviously he *hadn't* been having an affair.

No one had posted on the chat since the big fallout. She wondered whether anyone else was sticking to their resolutions still.

The new meal one had been really good. She should continue with it.

She *should* make sure that Declan was very much involved in Daniel's life. Maybe the next time she cooked something new she should invite him over to try it.

'This looks nice,' said Ankita when she came into the room. She sat down and picked up her cutlery and then cut a cherry tomato into two very precisely. 'I need to go to New York and Boston for work next week and I might be away for a fortnight, but I don't want to go if you won't be okay.'

'Ankita, of course you should go.' Poppy really wanted to ask if she was going to be going with Alex – she was *sure* there was a mutual attraction between the two of them – but maybe she should be subtle about the question. 'I'll be fine.' She probably would, she realised.

'I happened to speak to Beth and Declan, and Beth would love to come and stay for a few days and Declan will be around if you do need any help.'

'I'm *sure* I'll be fine,' Poppy said. 'Ankita, thank you.'

'Nothing to thank me for.' Ankita smiled.

'Soooo... is Alex going on the trip?' Poppy couldn't help asking about one second later.

'Yep.' Ankita spent far too long loading her fork. 'I might meet him at the pub this evening to discuss the trip.' Like she couldn't and didn't speak to him regularly during the day about work.

Poppy had to spend a long time sorting her own next mouthful to stop herself laughing. Ankita was *never* like this about men. It was very sweet.

* * *

After two days of guilt, she texted Georgie on Friday afternoon.

Hi, please don't feel that you can't meet Beth in the pub this evening because of me.

Georgie read the message immediately, and then maybe an hour later replied.

Hello! I hope you're well! Thank you so much but Max and I are busy today. Hope you have a lovely evening!

Sad. Very sad. They'd never been so distant in their lives. The exclamation marks made Georgie's words so fake-breezy.

She fake-breezily replied with 'Thank you!' herself. Sad again.

She suddenly decided that she'd like to see Declan later, if he'd like to see her and picked up her phone.

Would you like to come over half an hour early this evening so that we can both be with Daniel together? Nice for him?

His reply came straight back.

Love to, thank you.

Poppy wasn't sure whether she was devastated that he'd thanked her like that – that they'd got to that level of distance – or looking forward to seeing him or apprehensive about what they'd talk about.

* * *

It was a good job she'd been shopping for clothes earlier in the week because she felt a lot better about seeing Declan knowing that she looked okay (she'd bought a top in a size bigger than usual, and honestly she felt *so* much better).

'Is that a new top? You look lovely,' Declan said, as soon as he got inside.

'Thank you.' Poppy was pretty sure that if you had to describe the way she looked right now it would be *bashful*.

Luckily, Daniel, as soon as he'd learnt to crawl, had also learnt to pull himself up to standing and cruise around the furniture, and he kept making a break for freedom and the stairs, so they were too busy laughing with and about him to feel too awkward, and then it was time for Poppy and Ankita to go to the pub.

It had been nice seeing Declan.

23

GEORGIE

Georgie's thoughts were filled with Poppy the next morning as she drove to Melting to drop Max with Declan for the night.

Poppy had always been far more like family to her than her actual family. She missed her. A lot. She hoped so much that she was doing okay. She'd sent a few messages to say she hoped Poppy was alright and had then stopped because she'd had no reply and was worried that Poppy would feel harassed if she carried on messaging her. She wished so much, though, that they could somehow restart their friendship.

As she rounded the corner of the Duck and Grapes after dropping Max with Declan at the cottage where Declan had rented a room – he'd told her that he didn't want to rent a more permanent place for himself yet because he was hoping against hope that Poppy would take him back – she caught a glimpse of Raf, and on impulse stopped and rolled down her car window.

She missed him too (in a different way, obviously), and it wasn't like speaking to him was going to make things *worse*.

'Hi,' she called. 'How are you?'

Raf looked round and hesitated, really looking for a moment as though he was going to blank her, before walking over to the car.

'I'm good, thank you. I heard about your secret. Declan and Max. I see that that was a *big* secret.'

Georgie nodded.

'Yeah. I get why you would want to do anything, literally anything, to avoid Poppy finding out the way she did in fact find out.'

Georgie nodded again. 'Yep. I'm so sorry, though.'

'Yeah, no, all good. Totally understandable. You have to put old friends above new ones. Anyone would. Anyway. I'm glad you're well.' And off he walked while Georgie stared after him.

And *fuck* he clearly still thought that she'd only spent time with him in order to get the secret back.

Which obviously had initially been true, but it had very quickly changed into her just loving his company.

She rolled the window up as it started to rain horizontally into the car.

It was horrible to think that she'd hurt his feelings.

Maybe she should just get out of the car and walk over to him and tell him that he was wrong and that she'd really, really liked him.

Except that would be tantamount to telling him that she'd like a relationship with him.

And she wasn't sure that was true, because after a lifetime of being second-place in her parents' affections she *really* wasn't going to do that in a romantic relationship, and she'd always feel second best to his late wife. It was a recipe for getting hurt.

She couldn't do it.

24

POPPY

Poppy took a banana from her lovely well-stocked fruit bowl. Six weeks ago her mid-afternoon snack had been Hula Hoops and a Tunnock's Caramel. Maybe followed by a slice of cold pizza if there was any left from the evening before. It was amazing how fast you could get into a downward spiral and how hard, basically impossible, it could be to get yourself out of it without help from someone else.

Now she was sleeping and eating properly and, crucially, back at work one day a week and speaking regularly to *adults*, and she was *so much happier*.

Thank heavens for her friends. Ankita and Beth had been amazing recently. But so had Georgie. Ankita wouldn't have turned up in the first place if Georgie hadn't asked her to.

Poppy really missed Georgie.

Losing Declan was like losing her heart. And losing Georgie was like losing one of her limbs.

It was really weird, though, it was like she didn't know whether she could repair their relationship, even though she knew that Georgie had acted with the best of intentions.

It was almost like right now she only had the bandwidth to focus on trying to re-establish some kind of relationship with Declan. He had to come first because he was Daniel's father and her husband.

She'd been thinking about secrets and lies a lot. It wasn't as black and white as she'd been thinking. Declan *shouldn't* have gone behind her back to speak to Anya like that, but he *had* been doing it with the best of intentions. He hadn't wanted to upset Poppy if he didn't have to. Which had clearly spectacularly backfired but the saying 'it was the thought that counted' wasn't wrong. What might she, Poppy, have done if she'd been in his position?

She finished her banana, put the skin in the bin and took an apple. She was really looking forward to seeing Declan later when he came to help her do Daniel's bath and bedtime. And on reflection, she'd immediately felt when she met him that there was something different about him compared to anyone else she'd ever met. And if he'd felt the same way and wanting to wait before they had sex was one of his ways of expressing that, then... maybe it should be flattering rather than hurtful.

Maybe she should ask him if he'd like to go out for dinner. Almost... like a date.

Yep. She was going to do it. She was going to send a message right now. Maybe they could go out tonight. One of the neighbours would be happy to babysit, she was sure.

It was really annoying to have apple juice all over her hands because she wanted to text him immediately.

Okay, hands washed, message sent.

Waiting for his response she actually felt quite jittery.

Obviously, a watched phone never pinged.

Eventually, though, he did reply.

I'd really love to but could we speak later about which evening – could you do next Saturday instead?

While Poppy was standing looking at her phone, wondering what he was doing this evening, he sent another message.

I could also do tomorrow, Monday, Tuesday or Thursday if any of those would work for you?

Hmm. He did sound keen at least. And she'd been the one to ask him to move out. So if he had plans for tonight that was *entirely* his prerogative. She sent a reply.

Tomorrow would be great.

Eek. Now she couldn't decide whether she was more excited or nervous.

* * *

When Declan stepped inside the front door that evening, his smile – hesitant, hopeful, *gorgeous* – made something inside her click.

She loved him. He'd hurt her – a lot – but she still did, she loved him so much. And his smile told her that he *did* care. She was sure that he hadn't intended to hurt her.

Declan opened his mouth to say something, but was distracted by Daniel toddling down the hall to him, his arms stretched towards him.

Declan reached down and swung his son high up into the air while Daniel chortled hugely, and then held him against his chest in a close hug. Poppy felt her eyes fill. She shouldn't be preventing Declan and Daniel from spending as much time as possible together. And it was fully, fully understandable that a man who was as natural a father as Declan was would want to spend as much time as he could with the eleven-year-old he'd just discovered was his son. It wasn't just understandable, it was admirable.

'So, hello,' he said over Daniel's head, his smile the just-for-her one he'd always had from the moment they met.

'Hi.' Poppy smiled back at him. She couldn't really think of any other words right now.

Daniel began to struggle and pointed at the floor, and Declan laughed and put him down.

Daniel immediately punched his knee.

'Daddy knee,' he said very clearly.

'No way,' Poppy breathed. 'Oh my goodness. His first proper words.' She knelt down so that she was at Daniel's side. 'You're so clever,' she told him.

Daniel beamed, hit Declan's knee again and repeated, 'Daddy knee.'

'Oh my God, actual genius,' Declan said. 'I want to kneel down too but I don't want to put my knee out of reach.'

'Daddy knee,' Daniel said again.

Poppy had no idea how much time they spent in the hall with Daniel saying *Daddy knee* and the two of them just incredulous at the amazingness of their amazing son, but it was a long time. And it was a perfect time. And it was something that she could never have shared quite so wonderfully with someone who wasn't Declan.

Later, when Daniel was in bed and Declan was leaving, he said to Poppy, 'I'm really looking forward to tomorrow evening. Shall I book somewhere?'

'That would be nice.' Her face was going to split, she was smiling so hard.

'Great. Erm.' He coughed and his eyes slid away from hers briefly before refocusing on her face. He wasn't smiling now. Poppy felt suddenly shivery with worry. 'I'd have loved to have done this evening. The reason I can't is that Max is coming for a sleepover for the first time and I can't let him down. He was with me earlier in the day and is visiting his grandparents now so that I could come here.'

He paused and then continued. 'I wanted to tell you because I don't want you to think I wouldn't be fully open with you.'

Poppy felt her heart swell. That was actually lovely.

'Thank you for telling me. I hope you have a lovely time together,' she said, realising to her relief, really, that she meant it.

'Thank you.' Declan's arms moved forward a bit and then resettled at his side, as though he'd considered hugging her and then thought better of it. Poppy didn't know what she would have done if he had tried to hug her, but she did know that she suddenly just felt really overwhelmed again. Sad, really. It was all so much.

'Poppy? We're still going to go out tomorrow evening?' He had one eyebrow raised and his face twisted like an uncertain little boy.

'Yes.'

'Great. So I'll see you then. Eight p.m.?'

'Perfect,' she said, wishing that it didn't suddenly sound as if she was talking to a stranger.

Poppy felt lonely as soon as he'd left. She wasn't going to allow herself to feel miserable, though. She was going to do some reading for work and then iron in front of the TV and then get an early night.

* * *

Time dragged the whole of the next day. Finally, the evening and her date – for want of a better word – with Declan arrived. She was wearing a new dress that she'd recently bought, and even though she said it herself, it fitted well and looked nice and she felt confident in it, and she was looking forward to eating in a nice restaurant, and most of all she was looking forward to spending a whole evening with Declan.

He'd booked a Michelin-starred restaurant in Cheltenham, and had said he would drive them there.

As Poppy got into the car, he reached out at exactly the same time as her for the passenger door handle and their hands brushed. Back when they were together, they'd then have linked hands and sneaked a little snog up against the car. Instead, they both mumbled *Sorry* and withdrew their hands and Poppy climbed into her seat, very careful not to touch Declan again, and deflated all of a sudden about the evening ahead.

Their conversation in the car felt a little strained. Awkward. It wasn't normal, in Poppy's world anyway, to kick your husband out, not talk to him about anything other than your son for several weeks, and then go out for dinner with him. It was like they needed to catch up on all the little things that couples share, but they didn't know where to start. Especially since they *weren't* a couple any more.

Luckily Declan had always been able to make her laugh about things that really shouldn't have been – and, in fact, probably *weren't* – funny. He started talking about the roadworks on the way to Cheltenham and soon she was giggling madly.

She'd wondered if they should or would talk about their situation over dinner, but they didn't at all. And it was wonderful. They caught up on big and small things. Declan was delighted that she'd started working one day a week. He'd known about it but hadn't mentioned it. Presumably he hadn't dared, which felt very sad.

'I'm really pleased for you,' he said.

Poppy didn't know how to respond to the evident love in his eyes when he said that, so she changed the subject to the new shirt he was wearing.

'I think that's the first one you've bought for yourself since...' She stopped. They'd got all the way through a five-course tasting menu until coffee without mentioning anything controversial, and now she was messing it up.

'Since we met and we both realised that you like shopping a lot more than I do and have much better taste.' He'd managed to un-mess the conversation.

Poppy smiled at him. She really wanted to reach out and run her fingers through his hair. 'Your hair's longer than normal, too.'

'Do you like it?' He sounded slightly flirtatious.

'It does actually look very nice curling over your collar like that.' She kind of wanted to flirt back.

He was smiling at her in a way that in the past would definitely have led to a very nice end to the evening for both of them.

On the way back to the car they walked very close to each other. They both had their arms by their sides and Poppy's right hand and Declan's left touched a few times. She moved her fingers a little against his after about the fifth time it happened. It felt like one of the most daring things she'd ever done. And then he moved his fingers against hers, took her hand and laced his fingers through hers. And they walked the rest of the way like that.

Poppy had never seen or read any porn in her life, but she was pretty sure that this hand-holding was one of the most erotic experiences anyone had ever had, ever.

When they got home, she wondered for a moment whether she was going to do her best to seduce him, but then instead said, 'I'd love to do that again.'

'Me too.' Declan fixed her gaze with his gorgeous blue eyes for a long time.

He cleared his throat and moved towards her, and then stopped.

And after a drawn-out what's-going-to-happen moment, Poppy concluded that nothing was, and said, 'Goodnight, then. Thank you,' and went inside, not sure whether she was hugely relieved or hugely disappointed by the nothing-happening but sure that she'd had a lovely evening and that it felt as though bridges were being mended.

25

GEORGIE

'No way, no way, no way,' Georgie screeched. She swished through her phone for Beth's number and tapped. Please let her pick up. They *had* to talk about the photos Ankita had just sent.

'OH. EM. GEEEEEEEE,' Beth screamed down the phone a second later. 'I was just about to call you. I think it's for real.'

'I do too. I expanded the photos and you can definitely see rings on their wedding fingers.'

'Same.'

'Wow. Just wow. I mean *married*. In Vegas. They're bloody *married*.'

'I know. He's gorgeous, isn't he?'

'Well, of course he is. You'd expect nothing less from Ankita. Where are you at the moment?' Georgie knew that Beth had been spending a lot of time in Melting recently and she kind of didn't want to talk if Raf or Poppy were in the background.

'Having a cup of tea and doing some paperwork at the Duck. On my own, though.'

'Okay, cool. So Ankita said in her message that they're going to have a big wedding party soon and she wants to have a mini celebration next Saturday. And she sent the message to you, me, Poppy and her mum.' Georgie had felt a little twinge at the fact that Ankita had included her mum in the message group. If Georgie ever wanted to announce anything huge, she'd never include her own mother in the group. It would hurt too much when she didn't get round to reading it for several days, if not weeks (if ever).

And she'd felt a *big* twinge at the fact that Ankita wanted her and Poppy to come out together. How was that going to work? Ankita and Beth now knew about Declan and Max, and from what Ankita had told her recently Poppy had mellowed and understood now that of course a one-night stand twelve years ago had no bearing on her marriage, that Georgie had of course been planning to tell her immediately once she knew for certain if Declan was Max's father, and that she'd acted with the best of intentions. But she and Poppy still weren't communicating really. She'd sent a 'Congratulations on your job!' message (Beth had told her Poppy was now working one day a week) and had received a 'Thank you!' reply, and that had been it, really. Georgie didn't dare to say anything else and Poppy hadn't made any moves towards her.

'And you're wondering how you and Poppy are going to manage on Saturday evening?' Beth asked.

'Yes.' It felt like it would be extremely awkward for them to see each other again properly for the first time with others there.

'I honestly think it will be okay.' Beth paused for a second and then said, 'Okay, I don't like sounding as though I'm gossiping about any of my best friends but... Poppy went out for dinner with Declan the other evening. Everyone in the village knows because she had to get a babysitter, and you know what the Melting grapevine is like.'

'Oh, that's wonderful. I hope.' Georgie hoped so very much that Poppy and Declan would get back together. She'd love to get back together with Poppy herself but maybe that couldn't happen. But anyway. This wasn't about her. 'So, *Ankita*. Married. I can't wait to meet Alex.' She was definitely going to go on Saturday. She couldn't let Ankita down. And maybe it could be the start of a bit of a rapprochement with Poppy.

* * *

Georgie managed to arrive at the pub on Saturday a quarter of an hour early, to make sure she didn't arrive at the same time as Poppy, who was unbelievably punctual, never a minute late – or a minute early – for anything, even with a baby, it turned out.

No one else was there yet. Raf and Noah were both behind the bar.

Noah waved her over.

'I've reserved that table over there because it's busy this evening,' he said. 'And Ankita had champagne put on ice and asked for some nibbles, so I'll bring some over in a sec.'

Georgie could see Raf out of the corner of her eye. He was doing an expert-looking cocktail shaking thing for some blatantly besotted women. She really hoped that she hadn't looked so stupidly eyelash-fluttering when they used to talk.

She really missed his friendship.

Losing Poppy was even worse. It didn't seem likely that Georgie would one day meet another man as stop-the-traffic gorgeous and funny and nice as Raf, *if* she was interested in meeting anyone. But there was *zero* possibility that she'd ever meet another Poppy. You couldn't replace someone you'd been best friends with since you were five years old.

They'd got the bus to school together the first time they'd gone without adults. They'd bought their first bras together, with Poppy's mum because Georgie's had been busy. They'd tried on their first lipsticks together. They'd got drunk for the first time together. And they'd told each other everything. Until now. Now it seemed that they weren't ever going to tell each other anything again or do anything together again and it *hurt*, like a big, dull ache in her chest.

'Glass of champagne?' Raf had come over while Georgie had been staring at the table and she hadn't noticed him.

When you hadn't seen him up close for a few weeks his whole chiselled jaw, laughing eyes and perfectly-not-quite-too-long, thick, wavy black hair thing really made your stomach clench. Yeah, it was pretty bad not seeing him any more.

'Yes, please. And could I have a glass of tap water as well? I'll come to the bar to get it,' she said in her best 'you are just someone I vaguely know, not at all my ultimate crush' manner.

She definitely shouldn't drink too much or she'd end up doing something nightmarishly embarrassing, like propositioning Raf or begging Poppy through tears to be friends again. Or both.

'No, don't worry. I'll bring a jug and glasses for all of you to the table.' He turned round to go and Georgie tried not to sigh. Then he turned back round. 'So how've you been? All good?'

'Yes, great thanks.'

'How's Max? Still enjoying his sport?'

'Yes, loving it. We've got an end of season football tour in Wales coming up, which he's obviously *very* excited about.'

'That sounds like fun. And how's work?'

'Yep, all good. My Year Elevens seem to be just about ready for their GCSEs, thank goodness. And what about you? Are you still enjoying your gardening leave?'

Raf had had six months off between jobs, because apparently that was what happened when hotshot lawyers switched firms, and he'd spent a lot of time in Melting with Noah and helping out in the pub, because he liked being busy.

'Yes, I really am. I think—'

'Georgie!' Ankita had erupted into the pub with Alex behind her. He looked even more perfect-for-Ankita than he had in the photos she'd sent. He was tall, broad-shouldered, handsome and just *glossy*-looking. And then he laughed and Georgie understood why Ankita had fallen in love with him. An immaculate-looking banker like her with more than a hint of naughtiness and a twinkle in his eye.

Georgie stood up and hugged Ankita.

'Congratulations,' she said. 'I'm so excited for you.'

'Me too,' said Ankita. The way she'd been over Alex was possibly the least cool she'd ever been in the entire twenty-three years since Georgie had met her. It was lovely to see. 'This is my husband.'

'Your husband.' Georgie gave her a big nudge. 'You're sooooooooo grown-up.'

'I know. My *husband*.'

'Hey, Georgie. Pleased to meet you.' Alex had a lovely American accent. 'I've heard a lot about you. From my wife.'

'I'm very pleased to meet you, too. Congratulations. You're a very lucky man to have married our lovely Ankita.'

'Yes, I am.' Alex slung his arm round a still very un-coolly beaming Ankita's shoulders and pulled her in for a very cute hug.

'I really want the others to arrive so that you can tell us *everything*,' said Georgie.

'Ankita!' Beth practically sprinted across the pub and flung herself at Ankita. Poppy was following, smiling at Ankita and not catching Georgie's eye at all.

'Okay, we need details *right now*,' Georgie said, as soon as the girls had finished saying congratulations.

'I'm going to bring champagne and water for everyone and then I'm going to leave you all to it. Good luck, mate.' Raf smirked.

'Yep, I'm quite scared.' Alex was grinning.

An hour and a half later they had all the details. Georgie and Poppy weren't exactly interacting the way they used to, but it was doable being together, which had to be good news for the future.

Towards the end of the evening, Noah came over and joined them, sitting next to Beth. They knew a lot about each other's daily lives and shared little in-jokes, plus they were doing that thing that magazines said lovers did, copying each other's gestures and body language. Like if Beth bent her head in one direction Noah did the same.

Georgie snuck a look at Poppy out of the corner of her eye; Poppy had been looking at her out of the corner of *her* eye and she had her arms folded tight across her chest. Georgie didn't need a magazine to tell her what that meant.

She heaved a big internal sigh and then plastered a wide smile on her face and refocused on what Noah and Beth were saying. Rugby. Flowers. Noah's car repairs. New toothpaste. *Car repairs. New toothpaste.* All with great interest and enthusiasm and much laughter. They were like a lovely old married couple and Georgie was pretty much a hundred per cent sure they hadn't even held hands, let alone kissed. She *really* hoped they'd sort themselves out and get together. Maybe seeing Ankita and Alex so blatantly happy and *married* – bloody *married* – would give them ideas.

'Ankita,' she said. 'You're bloody married. You're Mrs McCarthy.'

'I *know*.' Ankita totally looked like the cat that had the best cream ever.

'So congratulations again,' said Raf, coming over and sitting down on the opposite side of the table from Georgie, between Alex and Poppy. Georgie immediately had a slight wave of that lonely-in-a-crowd thing. He'd sat down opposite her. Before, he would always naturally just have sat next to her. But whatever. It was Ankita's evening and Alex was lovely and it was fantastic that Poppy seemed to feel able now to be in the same place as Georgie so they wouldn't ruin social occasions for their friends.

She did miss talking to Raf, though.

26

GEORGIE

Two weeks later, at Alex and Ankita's (strictly adults only, no kids) wedding party, in a barn at the beautiful house that they'd just moved into in Little Bishop, Georgie discovered that Ankita also thought that Georgie could do with some more of Raf's conversation.

The evening started with a lot of champagne in the stunning and gigantic garden, followed by a sit-down dinner in the barn. Ankita had been uncharacteristically tactful recently when dealing with Poppy, but she'd gone for possibly the least tactful table plan in the history of tactless table planning. And she'd admitted it to Georgie during the drinks in the garden.

'I hear from Poppy that Beth and Noah are getting very close but nothing's actually happening, and I hear from Beth that Declan and Poppy went out for dinner but nothing's actually happening, so I thought I'd put them all next to each other on their table. And obviously you're sitting with them too but I didn't want you to feel like a gooseberry, so I've put Raf next to you.'

Georgie couldn't think of anything nice to say in response to that little bombshell – and anyway, you couldn't have a go at someone at their own wedding party.

'Oh,' she said.

'Love your dress by the way. I'll see you in a minute.' And the evil table planner was off, busy being Mrs McCarthy.

Georgie went off and did some very effusive mingling with old acquaintances, to avoid any accidental bumping into Poppy or Raf so that there wouldn't be any awkwardness. It was nice. It was a beautiful May evening, everyone was in a happy, party mood, and the champagne was extremely free-flowing at the hands of the black-suited waiters and waitresses (Alex had drafted in the teenage sons and daughters of some friends to help).

The barn had been set out with round tables of six for dinner. Ankita and Alex's table contained them, Ankita's parents, Alex's grandmother and his brother. Georgie's Table From Hell was right next to Ankita's. Meaning that there was no chance of changing anything around on the seating front.

'I had to have you all right next to me.' Ankita beamed at them all as she and Alex walked past.

To give Ankita her due, Beth and Noah had their heads together chatting and smiling away like an in-love couple, and Declan and Poppy were looking heart-stoppingly friendly with each other, which was a huge relief to see.

As Georgie sat down, she realised that since the other four were supposedly two couples, it looked like Ankita had put Raf there as her date, which was embarrassing, because Raf was clearly no longer interested in her. She was Norma No-Mates. Or Norma No-Dates.

Also, when you were going to be sitting next to someone for a whole evening, it felt like if there was an elephant in your room you ought to tackle it, but she couldn't because she still couldn't tell him that she'd *really* liked him, especially not when they were going to be sitting together for a good couple of hours.

So she said, 'Hello. What a lovely evening.'

'Yes, lovely.' Raf smiled politely and then looked slightly to his right. Poppy, who was sitting there, was busy talking to Declan, so Raf had to look back again at Georgie.

Georgie glanced around the table and said, 'Lovely to see everyone,' because the silence that had grown between the two of them was not comfortable.

'Yes.' He really did have very nice eyes. The colour was so deep and

velvety and his lashes were very thick. He suddenly relaxed and smiled –
maybe he'd accepted the inevitable and decided he was just going to have
to chat to her – and said, 'Good to see people looking happy.'

Georgie searched for words and found none, so picked up her champagne glass and emptied it in one for something to do, which made her feel
very warm inside and much more relaxed with Raf. 'Beth and Noah are *so*
perfect for each other,' she told him. 'I'm sure she's fallen for him. And he
looks besotted with her. And they're both single. They spend a lot of time
together. They know each other really well.' She smiled fondly over at them
both. 'They need to *snog*.' Oops, she'd said that really loudly, right into
some between-music silence from the string quartet at the end of the room.

All four of the others' heads shot round and they all stared at Georgie.

Raf was laughing so much that he nearly choked on his champagne. He
was still coughing a bit when the others resumed their own conversations.

'Serves you right,' said Georgie. 'That was *not* funny.'

'Actually, it really *was* funny. Beautiful timing.'

She pursed her lips at him and he laughed more.

And somehow, that had broken the ice, and suddenly talking to him felt
okay.

They carried on talking and laughing all the way through dinner. Beth
and Noah had their heads together the whole time, and so did Declan and
Poppy, with lots of smiles and low voices. It looked like they might perhaps
get back together again, the thought of which made Georgie's heart sing.

Alex's speech was heartwarming and almost laugh-out-loud funny in
places. And Ankita's speech was full laugh-out-loud funny most of the way
through and just *clever*. The whole time she was upstaging him on the
speech front, Alex sat and looked at her adoringly, and it was just *gorgeous*.

As Ankita finished and they all clapped, Georgie glanced at Raf and saw
that the broad smile she felt on her own face was mirrored on his. He
looked at her and his smile widened even further. Georgie couldn't take her
eyes away from his until it was time to raise her glass for the toasts. Her
gaze went to his large fingers holding the delicate stem of his champagne
flute, and there was something about looking at his hands and – if she was
honest – imagining *very* naughty things that he might do with them (where
had that thought *come* from?) that made her suddenly very hot.

Raf leaned in and spoke close to her ear. 'What were you thinking just then? You had a very cheeky edge to your smile.'

Nooooo. What if he'd *guessed*?

'Nothing!' Georgie squeaked.

Raf rolled his eyes a little and nudged her thigh very fleetingly with his, and honestly, the brief touch made her almost spontaneously combust.

* * *

'And *now*, it's time for the first dance.' Ankita's mum had done the last speech. 'And once my daughter and her husband—' everyone cheered '— have shown you how it's done, they'd love you all to join them on the dance floor.'

On Georgie's left, Noah leaned into Beth and spoke quietly to her, his neck going scarlet as he did so.

'I'd love to,' Beth said in response, and they stood up together and moved towards the floor.

Out of the corner of her eye, Georgie saw Declan and Poppy look at each other and then stand up together. Georgie sat completely still, not wanting even to twitch, in case any movement might pierce the little bubble the two of them seemed to be in. It would be wonderful if they got back together, and maybe tonight would be the catalyst. She and Poppy might not be speaking much at the moment, but Georgie still loved Poppy and was desperate for her to be happy again, and it was so obvious that Declan and she were wonderful together.

'Would you like to dance?' Raf put his hand out theatrically and Georgie smiled and laughed as she put her hand in his because there was no other option. And who was she kidding? Obviously it wouldn't exactly be a hardship.

'Why, I'd *love* to.' She hoped she'd sounded ironic or comedic or *anything* that would disguise the way her heart was suddenly banging against her ribcage.

They all clapped and cheered as Ankita and Alex finished the most amazing quickstep, and couples began to crowd onto the dance floor as the band struck up some Dusty Springfield.

Raf held an arm around Georgie's shoulders as they were jostled on all sides as they tried to find a space. When they'd found their own little spot, they went for a waltz hold exactly as everyone else was doing.

'If I'm honest,' he said, 'I'm not the world's most gifted dancer. There's some serious ballroom dancing going on here. I'm probably just going to go with swaying.'

'There's a lot to be said for swaying,' Georgie told him. 'It keeps everyone's toes safe, for a start.'

'I wouldn't be so sure about that.' Raf grinned down at her and then his smile became more serious. Georgie couldn't take her eyes off his face. He was just gazing at her as though she was someone very special, which she knew she wasn't, but it felt lovely that someone would look at her that way.

They carried on with the not-very-waltzy swaying all the way through the waltz and the next couple of dances, and it was just magical. Georgie felt like she belonged in Raf's arms. She could have carried on like that all night, and was pretty sure she *would* have done if someone hadn't begun a conga. Soon they were all dancing and kicking their heels up, with Raf behind Georgie in the line. She could feel incredibly deeply where he had his hands on her waist, almost to the extent that she wasn't really aware of anything else.

When the line ended, somehow Raf's arms slid round her and they were back to the swaying before going more adventurous and doing some spins, which made them both laugh a *lot*.

* * *

They danced together the entire time until just before midnight, when everyone went out into the garden to watch the fireworks.

They weren't normal fireworks. They were mega fireworks, because apparently Alex knew someone who was huge in pyrotechnics. The barn and the main house were at right angles, along the edge of a massive, probably about two-acre-plus lawn which stretched towards a wood, and beyond that apparently some fields, all belonging to Alex. And now his wife, Mrs Ankita McCarthy.

Again, married, wow.

All the guests stood outside the barn to watch the fireworks. It seemed completely natural that Georgie ended up standing with Raf, as if they were their own little world inside the crowd.

When the final burst of fireworks finished after a solid twenty-minute quite phenomenal display, the band started up again inside the barn. Some people went back inside but others started to drift off around the garden. There was an almost full moon and the sky was clear, so you could see well enough to walk but not well enough to make out exactly what anyone not close to you was doing, or who people were.

'Shall we explore the garden?' Raf's voice in Georgie's ear sounded almost purry.

'Yes, it looks gorgeous.' Much like Raf.

Alex had very proudly shown them his ride-on mower at the beginning of the evening – to much laughter from Ankita – and he'd definitely done a good job on the lawn because it wasn't too hard to walk on in three-inch stilettos. But when they got into the woods, it was a lot trickier and a lot darker.

'What's that?' Georgie screamed, batting manically at something that had touched her face.

'I think it was a cobweb,' said Raf, brushing it gently away from her cheeks. She nearly jumped a mile at his touch. Thank goodness it was fully dark in here and he hadn't seen. Honestly, her skin was tingling like mad where he'd touched her.

Help, there was something else touching them.

'What's that?' she shrieked.

'A leaf, I think.'

'Oh.' Georgie peered through the dark. 'Stop laughing.'

'Sorry.' He was laughing even more now.

'Max and I watched a horror movie last weekend. It was only rated 12 but it was so frightening that I had to sleep with the light on afterwards. Terrifying. This is like that.'

'Didn't you say Max is eleven? Was *he* scared?'

'He's actually nearly twelve and no he wasn't scared, though I have no idea why. Like, I don't know why you aren't scared now.'

'Yes, you're so right, I should be. Adults regularly get horribly murdered by ghosts or lions in woods in Gloucestershire. Who *knows* what might happen next?'

As Georgie opened her mouth to tell him to shut up, something tapped her on her back. Proper tapping. Like possibly an actual ghost, even though she was pretty sure that ghosts did not exist. The tapping happened again. She screamed. And screamed. And kept on screaming. This was just like the poltergeist in the forest in the film. And then she realised that *obviously* it had been Raf tapping and now he was almost doubled up he was laughing so much.

'Sorry,' he gasped. 'I shouldn't have done that. I think I might have under-estimated your imagination.'

'Have you finished being juvenile?' asked Georgie, aiming for haughty and dignified.

'Yep.' He hadn't. He was still sniggering. 'Sorry. Have you recovered?'

'Totally. I was just humouring you.'

'Course you were.'

'Oh my goodness, what was that?' Georgie yelled. 'On my foot. A small animal, I think.'

'Would you like to leave the wood?'

'Yes, I really would.'

'Come on.' He took her hand and they walked back the way they'd come. When they got to the edge of the wood, they were still holding hands. Raf stopped walking. 'It might be a little too scary for some people, but it's beautiful, isn't it?'

'Mmm.'

Now that they were out of the woods and she could see him properly again *and,* crucially, she wasn't worried about animals and ghosts any more, Georgie couldn't think about anything except the fact that they were still holding hands, and his hand felt very big and warm and strong. Just exactly right for her. The Goldilocks thing. She was staring up at his face, she knew she was, but she couldn't help it.

He looked back at her. His eyes moved from hers to her lips.

'Georgie,' he said.

'Yes?' Her voice sounded weird.

'I...' He was still gazing at her intently.

He drew her even closer to him, and bent his head.

They were going to kiss... and Georgie couldn't until she'd explained properly to him about before. She couldn't bear him to continue to think that she'd been using him. Whatever her admission might or might not say about what she wanted now.

'I need to tell you something,' she said, the movement of her lips almost causing her mouth to brush against his, they were standing so close together.

'Now?' His voice was hoarse.

'Yes.'

'Oh-kay.' Raf let go of her and took a step backwards. 'Would you like to go back now?' His voice sounded clipped. Well, maybe he thought she'd looked like she wanted to kiss him and had changed her mind. Maybe, if Georgie wasn't flattering herself, that might have made him feel disappointed. It would definitely have disappointed her if it had happened the opposite way round.

'No,' she said, fast. 'I wanted to explain that, yes, initially – *very* initially – after New Year I needed to spend time with you to get my secret back, but very quickly I just started loving being with you and, yes, the secret was still there, hanging over me, but when I was with you... I mean, I just loved your company.' And fancied the pants off him, but there was a limit to how much she could own up to right now.

'Is that so?' His voice was warmer again.

'Yes, it really is.'

'And you're sure you don't want to go back to the house yet?'

'Mmhmm.'

He slid an arm round her waist and she put her arms round his neck and now they were gazing into each other's eyes again and Georgie's heart was crashing around inside her chest like nobody's business.

He lowered his head towards hers and then, just as, *finally*, she was parting her lips in huge anticipation, he said, 'I have a confession too.'

'You do?' Georgie almost wanted to stamp her foot.

'I have to own up to the fact that I only ever agreed for you to cat-sit because I wanted to spend more time with you. I totally had other cat-sitters available.'

'Hunh.'

'Yeah.'

And then, very slowly and very deliberately, he moved his head towards hers. He stopped for a moment just before their lips met and then, just as Georgie wondered if she was going to *scream* with frustration, he moved further and she did too, and then they were kissing – it was almost better this time because this time they knew how well they fitted together – and everything ceased to exist except where they were touching.

Georgie had no idea how long they stayed there, but after some time she became aware that it was raining and moved back a little.

And then the heavens opened.

Raf took her hand and they ran (as much as she could in stilettos) across the lawn until they got to the shelter of a doorway at the back of the house.

'I'm staying here tonight,' she told him, not really sure where she was going with that comment, and kind of wanting to leave things to fate.

It turned out that Raf wasn't so keen to leave things to fate. He kissed her hard, really hungrily, in the doorway, before drawing her inside the house and whispering, 'Where are you sleeping?' in a way that made her entire insides turn to complete liquid.

Unbelievably, Georgie couldn't remember where the bedroom was. And the house was enormous.

'We can't just try other people's bedrooms, can we?' she whispered to Raf, in the middle of the bigger-than-most-people's-entire-upstairs landing, standing next to an actual suit of armour (apparently the owner had begged Alex to buy a lot of their furniture and he'd agreed and was now regretting it).

'Come back to Noah's?'

'But Noah will be there?'

'No, he texted me earlier and said he was staying here.'

'Oh my goodness – with Beth?'

'Maybe. Probably.' Raf put his arm round Georgie's waist and kissed her on the lips again.

Perhaps fate was trying to tell Georgie that this whole thing with Raf was a bad idea. She didn't want to get hurt, and if he hadn't lost his wife he wouldn't be here with her now, would he? But, also, *where* would she sleep if she stayed here?

'Let's get an Uber back to Melting and maybe have a coffee at Noah's?' she said.

While they were waiting for the cab, they kissed quite a lot, and they also talked, in whispers, sitting on a bench in Alex and Ankita's stunning and enormous wood-panelled hall.

'And that is why I'm going to *watch* when Max goes kayaking.' Georgie finished describing her one and only (nightmare) brush with canoeing.

'Wow, yes.' Raf twisted his mouth a bit. 'I'm trying really hard not to laugh.'

'You're failing,' Georgie informed him.

'Yeah. But in my defence, *anyone* would laugh. What did your parents say when you got home?'

'Well, it was Poppy's parents, because I was kind of living with her at the time. And, yep, they *really* laughed.'

'Were your parents working abroad?'

'Nope. My dad was living in Cheltenham and my mum was in the house she's in now.'

'Oh.' Raf raised his eyebrows very slightly but didn't ask anything further.

And suddenly, Georgie did something that she never normally did. She told him.

'Basically, when my parents split up, they each met new partners – who they're both still with – and they argued over custody of me but in the exact opposite way from normal; neither of them wanted me, although my dad didn't mind having me for a night or two during the week. Poppy told her mum, who was aghast, and invited me to stay for a week or two while every-thing got sorted, and in the end I stayed for months and effectively just visited my parents for a few nights here and there. Poppy's parents have always had a room in their house which Poppy's mum says is for me and Max, although I don't stay with them that often now because I like to try to pretend to Max that I'm from a regular family who love me.'

Raf didn't say anything for a few moments and then, just as Georgie was *really* wondering why she'd blurted all of that out, he said, 'If there's one thing you learn in my line of work it's that families can be *shit*. Poppy's mum sounds amazing and I think any parent should be incredibly proud to call you their daughter. And I'm so sorry that things are difficult between you and Poppy at the moment. I hadn't appreciated quite how much your friends are your family.'

'Thank you.' Georgie never told anyone that kind of stuff; the only people who knew were Poppy, Ankita and Beth. And Raf had managed to make it feel okay – good, even – that she'd told him.

Enough was enough, though.

'You know what,' she said, 'it's probably been good for me. Like, I'm quite good at moving on.'

Except from Poppy. She really wasn't doing well at moving on there.

'If I have a situation at work or whatever I'm quite good at dealing with it and just getting on with things,' she continued, pushing the Poppy thought away. 'In fact, I'm excellent at it. I just think about different things and don't let myself think about anything tricky.'

Which was *obviously* what she needed to do about Poppy. Just not think about her at all.

'I think that's natural if you're going to survive traumatic things.' Raf hesitated and then said, 'Coping with losing Anna has probably made me more resilient to other, lesser things.'

'I can't even begin to imagine. I'm so sorry.'

'Yep. But you do come out the other side eventually.'

Raf's phone buzzed. 'Uber's here.'

They held hands in the taxi all the way back to Melting with their fingers all entwined round each other, and the drive back was pleasurable torture: *what was going to happen next?*

Once they got inside Noah's kitchen, Raf put the kettle on.

'I think I can offer you a choice of gourmet instant coffee, or English breakfast or peppermint tea.'

'I would love some instant coffee.' Georgie didn't really care what drink she had because now she was alone here with Raf she was thinking about much more interesting things than hot beverages.

'Okay,' Raf said.

Except he didn't get mugs and coffee granules out. Instead, he walked over to where she was standing just inside the kitchen door and pulled her against him and kissed her, hard.

They kissed for a long time. And then Georgie stayed the night, and they didn't get much sleep. And when they were both dragged awake by her alarm clock, which she'd set for nine o'clock so that she could get back to Bristol to pick Max up from his sleepover, they lay next to each other smiling stupidly. Well, Raf was smiling stupidly and she was pretty sure that she was too.

She didn't know where they would go from here or where she *wanted* them to go, but she did know that she'd had an *amazing* night.

27

POPPY

There was nothing like waking up thinking about your estranged husband and how much you loved him and how maybe you could get back together and how much you were looking forward to seeing him later that day...

And then looking out of the window after breakfast and seeing him with the son he shared with your ex-best friend. Max must have had a sleepover at Declan's last night.

Poppy felt like she'd been physically punched, actually physically winded.

She stood frozen to the spot until Daniel, who she was holding, accidentally hit her in the face. He was waving manically at Declan and Max, and beaming away like nobody's business, his four little teeth on display. 'Daddy. Mak,' he yelled. He was *so* clever. He could wave. He could grow teeth. He could say people's names.

Now he was banging on the window and yelling even harder. Okay. She had to open the front door and call to Declan and Max. She couldn't let Daniel think that they were ignoring him.

They heard her as soon as she called. Max ran straight over and gave Daniel a hug. Poppy could feel her shoulders going completely rigid. She wanted to be nice about things, for Daniel's sake, she really did. But she *couldn't*. And then she looked properly at Max. He was pulling faces at

Daniel like he always did and Daniel was laughing and laughing. Then she looked at Declan. He was smiling at his two sons and she could see the love and pride on his face.

Then Declan looked up from the boys and at her and his face changed. His smile got smaller and his eyes got a bit wider and his eyebrows rose a bit. He looked... nervous.

Okay. She had to get a grip. Max was Daniel's brother and Declan's son. He hadn't hurt anyone. Daniel hadn't hurt anyone. And Declan hadn't hurt her on purpose. She had to pull herself together right now and make sure that the boys never got hurt by this situation.

'Do you have time to come in and play with Daniel for a bit? Together?' Now she was the one feeling nervous. It felt incredibly important for Declan to understand how big this was from her perspective.

He was smiling properly at her. That was good.

'Max, do you know if your mum had any plans for you this morning?' he asked.

'Don't think so. I've got a match this afternoon. I think she just wanted me to do my homework this morning.'

'I'll ask her.' Declan kind of chewed his lower lip as he took his phone out of his pocket.

'Okay, thank you.' Poppy wasn't totally keen to hear him talking to Georgie.

But, actually, it was alright. Fine, in fact. He sounded spectacularly business-like on the phone to her, like he was talking about a wardrobe delivery or something.

It was also fine – lovely, even – having Max with them. And watching Declan being the fantastic dad he was, with both his sons together, and Max and Daniel having fun together, made her realise that for Daniel's sake, for Declan's sake and for Max's sake, they had to do this regularly.

'Maybe we could all go out somewhere next time you have a weekend together.' It was worth it just for Declan's smile. 'Are you coming over for bath-time later?' she asked, really wanting him to say yes.

'Yep, looking forward to it. Do you fancy maybe watching a film together or something afterwards? If you like?' He sounded a little bit breathless.

'That would be lovely.' She felt as breathless as he'd sounded.

Poppy felt jittery all afternoon, desperate for Declan to turn up. It felt like they should *talk*. It had felt like that since the wedding party last weekend.

It had been a really good night. She and Declan had chatted all evening, in a cocoon of togetherness over dinner, and then danced for hours.

And they weren't the only ones. Beth hadn't said anything since, but she'd been in Melting all week and permanently looked as though she was brimming with news. Either she'd developed a serious drinking problem or she and Noah were seeing each other.

Poppy was fairly sure that Georgie and Raf had kissed that night too, although she obviously hadn't seen Georgie since to gauge whether or not things were happening in that way. She'd realised, the day after the wedding party, that she hoped for Georgie's sake that she *had* got together with Raf, because, irrespective of what had happened, she'd like her to be happy.

So everyone else seemed to have been kissing that evening. She'd have liked to have seen a bit of action too, but Declan hadn't made a move, despite some *amazing* slow dances where she could feel his whole body against hers, making her remember how they used to be.

So this evening... she'd cooked what she'd have to describe as a seduction meal...

When Declan came back downstairs after putting Daniel to bed, Poppy had dinner completely ready. She'd made a chicken dish with a cider and cream sauce that she'd been making for years, the one that Declan had set on fire. It was Declan's second-favourite recipe of hers. His top favourite was a prawn curry. She'd decided on chicken because, if the evening panned out the way she hoped, it would be better if Declan hadn't eaten curry.

'Wow, thank you,' said Declan, when he walked into the kitchen and saw the table laid for the two of them. 'This looks nice. Napkins and everything.'

'I miss cooking for you.' What she really meant was *I miss you* full stop.

'I've missed you cooking for me.' He was smiling at her in the way that in the past would have preceded a long kiss. She smiled back. And neither of them moved. Yep, awkward.

'Help yourself to rice and broccoli and I'll bring the chicken over,' she said, pouring him a glass of Chablis.

'I love this meal,' Declan said as he sat down.

'I know you do.' Did cooking some of someone's favourite food show that you wanted to bridge the gap between you? Hopefully. She'd also made a Key lime pie, his all-time top favourite, for pudding.

She really liked the way he held his knife and fork.

'What?' he asked, looking at her staring.

'I like your hands.' Hmm. In one short sentence she'd managed to be weird and stalkery *and* sound like she was flirting incompetently with her own estranged husband. She needed to up her game. She smiled at him. You couldn't go wrong with a smile.

'Thank you.' He grinned.

She liked his smile a lot, too. She could feel her own lips curving more widely in response.

It was a long time since they'd just sat and smiled at each other like that. She kind of didn't want to break the moment but she also kind of suddenly just really wanted to get on with what she had to say.

'So I thought that it would be good to talk.' Her heart was beating really fast, thudding in her ears. 'About our situation.'

'Good idea.' Declan didn't *look* like he thought it was a good idea. His smile had gone and he had his lips pressed together and his eyes had gone really hard. He never looked like that. Poppy opened her mouth to speak but Declan beat her to it. 'Could I possibly say something first? If you wouldn't mind? Quickly?'

Maybe she'd been too awful recently. Maybe he was going to say that he wanted a divorce. Please no.

'Yes, of course,' she said.

Please, please, please let it not be a request for a divorce.

What if he'd met someone else while they were separated? Everyone loved a doctor. And he was a particularly gorgeous doctor. And very nice. And very funny. Please, please, please no.

He was clearing his throat like he couldn't get any words out. She closed her eyes. He was going to say something awful. Obviously he was.

'I love you, Poppy. I love you so much. I never wanted to hurt you. From the moment I met you I just wanted to be with you. I'm so sorry for how much I hurt you. I love you.'

Poppy opened her eyes in shock. They were suddenly full of tears. She couldn't speak at first.

'I love you too,' she whispered, finally. 'And I'm so, so sorry for asking you to leave.'

'Please don't apologise.'

A tear dribbled down Poppy's cheek. She was fairly sure that some mascara would have gone with it. She'd never been good with make-up. Annoying to have made a big effort to look as good as possible for Declan this evening and to end up looking like a panda.

Declan stood up, walked over to the work surface and got a piece of kitchen roll. Then he moved over to Poppy and put one hand under her chin and wiped her cheeks with the paper. It felt like the most romantic gesture anyone had ever made in the history of the world, ever.

He looked at her eyes and then at her lips and Poppy held her breath. He was going to kiss her. He definitely was. *So* exciting.

And then he *bloody* sat back down and said, 'Thank you very much for making this chicken. It's delicious.'

And then he bloody, *bloody* picked up his cutlery and started eating again.

Poppy sat and stared at him. What? Why was he *eating*? They were in the middle of an enormous conversation.

He looked up from his plate. 'What?'

'Nothing,' she said.

'So you said there was something you wanted to talk about?' He was being very weird the way he was loading his next mouthful onto his fork. He was doing it very over-carefully.

'I've kind of said it already.'

'So what exactly was it, though, that you wanted to say?'

Seriously, he was still loading the same mouthful onto his fork. It was going to be the most well-balanced mouthful anyone had ever eaten any time, anywhere. He couldn't have done it more carefully if he'd used weighing scales.

'I love you and I'm sorry for asking you to move out, and I understand all your points...'

Declan put his cutlery down, *still* with the well-balanced mouthful on his fork, and cleared his throat. Twice.

'And I think my question would be, where would you like to go from here?' he said.

Actually a good point. She just wanted him to move back in. She wanted to have *sex* with him. She wanted them to be properly married again. And she hadn't said that.

He was looking really hard at her now.

'If you'd like to, and I totally understand if you wouldn't—' which was a lie; she would not feel understanding, she'd be really, really upset '—I'd like you to move back in.'

'Where would I sleep?'

'With me? If you'd like?'

Her heart was galloping away again.

'I would really like that,' said Declan. He was smiling a little bit and he hadn't touched his cutlery since he put it down. 'When would you like that to happen?'

'Tonight?' Poppy was whispering. It felt like an incredibly big deal, effectively propositioning your own husband.

Declan's smile got a lot bigger and he pushed his chair back and walked round the table to her.

'Could we have a hug?' he asked.

'Yes, please.'

The hug was just what she needed and she cuddled into his warmth. They didn't kiss or anything. They just clung on to each other.

'I thought at one point that you were going to ask me for a divorce,' said Declan. 'I don't think I could have borne the pain. I've really hated being separated. I'm so relieved. And so happy.'

'Me too.'

And then he kissed her and it felt like they'd come home together.

When Declan suggested going upstairs, Poppy said, 'But I spent ages making one of your favourite meals for you.'

'Yes, of course,' Declan said. 'Let's finish eating first.'

'Joking,' said Poppy, pulling him towards the door. 'I've got Key lime pie for pudding, though.'

Declan stood still for a moment.

'Now that's a tricky one,' he said.

'*What?*'

'Joking.'

28

GEORGIE

DECLAN AND POPPY BACK TOGETHER!!!!! DECLAN'S MOVED BACK IN!!!!!
And I have something to tell you, will call later.

Georgie was pretty sure that she knew what Beth's text was referring to, but she still wanted to hear it.

As soon as they spoke a couple of hours later, Beth squealed, 'I'm with Noah and I'm moving in with him.'

'I'm so pleased for you. Noah's lovely and sweet and gorgeous, just like you. You're perfect for each other,' Georgie told her. 'I honestly couldn't think of a better partner for you if I tried to invent one.'

'I know.' Beth *never* sounded smug, but she did today. With good reason. It wasn't every day that you officially hooked up with your soulmate. 'And it's Noah's fortieth in ten days' time and I'm going to have a party for him here at the pub. I'm inviting all his best friends and family, obviously. Ankita and Alex. And also Declan and Poppy. Which should be okay, shouldn't it? Like at the wedding party?'

'Yes,' said Georgie firmly. She was going to have to get used to being in the same place as Poppy in this weird polite-but-not-good-friend way, and hopefully one day they might even become closer again.

'Wonderful. It's going to be so nice, all four of us being together with our other halves.' Okay, that was slightly cloud cuckoo land. Obviously Declan and Poppy were happily back together, thank *goodness*. And Beth and Noah were very happily newly coupled up, also lovely news. And obviously Ankita and Alex were married.

But it still made Georgie sad seeing Poppy. And Noah and Raf's whole family and a lot of their friends would be at Noah's birthday party, and while she and Raf were now seeing each other regularly, Georgie was kind of thinking they were just having fun together for the time being, and the party would not be the best first place for them to go public as a couple. Beth's positive thinking was one of her most endearing qualities, though.

'I can't wait,' Georgie lied.

* * *

Georgie and Max stayed with Georgie's mother and stepfather for the party.

'Darling,' her mum said, 'you won't mind, I'm sure; we're going out this evening and the cleaner's coming to babysit Max.'

Obviously Max would be safe with the cleaner, who he knew very well, but his grandmother had promised him a fun evening.

'I thought we were going to play tennis at your club this evening?' Max's gorgeous, sweet, still-innocent, eleven-year-old face had fallen.

'Next time, darling, and I'll buy you hot chocolate as well to make up. How does that sound? In fact, why don't I buy you hot chocolate at a café tomorrow morning? And maybe slip in some tennis, too?' Max was easily bought and was smiling again. So now Georgie was going to have to choose between disappointing Max over playing tennis with his granny at her very swish club, or letting Declan down over seeing him in the morning, or getting back to Bristol later than expected and having to go straight to Max's football match and not getting his homework or her marking done. All without mentioning Declan to her mother because she still hadn't told her about that.

'Granny, I have to tell you all about school this week. So many cool things happened. On Tuesday—'

'Darling, shh, maybe tomorrow morning. I have to get ready to go out now. We're going for dinner with Lauren, a lovely last-minute invitation.' Lauren was the older of Georgie's two half-sisters.

Max looked as though he was going to cry. It was fortunate that there was no obvious weapon handy because if there had been Georgie might have brained her mother with it.

It was *shit* being second best to your own half-sisters. It had been shit for twenty-four years now since her parents had split up, and it never got better, although she was used to it. And it was *really* shit, beyond shit, when your beautiful son got upset by his grandmother having close to zero interest in him *again*. Being second best was terrible.

Georgie was a little bit late for the party because before she left the house she spent ages listening to a practically real-time account of Max's school football practice the day before. It wasn't like her listening to him that evening was *actually* going to make up for her mother's almost complete lack of interest, but she just couldn't be the second adult in one evening to tell him to stop talking because she had somewhere better to be.

The party was in the pub's garden. Beth had had the dining room on hold in case it rained but it was a beautiful cloud-free evening, and in fact fairly warm, which was actually quite rare for a June evening in the Cotswolds. Some people even had strappy dresses on, with bare shoulders on display.

Raf was waiting for her outside. He immediately slung an arm round her shoulders and pulled her in for a big kiss on the lips. Half of Georgie was swooning, because as always it was a *good* kiss, but the other half was going *What, what, what?* This was in full view of, well, everyone?

'Let's go for a quick walk first.' He took her hand.

'Okay. Although not *quick* quick, because of my shoes.'

'I will bear your shoes in mind.'

As they walked slowly round the green, he said, 'I haven't felt this close to anyone since Anna died. I didn't think that I'd ever have this much fun again.'

As Georgie's lips formed into an oh, he continued, 'We met when we were twenty and we got married when we were twenty-four. A lot of people thought we were too young but we weren't. It was great, for seven years. And then Anna found a lump in her neck.' He paused for a moment and then went on, his voice sounding tight. 'And we found out that she had cancer. And she died five months later.'

Georgie squeezed the hand she was holding and he returned the pressure.

'Thank you. Anyway, I couldn't face sympathy from people so I moved to New York and started a new life there. I stayed there for six years until eventually I felt that I was ready to see my family and friends again, so I came home. But I still didn't think I'd ever want another relationship. And then I met you. And I realised that I am ready.'

Wow. Georgie was pretty sure that he was officially asking her to commit, and she didn't know what to say.

'I'm falling in love with you, Georgie.'

Georgie looked at his kind, gorgeous, now-so-familiar features and knew that she'd totally fallen completely in love with him, ages ago. So when he stopped walking and smiled at her and pulled her into his arms and started kissing her, she kissed him back. *Obviously.* Because he was the most gorgeous man she'd ever met, she missed him when he wasn't there, he made her laugh like a drain, and, basically, she loved everything about him. Except the enormous fact that if Anna hadn't died he'd still be happily married to her.

And then, before she could think, he took her hand and said, 'Party time.'

* * *

The guests were all milling around outside, drinking Prosecco and beer, eating nibbles and exclaiming over what an amazing evening it was.

Georgie and Raf bumped into Poppy and Declan as soon as they arrived.

'Hello,' they all said.

'Lovely evening,' Georgie said.

'Absolutely,' Poppy agreed.

There was a tiny silence and then Raf said, 'Excuse me, I'm going to steal Georgie away to meet some of my family.'

So – while trying hard not to mind about the weirdness with Poppy –

Georgie met Raf's father for the first time and re-met his mother, which was pretty much as excruciating as she would have predicted after the search-ing-for-secret incident. And she met his grandmother. And Noah's parents. And a lot of aunts and uncles and cousins. And some lifelong friends. All while panicking.

They were all very nice and a lot of fun.

If she hadn't had the I-don't-think-I-can-be-second-best-to-his-late-wife-plus-it's-awkward-being-at-the-same-party-as-Poppy   thoughts whizzing round her head, she'd have had a lovely evening. As it was, though, she didn't love it.

Just after midnight, when some people were starting to go home, Raf asked her if she'd like to go for another walk.

'We can look at the stars. And hopefully not rescue any cats,' he said.

Georgie laughed uneasily, trying to ignore how the way he had his hand touching the small of her back was doing all sorts of things to her insides; she had a nasty feeling that he was going to want to continue the conversa-tion from earlier.

Raf steered her round the corner of the pub and over to the stile along the lane, where six months ago she'd thrown up on his feet.

'I have something really important to say to you and I thought that here would be a nice place to say it.' He was standing with his back to the stile, holding her hands and smiling down at her. 'I think that it was probably right here on this spot that I started to fall in love with you.'

'Oh.'

'Georgie—'

'The only other time we've been here together, I vomited on you.'

'Yep. So as I was saying—' he took her hands in his and looked into her eyes '—I'd love us to become more serious. I mean, I know it's very early days but I just *know* and one thing I've learnt from my bereavement is that life can be short and we should make the most of every moment.'

Georgie couldn't speak.

It *was* early days, but she was pretty sure – certain, really – that she loved him too.

But.

It was bad enough being second best to your younger half-siblings, who at least messed up sometimes. Being second best to a dead person, you didn't have a hope of competing with them. And if Georgie had children with Raf, what if Max felt second best to them? He'd never be second best in her eyes, but what if he was for Raf? She couldn't do it.

'I'm so sorry.' Georgie knew without a shadow of a doubt that it was the right decision. 'I just... I don't think we should see each other any more.'

Raf pressed his lips together and then let go of her hands, and then after a pause said, 'I wondered, um, if you had a reason?'

Georgie couldn't do more than shake her head because she really wanted to cry.

'Could I ask...? I... No. Sorry.' He took a deep, juddering breath and then shook his own head.

No. This was awful.

'I do love you,' Georgie told him. 'But I need to go. I'm sorry.'

She turned round. She had to leave before looking into his lovely, *sad* eyes broke her resolve.

She'd been an idiot. This was clearly never going to have been just 'fun'.

29

GEORGIE

Late afternoon the next day, when they finally got home after Max seeing Declan for a walk, Georgie said Max could watch TV and considered for a moment allowing herself to *massively* wallow in self-pity. That would be *crap*, though.

'Come for a run with me,' she wheedled, until Max gave in and joined her on a 5k (who'd have thought that would be the one resolution she'd stick with when she didn't need to?) before settling in front of the TV again while she made their dinner and arranged with some local girlfriends to go out the following weekend, before getting on with work until bedtime. She did not need a man, she did not need her oldest friends, she did not need her mother; she could totally, *totally* be happy without all of them.

* * *

She had, basically, a shit week, and then, on Thursday, she found a voice message on her phone from Poppy. It took her a couple of minutes to make herself listen to it. Was it a butt call and she'd just be listening to ten minutes of Poppy's daily routine? Or was she calling to tell her to stay away again?

'Hello. Er, it's Poppy,' the message said. 'I'd really like to talk. Could I come over? Tomorrow evening if possible?'

Oh. Wow. Maybe Poppy wanted to spend time with her again. Or maybe it was something boring. Or maybe something about Max and Daniel. It *might* be positive, though, it definitely might. She could hope. She texted Poppy her reply:

Yes of course, please do come over.

* * *

It was harder choosing what to wear to see Poppy, her *oldest friend*, than it had been choosing what to wear on dates with Raf. She didn't want to look like she had no respect for Poppy so she didn't want to dress down. She didn't want to look like she was dressing really smartly for her, either; that would look stupid. It was really tricky. In the end she went for her new favourite going-out top, but with boyfriendy jeans and flip flops.

When Poppy rang the doorbell, her heart actually lolloped.

'Hey, Georgie.' Poppy was dressed pretty much identically to her style-wise, hooray. The first thing she'd got right with regard to Poppy for a *long* time.

Georgie had sent Max on his umpteenth sleepover of the year with a friend round the corner, because if there was one person whose presence probably wouldn't help a conversation between her and Poppy, it was him. So they were able to get talking immediately. Eek.

Poppy began as soon as they'd sat down at the kitchen table, opposite each other, quite formally, with drinks that Georgie had just made, really clumsily, nearly pouring boiling water over herself and nearly spilling milk everywhere. Shaking hands weren't ideal for tea-making.

'I've come to see you because Beth told me that you and Raf got together for about five minutes and then split up. She said you don't want to be second best and that you're really miserable. I've been thinking a lot about you. Georgie, I'm sorry. So sorry. Finding out about Declan and Max came at a bad time for me and I reacted badly. To be fair, I was probably never going to react well in the short-term, but I can now see everyone's point of view and good intentions. And thinking about how important our friendship is to you in place of your family, I understand why you, maybe even more than all of us, couldn't bear to break it up and panicked when you suspected about Declan. And I just want to say that you aren't second best to me. You're almost more to me than Declan, and that's why I've found it so hard to find my way back to you. I mean, you aren't more to me, he's my husband, but you know what I mean. I hope. We've known each other forever.'

Georgie was staring at Poppy. It was like her mind had gone all treacly. She couldn't work out what exactly Poppy was saying.

Poppy was looking at her like she expected her to reply, but nope, still treacle. So she just sat there and blinked a little.

'You know none of us are the same people now that we were ten, fifteen, twenty years ago,' Poppy continued. 'Who you are is shaped, at least to some extent, by your life experiences. Raf's a widower who's lived, worked and partied in New York for several years. He's a lot older and almost certainly a lot wiser than he was when he was younger. So are you. Maybe if you and Raf had met when you were much younger you wouldn't have fallen in love with each other. Maybe you would have. Maybe he wouldn't fall in love with Anna if he met her now. Maybe he would.'

It *seemed* like Poppy had a point, but the treacle effect was ongoing in Georgie's brain and she still couldn't think of anything to say.

Poppy wasn't finished, so it didn't really matter that Georgie couldn't speak.

'For example, if you and Declan met now, you wouldn't shag each other, would you? I know that. We all know that. And not just because he's married, but because you're both older and different.' Poppy had to feel really strongly about her point if she was prepared to use Georgie and Declan shagging or not shagging as an analogy. 'And I am not second best because he slept with you first. And second children are not second best to their older siblings.

'Basically, Georgie, you aren't second best in Raf's eyes. He told Dec and Noah over a drink last week that he'd never wanted to do romance again because he didn't want to be in a position where he could feel grief-stricken, and then meeting you changed his mind. He's ready.' She picked up a teaspoon and pointed it at Georgie. 'You. Are. Not. Second. Best. To. Raf. You are to your mother, yes, but that's her problem. You are not second best to Raf. It's so fucking obvious it's untrue.' Poppy paused for breath and then asked, 'Are you listening? Are you fucking listening?'

'Yes.' Of course Georgie was listening; the new sweary Poppy was scary.

'So what are you thinking?'

'I'm thinking that maybe you're right. And I'm also thinking that there's something I'd like to say to you, if I may.'

'What's that?'

'I love you, Pops. Please, please could we be friends again? I know that I shouldn't have written that secret and that I could have handled things differently but I never, ever meant to hurt you. I wouldn't.' Georgie sniffed loudly. Any minute now she'd be a blubbering wreck.

'I know that. I love you too.'

Some of the best words Georgie had ever heard. Maybe *the* best.

Georgie stood up and held out her arms and Poppy stood up too and they had a big hug. They were both full-on sobbing by the end of it.

'Raf loves you too, you know. You aren't second best to him, you idiot,' said Poppy, wiping underneath her eyes. Poppy had never been good on make-up knowledge – that was the kind of thing you knew about someone you'd been best friends with forever – and as usual she was wearing rubbish non-waterproof mascara and now had black rings under her eyes. 'Seriously. You're so obviously made for each other.'

'I think I need to call him.'

'Do it now. Pleeeeeeease.' Poppy really looked like her fourteen-year-old self at that point.

'Do you remember when you made me call Harvey Green? Twenty years ago. I think that was the last time you made me call a boy.' That had *not* ended well.

'Yeah. Sorry about that. But this is different. Harvey Green was a shit and Raf is lovely, and we're a *lot* older.'

'Okay. That is true.'

'Right. In recognition of the fact that we *are* a lot older, I'm going to go now instead of giggling in the background, but please, please phone Raf.'

They shared another big, fantastic, superb hug before Poppy left.

And then Georgie sat down at her kitchen table and stared at her phone. When it pinged about three minutes later, she physically jumped in shock. It was always weird when your phone did something when you were watching it. Kind of like you were psychic, but not.

It was a message from Poppy.

PHONE HIM.

Then she got another one.

LOVE YOU LOADS. BLOODY PHOOOOOOONE HIM.

30

GEORGIE

It was a good job that Raf didn't pick up when Georgie phoned because, just as her call went to voicemail, she realised that she didn't know what to say. *Hi. You know you said you loved me and you'd like to get more serious? Do you still mean it? Can I just confirm whether I'm second best or not?* No. So she ended the call without leaving a message.

Then she realised that her number would show up as a missed call. So she sent a text saying, 'Just tried to call you.'

And then she sent another one saying, 'I wondered if we could talk.'

Okay. Done. Ball in his court. If he didn't phone back, all good, she'd know that he was regretting his suggestion and it was therefore very lucky that she'd said no. If he did call back, she'd think about what to say then.

She hadn't heard from him before she went to bed at midnight. Which felt pretty depressing if she was being honest, *but* she did have the huge joy of having Poppy back in her life. She texted her just before she put the light out to say that she'd messaged him and had had no reply.

And Poppy replied saying, 'He's probably out. Try him tomorrow. Lots of love,' just like she would have done in the past. Which was so nice that Georgie went to sleep smiling despite Raf.

She was woken at seven in the morning, by Raf phoning.

'Hi, Georgie.'

'Hello.' This was a very heart-beating-fast way to wake up.

'I got your messages.'

'Thanks for calling back.'

'Not a problem. I would have called yesterday but I was in an underground restaurant which had really bad reception.' He'd been out. Probably having a lot of fun. Which was *totally* fine. 'With clients.' Yessss, such a relief that it hadn't been a date. 'So, was it something important?'

'Yes, quite important.' Understatement.

'Okay. So would you like to talk now?'

'Maybe we should talk in person? If that's okay?' Then she might be able to tell if he still felt the same way about her.

'Yes, of course. Now? I could come round? If you're free?'

Now? What. No. She needed to have a shower and put some make-up on.

'Maybe in about an hour's time? If that's okay?' It was weird being this polite and pussy-footy with Raf.

'Perfect.'

An hour was good. In an hour, as it turned out, working at extreme speed, she had time to have a shower, dry her hair, do her make-up, decide what casual but flattering top to wear and sprint round the house making it as immaculate as possible. In fact, by the time Raf rang the doorbell, the kitchen and sitting room were practically ready to audition for an appearance in a *Beautiful Home* type magazine. She had to stop herself from switching the oven on and sticking a loaf of bread inside to go full estate-agent's-dream.

When she opened the door, Raf took her breath away. He was wearing nicely-worn-in jeans, with a slim fit navy shirt open at the neck, and he looked gorgeous. Even better than in her dreams.

He smiled at her and her tummy did a little dip. Please, please let him not have changed his mind.

'Good morning,' she said.

'Good morning.'

'Come in.' She walked ahead of him into her excellently tidy sitting room and then wished they'd gone into the kitchen so she could offer him coffee without having to go to a different room to make it. Okay, fuck it, no coffee, she should just get on with it. 'Thank you for coming.'

'Thank you for asking me to come.' This politeness was getting *ridiculous*. 'So what did you want to talk about?'

That was better. More like normal Raf.

'Basically, I wanted to say that I wondered if you, erm...'

Asking if he did indeed love her had sounded a *lot* better in her head than it did out loud. Maybe she should have spent some time planning what to say instead of plumping up cushions. Raf wasn't even looking at the cushions. He was just staring at her. Not moving.

Then he said, 'Yes?'

Oh, fuck it again.

'I love you,' she told him.

'You do?'

'Yes.'

'Oh-kay.'

Right. She'd hoped for a bigger response than that.

Oh, fuck it once more.

'If you were still interested in... um... becoming serious then I would actually also be interested.' She really wished that he wasn't looking so inscrutable right now.

'You would?' He was sticking with his inscrutability.

Georgie nodded.

And then his inscrutable mask cracked and his face spread into a broad, broad smile.

'I love you, Georgie.'

Oh, thank God.

'I love you too.' She was smiling and tearful at the same time.

And then he opened his arms very wide and she walked straight into them.

They hugged hard for a moment and then she looked up at him and suddenly they were kissing.

And Georgie did not feel remotely second best.

EPILOGUE
POPPY – 30TH DECEMBER

'Oh my goodness. I am *ready* for this sofa.' Poppy sank down next to Declan and took the glass he was holding out to her. 'Busy day.'

She'd done a full nine hours at the surgery and then picked Daniel up (her parents had been looking after him) and had dashed to the shop in Little Melting before coming home and giving him his bath and putting him to bed (her mum had very kindly given him dinner).

Declan pulled her right in against him and slapped a big kiss onto her cheek.

'Mmm,' she said, snuggling in.

'New Year's Eve again tomorrow,' he observed. 'A lot's changed in a year.'

It had. Poppy was now working two days a week and was loving it. Daniel was doing one day a week with a childminder and one with Poppy's parents. And they'd managed to buy a small house in Melting and had moved in in October.

'Not least this sofa.' Poppy wasn't just snuggling into Declan, she was snuggling into the sofa, too. They hadn't been able to afford it until this month, and it had been delivered two days ago. They both *adored* having something other than the floor to sit on when they were watching TV.

As he pressed buttons on the remote, Declan said, 'Soooo, how are you feeling about tomorrow evening?'

They were going to be meeting the same group as last year.

'Good. Very good.' Poppy was still ecstatic to be back on best-friend terms with Georgie. The few months where they hadn't been speaking had been awful. 'I'm just kind of—'

'Not wanting to read your secret out but you haven't kept your resolutions?'

Poppy nodded. 'Basically. Yep.'

'I was sort of wondering if that might be the case for you. It is for me. I had a little suggestion.'

'Yes?' Poppy really hoped he was going to suggest what she wanted to hear.

'Maybe just teensy little lies from both of us?'

'I would be *ecstatic* to lie our way through the evening.'

A little silence grew between them as the opening credits of the film they were watching began to roll.

Poppy wriggled herself round to look into his face. 'Do you think it would be better if we shared our secrets, if we both feel able?' She knew *she* could.

'Yep. I would like to do that if you would.' He looked uncertain. But, thank heavens, he surely wouldn't want to share it if it was *truly* awful. And, frankly, if it was, she kind of needed to know that he'd ever felt like however he'd felt.

'Okay. You go first? Or I could?'

'You go,' Declan said.

'Well,' she said. 'I wrote that I thought you were having an affair.' She couldn't really believe that they hadn't told each other their secrets before.

'Oh, Poppy.' Declan wrapped his arms tightly around her and buried his face in her hair.

Poppy screwed her face up. 'What was your secret?'

'Well, you know what my actual secret was. And another one that I was carrying was that I was worried about you. But what I put was that I was worried that you were getting addicted to Tunnock's Caramels. Which I immediately regretted because it sounded so patronising, but I was panicking because I was sober and therefore realised that it was a really bad idea writing big secrets down.'

'I love you. Thank you for being such an amazing husband.' Poppy kissed him on the lips, softly at first and then much more deeply.

'I'm thinking let's not bother with the film this evening?' Declan said after a while. 'It would be a good New Year's Day watch?'

'Mmm,' Poppy said.

As they went upstairs, hand in hand, Declan said, 'So we're agreed: lie through our teeth about the resolutions tomorrow evening?'

'Perfect,' Poppy told him as she pulled him towards their bed.

EPILOGUE

GEORGIE – NEW YEAR'S EVE

Georgie beamed at her three best friends. And their lovely other halves. Including her own. It was wonderful being here with them. Wonderful that she and Poppy were back together with their friendship as strong as ever, stronger even than before.

'A toast.' She raised her glass. 'To friendship.'

'To friendship,' everyone echoed.

Ankita raised her whopping-diamond-ring laden left hand and said, 'It's time, everyone.'

Georgie nearly choked on her Prosecco in trepidation. 'For what?'

'Resolutions and secrets.' Ankita looked at Noah. 'Do you have the Resolutions sheet?'

'Yup. Hang on.' Noah stood up and went over to the bar before coming back a minute later with the envelope that Georgie and Raf had unsealed and... yes, re-sealed very well.

Georgie wanted to mouth *Well done* at Raf, but better not. Also, why was she thinking about envelopes and glue when she needed to be playing down what she'd written? Everyone knew that Declan was Max's dad, of course, but she really didn't want to remind everyone about how it all came out.

'So let's read them,' Ankita said.

'We don't have to do this,' Noah suggested.

'What?' Ankita said.

'Should we maybe vote on whether or not people are happy to do it?' Beth asked.

'Okay. Who *isn't* happy?' Ankita looked at them all in turn.

Georgie tilted her head down and peeked through her eyelashes at everyone else. No one was going to want to be the one to say they weren't happy to do it. She was pretty sure that if one, or at least two, people said they were unhappy about it then at least half of them would agree. But Ankita had played a blinder acting like she was almost daring them to say they weren't up for it.

'Right, then,' Ankita said after a couple of seconds. 'Let's go.'

She opened the envelope.

'The first one is Poppy's.'

'Maybe everyone should read their own one out,' Georgie said, before Ankita could start.

'Good idea.' Ankita handed Poppy's sheet to her.

Poppy cleared her throat. 'Okay. No dessert, lose two stone, have Daniel sleep through the night by May, cook a new dish every week, and learn how to hula and do the splits.' She looked around the group, very much looking everyone in the eye in a completely fake I-am-looking-you-in-the-eye-because-I've-heard-that-liars-cannot-meet-people's-eyes-and-I-want-to-prove-I-am-not-lying-but-totally-am way. 'And I kept them all! Yay me!'

'Oh wow,' Beth said. 'Can you do the splits for us now?'

There was a slightly-too-long pause and then Poppy said, 'Certainly not. It's very undignified doing the splits in public. It's something that no adult should ever do other than at home or in an Olympic competition. And that is why I did not ever post any pictures of myself in my perfect splits. Which I can totally do.'

'Amazing and fair enough,' Georgie said quickly. 'So who's next?'

They should definitely move on; Poppy clearly had *not* kept her resolutions but clearly did not want to read out her secret. And why would anyone want to make her?

'Raf.' Ankita handed his piece of paper to him.

'I just had: Move back to the UK, be in bed before midnight at least five nights a week and stick to one cup of coffee a day. And I did them all.'

'Hmm, I think we should have made everyone learn a new skill,' Georgie said. 'Those were *easy*.'

'Oh, yes.' Raf nudged her. 'Your new-skill-learning went fantastically, didn't it?'

Dammit. She'd set herself up for that one.

'Yes, it did actually.' She kicked his ankle under the table and he grinned.

'Mine next.' Ankita held hers up in front of herself with a flourish. 'Give up caffeine, see my friends more, visit twelve new countries, learn how to mix cocktails.'

'My goodness.' Beth's eyes were on stalks. 'What countries did you visit?'

'Only America and Mexico, and I'd already been to America. And I can't actually live without caffeine. And I don't really want to mix cocktails because if I ever have guests I just want to talk to them.'

'So what was your secret?' Beth was the only one who asked the question, probably because most of them *really* didn't want to go there because they didn't want to go anywhere near discussing their *own* secrets.

'Um, that I'd slept with my boss before I realised he was my boss.'

'Ankita!' Beth did a big eye swivel in the direction of Alex.

Ankita sighed out loud. 'Darling Beth. *Alex* was my boss.'

'*Oh*. I see.' Beth reached out to hug both of them. 'Well, that is cute.'

'It certainly is.' Alex was still looking like the cat that got the cream.

'Beth, the next one is you.' Ankita passed her list to her.

'I only had one. And I succeeded.' She put her hand on her rounded tummy and smiled at Noah. 'And it was half my secret and I really don't mind telling you the other half, because you all know anyway.' Around her friends, Beth was still a complete open book. 'My resolution and the first half of my secret was to get pregnant this year, although I thought I was maybe going to have to do it by IVF with a sperm donor. Because the second half of my secret was to think about leaving Dominic.'

There were lots of choruses of words to the effect of '*That's so wonderful*.' They had indeed all already completely known.

'Yours next,' Ankita told Noah.

Noah's resolution was staying off alcohol and his secret was that he had a very loudly ticking biological clock, so he'd done very well on both.

'We started trying for a baby almost as soon as we started going out,' Beth told them.

When everyone had stopped exclaiming even more about how happy they all were for Beth and Noah, Declan whizzed through his flower-buying, getting Daniel on the Irish foreign births register so he could get his Irish passport and Spanish-learning resolutions.

'And I did them all, *hola y gracias*, haha,' he concluded. 'Who's next?'

'Must be me,' Georgie said, really fast again, so no one could challenge Declan with any Spanish beyond hello-and-thank-you because again why should anyone be forced to share a secret if they didn't want to? The whole thing had been a *stupid* idea. She took the piece of paper from Ankita. 'Mine were go running, give up chocolate, crisps, cake and pizza, don't pull my grey hairs out, go to bed before eleven at least four times a week, do yoga at least once a fortnight, learn Italian—' there was no need to mention the taking-a-GCSE aspect '—and learn how to do a jump while ice skating and—' *eek* no *way* did she want to mention that she'd resolved to cheer Poppy up '—that's it.'

She screwed the piece of paper up and stuck it in her handbag.

'You can't have managed all of that?' Ankita stated.

'I actually did,' Georgie lied. 'I'm a new woman.'

'It's midnight,' said Noah. 'Happy New Year, everyone.'

Thank goodness for that.

'*Buon Anno*,' Georgie said. She'd learnt minimal Italian as it had turned out, but she'd done very well on the 'festival' section of Duolingo.

When all the glass clinking and kisses had finished, Beth said, 'Let's not do the resolutions and secrets thing again.'

Everyone clinked their glasses even more than before in agreement to that.

* * *

Two hours later, as everyone said goodnight, Raf said to Georgie, 'Walk around the green before bed?' They were staying with Noah that night.

'Yes, good idea.' It was a gorgeous, frosty, clear night and there was something lovely about being out on your own.

'So,' Raf said when they were right in the middle of the green. They were standing under the same tree they'd rescued the cat from on New Year's Day. 'Do you want to know what my secret was?'

'Only if you want to tell me.' Georgie really did not like the secret revelation thing.

'Well, obviously I do or I wouldn't have said. And I don't want to have secrets from you.'

'Oh-kay.' Georgie still wasn't sure.

'My secret was, "I fancy Georgie". Very teenage. But very true.'

'Aww.' Georgie beamed in the moonlight with happiness and relief. 'I fancy you, too.'

'So. Georgie.' He moved so that he was facing her and then went down on one knee and took her hands in his.

Georgie gasped.

'I love you. And I'm pushing forty. And I know for absolute certain that I want to be with you forever and I feel the luckiest man in the world to have met you. Will you marry me?'

Georgie couldn't speak around the enormous lump in her throat.

'Erm. Georgie?' He gripped her hands a little more tightly.

The word, 'Yes,' suddenly burst out of her.

'That is such a relief,' Raf said, as he stood up and put his arms round her. 'For a horrible moment I thought you were going to say no. I love you.'

'I love you too. So very, very much. Happy New Year.'

ACKNOWLEDGEMENTS

This story began life as the first book that I wrote, and so is very close to my heart. Huge thanks to all those who helped it become the story that it is today.

Firstly I have to thank my wonderful sister Liz, who was the person who inspired me to begin the story and has cheered me on the whole way (and is one of the very few people to have read the very first draft).

Many thanks also to my amazing agent, Sarah Hornsley at PFD, for her always pertinent and perceptive support and advice, and also to Sam Brace at PFD for her much-needed and much-appreciated help during my mid-edit wobbles during Sarah's maternity leave.

Enormous thanks, of course, to the lovely team at Boldwood. Thank you in particular to Emily Yau for her superb insight and determination to make the story the best it can be. Thank you also to Gary Jukes for copyed-its, to Rachel Sargeant for proof-reads and to Clare Stacey for the beautiful cover.

And last but not least, thank you so much to my family and friends. Thank you to Dave and Fiona and my husband for many fantastic New Year's Eves (especially the legendary French supermarket fireworks one) and thank you to my in-laws for all the special times in the Cotswolds. Thank you to Lynn McInnes for the cat injury details (ouch!). And thank you to my children for allowing me to drag you out on New Year's Day for my go-running resolution (never lasts). And thank you more widely to my husband and children for putting up with my writing spurts! All very, very much appreciated.

ABOUT THE AUTHOR

Jo Lovett is the bestselling author of contemporary rom-coms including *The House Swap*. Shortlisted for the Comedy Women in Print Award, she lives in London and was previously published by Bookouture.

Sign up to Jo Lovett's mailing list for news, competitions and updates on future books.

Follow Jo on social media:

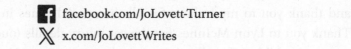

facebook.com/JoLovett-Turner

x.com/JoLovettWrites

ALSO BY JO LOVETT

Another Time, Another Place

Can You Keep A Secret?

LOVE NOTES

LOVE IN EVERY CHAPTER

WHERE ALL YOUR ROMANCE
DREAMS COME TRUE!

THE HOME OF BESTSELLING
ROMANCE AND WOMEN'S
FICTION

 WARNING:
MAY CONTAIN SPICE

SIGN UP TO OUR
NEWSLETTER

https://bit.ly/Lovenotesnews

Boldwood

Boldwood Books is an award-winning fiction publishing company seeking out the best stories from around the world.

Find out more at www.boldwoodbooks.com

Join our reader community for brilliant books, competitions and offers!

Follow us
@BoldwoodBooks
@TheBoldBookClub

Sign up to our weekly deals newsletter

https://bit.ly/BoldwoodBNewsletter

Milton Keynes UK
Ingram Content Group UK Ltd.
UKHW042029070324
439026UK00002B/6